WRAPPED UP IN LOVE

A HOLIDAY ANTHOLOGY

DIANE BENEFIEL

M. TASIA

L.P. MAXA

EMILY MIMS

JOAN BIRD

ELLE WRIGHT

Boroughs
Publishing Group

www.BOROUGHSPUBLISHINGGROUP.com

The Gift of Us, Brighton Holidays, Grey, Mission: Acceptance, A Home for Christmas, The Vow
Copyright © 2024 Diane Benefiel, M. Tasia, L.P. Maxa, Emily Mims, Joan Bird, Elle Wright

ISBN 978-1-957295-76-3

WRAPPED UP IN LOVE

THE GIFT OF US

DIANE BENEFIEL

CHAPTER ONE

Juliette sat back in her chair at the nurse's station logging notes in her tablet. She glanced at the clock. Five a.m. A light up snowman danced with elves next to a gingerbread house in the holiday display at the end of the counter. She frowned at the incongruity. Didn't elves hang out with Santa?

Anayah slouched in the chair next to hers.

"Two hours until end of shift. It's been quiet. I hope—"

Anayah whipped up her hand. "Stop. Don't say it."

"What? That it's been quiet, and I hope it stays that way?"

"Oh good lord, you've jinxed us."

Juliette rolled her eyes. "That's a superstition. Saying the words doesn't make stuff happen."

"Incoming, ladies," Tupu sang in his deep baritone as he stopped at the station.

Anayah hissed at her. "See? You don't say that kind of thing out loud."

Ignoring her friend, Juliette asked, "What's the status?"

Staff loved Tupu because of his flowery language and incredible voice. He was a giant of a man who stood at six and a half feet with intricate tattoos in geometric patterns on his arms that reflected his Samoan heritage.

"I will tell you what I know." Tupu cleared his throat. "Our current drama was caused by juveniles hell-bent on endangering the public by street racing. Incoming Speed Racer crashed his tiny little sports car through a guardrail and rolled to a steep drop-off where he hung precariously at cliff's edge. At great peril to themselves, stalwart members of our own Sisters FD rescue squad rappelled over the side to reach the vehicle and the young idiot trapped inside. The driver, and the firefighter injured in heroic service to the public, are on their way in with flashing lights and sirens."

"Firefighter?" Juliette tightened her grip on the tablet.

"I'll take the juvenile delinquent so you can take the firefighter in case it's your cutie-pie," Anayah offered. Her voice held a beautiful lilt reflective of her native Kenya.

"He's not my cutie-pie."

Tupu shot a finger at her. "Stop lying to yourself, my redheaded friend. You *like* him." He sang the word "like" with a soul vibe.

The doors from the ambulance bay slid open and the team pushed in a gurney. "That's Speed Racer. I got him." Anayah directed the team to a room and Tupu followed her in.

Juliette stepped outside to the bay area as the ambulance that had brought the injured teen rolled out. The wail of sirens grew nearer.

With her arms crossed against the biting wind, and her hair flying, she paced while waiting for the next ambulance. That evening when she'd been driving to the clinic, she'd seen the rescue truck speeding up Main Street with Mateo at the wheel, so she knew he was working a shift.

It's not like she and Mateo had anything going other than a flirty acquaintance. As a firefighter, he was at the emergency clinic several times a week. Her very first shift he'd come in with a squad member who'd injured his ankle. One look at Mateo and Juliette had felt her heart rate kick up and her face flush. She'd been irritated with herself. What could be more cliché than falling for a hottie firefighter?

That he seemed to reciprocate was exciting. When he was in the ER, he sought her out, always flirting, smiling that wonderful smile of his, and recently he'd asked her to hang out. Which was great, but the more she got to know him, she realized he was open and friendly with everyone, especially women.

An elderly woman coming into the ER? Mateo offered an arm. A frazzled mom dealing with a cranky toddler? Mateo would hold out his hands and the toddler would reach for him without hesitation. And young, single women? If his magnetism didn't captivate them, they'd have trouble finding resistance to his delicious package: thick black hair, gorgeous brown eyes, and a slightly naughty grin.

Mateo was attractive and charming, and everyone loved him. Which was great. Terrific even. But a caution for her not to let her heart get tangled up over him. Attractive and charming had burned her before.

The Sisters FD rescue truck pulled into a parking space, followed by the ambulance backing into the bay. Juliette opened the back door.

Scott, the paramedic, hopped out, and he and the EMT, Nicole, pulled out the gurney and dropped the wheels. Juliette's heart gave a hard lurch when she saw the man on the stretcher.

"Patient is Sisters FD engineer Mateo Reynoso," Scott reported. "Laceration to the ass, right butt cheek."

"It's my hip, not my ass." Mateo's voice sounded muffled because he was lying face-down on the gurney, his head turned away from Juliette. "And cover me up. Is my ass hanging out?"

Scott tugged up a blue drape, winking at her. "You're covered, my man. Your girl won't see a thing."

"Is she here?"

"Take him into room four," Juliette directed.

Mateo propped himself on his elbows so he could turn his head. He caught sight of her. "Dammit."

"Nice to see you too, Mateo. I'm sure your girl will be disappointed she missed you." Go figure, he had a girlfriend. Now she really felt like an idiot.

"Shoot me now," he muttered. Scott and Nicole rolled the gurney into the clinic.

Once he was transferred to a bed, Juliette lifted the drape. His pants had been cut away and bandages were taped from his right butt cheek to his hip.

Mateo buried his face in the pillow. "Can I request a different PA? Or Doc Hanson?"

As physician assistants, Juliette and Anayah worked under the supervision of the elderly Doctor Hanson.

"I'm afraid not. Anayah is with the guy you rescued, and the doctor is setting a bone fracture."

"Maybe you could switch? Or send in Tupu. Nurses do stitches, don't they?"

"Really, Mateo? You don't want me to stitch up a cut on your ass?"

"It's my hip, not my ass. But I didn't want the first time you see me down there to be when I'm all bloody."

"Since this will be the only time I see you down there, I think we're good." She tried to dampen the hurt. Keeping her tone professional, she said, "I'm afraid you're stuck with me."

"You'll never go out with me after you've sewn up my ass. The magic will be gone."

He sounded so woeful she couldn't help a smile. She reminded herself about the girlfriend and not to take his flirting seriously. Juliette wondered who the girlfriend was. "I haven't gone out with you yet, so stitching your posterior won't change anything."

She took a minute to study his chart on her tablet. Mateo Reynoso, thirty-three years old, skimmed in a half inch under six feet, and weighed a hundred eighty pounds. Both blood pressure and heart rate were a little elevated, as would be expected with an injury. No known allergies. After putting on gloves, she pulled the rolling tray table to the bed and opened the laceration kit.

"Anything you want to warn me about before I start? Fear of needles? Tattoos you don't want damaged? Any unusual piercings I should know about?"

"I'm not scared of needles. I don't have a piercing on my ass. Or a tattoo, for that matter."

"Good. That makes things simpler. I've had patients cry when their tattoo got messed up by an injury. Let's see what we've got here." She removed the bandages and winced in sympathy. "That has to hurt."

"Yeah, it hurts." He glanced over his shoulder, dark eyes reflecting pain that dulled their usual spark. "But I won't ask you to kiss my ass and make it all better."

"That's a relief. Tell me what happened."

She listened while preparing the lidocaine syringe and irrigating the wound.

"We got the kid out and he's being hauled up the incline to the road. He's damn lucky the car stopped when it did. Another couple feet and he'd have been at the bottom of the mountain as opposed to hanging on the side.

"We had a cable on the vehicle, but the car was in a bad position and it shifted. I was the last one up and a torn piece of metal caught me right between the harness straps." He rested his forehead on his folded arms.

She swabbed the area and covered all but the wound with sterile drapes.

"Sounds like a risky rescue, especially in the middle of the night." Keeping the syringe out of his line of vision, she injected lidocaine to numb the area.

"The kid's alive, and that makes the risk worth it."

Mateo's comment was exactly what made him heroic.

"This will keep you off duty for at least two weeks," she murmured as she used the needle driver to insert the curved needle and pull through the suture thread.

"Two weeks? I can't be off duty for two weeks."

"That's how long this will take to heal. You'll need to come back to get the stitches out." She concentrated on her sewing skills, making a neat row of stitches. "I'm putting two weeks in the off work orders I'll submit to your captain."

Mateo's shoulders slumped. "C'mon, Jules. Can't you make it one week as a favor for a friend?"

She glanced at his bent head. She'd love to run her fingers through all that thick hair. That is if they were anything more than verbal sparring partners.

"No, and you'll need to keep the stitches dry for at least two days so that means no showers." He shifted again so he could see her.

"Face down, hotshot, so I can make the awesome scar you'll have nice and straight."

He shifted to face-down again with a sigh. With the wound closed, she knotted and snipped the thread.

"Will I be able to sit?" Even muffled his voice sounded pathetic.

"You'll be sore enough that sitting will be uncomfortable for several days, though the injury is more toward the hip so you'll be better off positioning yourself with your weight on your left side. You'll want to watch for infection. Any redness, swelling, drainage, pain, you come back and we'll put you on antibiotics."

"Got it, doc."

"I'm not a doctor," she said crisply. "We'll send you home with care instructions and anything else you'll need."

"How can I see my ass to check if it's infected?"

"Any person in this community would be happy to check on your ass for you." That was no exaggeration; the people of Sisters looked after their own. "Or ask your mom. She's awesome." He groaned.

"I don't want my friends looking at my ass. I certainly don't want my mom looking at my ass. I only want you." He perked up. "Hey, you can come over and give me some TLC. Check my injury, have dinner with me. We'll do takeout.

"We can watch a movie, and since I have to lie down, I can rest my head on your lap while we're on my couch. You could play with my hair." She'd bet money the smile he aimed at her had gotten him what he wanted all his life. She wished she could accept his invitation at face value, not overthink it, simply hang out with Mateo without involving her heart. But the risk of heartbreak was too great.

"That's very specific."

"Yeah, it'll be great. I'll get the food from Easy Money and ask Owen to set aside a couple slices of the lemon meringue cheesecake everyone's crazy for."

"Is this your way of asking me out, by luring me with amazing cheesecake?"

"Is it working?"

"I'm not dating you, Mateo."

"But you're getting close to accepting. Your resolve was weakening. I can feel it." He was right. Her resolve was weakening. She liked Mateo. As in really liked Mateo. But he had a girlfriend so either he wasn't serious about the invitation, or he was a player. She'd hoped he had more substance than that.

Tupu came in carrying a bag.

"How's the kid?" Mateo asked.

"Lucky to be among the living. His mother and father have arrived. The mother is crying over his injuries. The father is glad his son is alive and that his injuries aren't more serious, but you can tell that boy will be paying for his lack of judgment." He put the bag on the bed next to Mateo. "Here, sir, is a change of clothes brought to you by your compadres."

"Thanks, man."

Someone called out from the hall and Tupu stepped out.

Juliette moved to the head of the bed so Mateo could see her more easily. "Tupu will finish up and go over the care instructions. Take the meds as prescribed to help with the pain. It's going to hurt when the lidocaine wears off. I'll leave you to get changed. Wait until Tupu is here to get up."

Mateo propped himself on his elbows. "If you're not going to kiss my ass to make it better, you can give me a kiss right here." He tapped his cheek.

Maybe it was because it was the end of shift and she was tired, or maybe he was just so appealing, and she hated that he'd been hurt, but she leaned down and gave him a brief kiss. "Feel better, hotshot."

His dark eyes gleamed. "I knew you liked me."

CHAPTER TWO

After Juliette gave the firefighters in the waiting room an update on Mateo's condition, Shawna, an RN, directed her to a room. "Emery Keller just came in. She's at thirty-seven weeks gestation and presenting with vaginal bleeding."

That was never a good sign.

"I'll check for a heartbeat with the doppler first. Bring in the ultrasound machine." While Juliette enjoyed ER work, obstetrics was her true calling.

Because she was needed, she worked shifts in the emergency clinic, but her primary specialty was obstetrics and gynecology. While Sisters Medical didn't have all the specialties of a full hospital, they did have an obstetrics department and a labor and delivery wing. Juliette worked with Helen Tran, the only obstetrician in town, so sisters Delaney, Emery, and Cam were her patients.

When she'd first moved to the picturesque mountain town of Sisters, the clinic staff had been abuzz with the pregnancies of the three sisters. She'd learned the town had been named for three sisters from gold rush days who'd defied gender stereotypes and operated a mine on Payback Mountain. With that history, the townsfolk were enraptured with the more recent story of three sisters. There'd even been articles in the local newspaper.

Growing up, the modern women—same father, different mothers—hadn't known of the others' existence. They'd found each other through the efforts of their paternal grandmother, the matriarch of the local Cider Mill Farm. The dangerous challenges that had brought the sisters together, and ultimately to their husbands, made their journeys fascinating. The cherry on top of the saga was all three had gotten pregnant around the same time, and were due in the next several weeks.

Juliette entered the room where one of those sisters reclined on the exam table, her husband Shane at her side, their hands firmly gripped together. Their faces reflected their fear that something was wrong with their baby.

Juliette went to the sink to wash her hands, then moved to the side of the exam table opposite Shane. "Tell me what's going on."

Emery shifted her pregnant belly trying to get comfortable. Her hair was pulled into a messy bun, and her sky-blue eyes were clouded with worry. "Little girl was moving around so much I couldn't sleep, so I got up to make some tea. Then I felt wetness." She brushed a tear from the corner of her eye. "I thought my water must've broken. But when I went into the bathroom, it was blood." Emery's voice cracked. "I haven't felt her move since then."

Shane brushed her hair back and pressed his lips to her forehead. "We'll be fine, darlin'."

"How long ago was that?"

"About an hour," Shane replied. "Maybe a little less. We came right in."

"At this point, I wouldn't worry about her not moving. She's probably asleep. You presented with placenta previa with the placenta covering the cervix and sometimes that results in bleeding." Juliette did a quick general assessment, then reached for the doppler fetal monitor. "Let's start with the easy stuff and listen for a heartbeat."

She had Emery pull up her baggy sweatshirt and push down her leggings to expose her rounded abdomen. After manipulating her belly to determine the position of the fetus, Juliette added gel and pressed the fetal doppler probe to where she'd determined a shoulder was located. Immediately the whoosh-whoosh sound of the fetal heartbeat filled the room.

"That's a good healthy one hundred and thirty beats per minute, so baby girl is going strong."

Emery burst into tears and Shane dropped his head to hers, murmuring quietly.

Shawna rolled in the ultrasound machine and began setting it up.

Juliette rubbed Emery's leg. "Next step, we'll do an ultrasound to see what we can see. The last ultrasound showed the placenta has moved up as the baby's grown, but there was still partial obstruction of the cervix. Let's see where you're at now." With another squirt of gel on her belly, Juliette began the procedure.

What they saw was what Juliette suspected. She finished and set aside the wand and wiped the gel from Emery's abdomen with a warm cloth.

"Good news is the placenta no longer covers the cervix, so that makes delivery less complicated. A little bit of the placenta likely tore loose, causing the bleeding, but everything is looking good. If you have any more bleeding, don't hesitate to come in."

"Can placenta previa return?" Shane's voice was gruff.

"It's possible, but not likely." She smiled at the tired couple. "You two go home and get some rest. Your little girl is doing fine."

***

By the time Juliette drove her Subaru home through the early morning darkness, she was exhausted. Her stomach rumbled loudly. Make that hungry and exhausted. If she'd been in any town larger than Sisters, she could have stopped for an Egg McMuffin on her way home. But part of Sisters' charm was the mom-and-pop shops. Charming as they were, they didn't lend themselves to early morning takeout.

Locking her car, she slung her backpack over her shoulder and contemplated the stairs to her second-story apartment. They seemed extra steep this morning.

When she got to her door, she found a plastic bag hanging from the knob. Frowning, she picked it up by the handles and opened wide to peer inside. The scent of bacon wafted up from a foil-wrapped bundle. There was a small plastic container of what looked like salsa.

She pushed open her door, turned the deadbolt to lock it, and took off her coat, scarf, and shoes before making her way to the kitchen. Flipping on the light, she put on the electric kettle. She set a tea bag in a mug then gave in to temptation and unwrapped the bundle.

A burrito. Steam rose as she unfolded the tortilla to examine the contents. Someone had left a giant breakfast burrito hanging on her door.

A breakfast burrito with eggs, bacon, cheddar cheese, and what looked like pan-fried potatoes. It even had chopped cilantro and green onions. She swallowed as her mouth watered. If she was anywhere other than Sisters, she'd guess that a delivery service had left takeout at the wrong address.

She poured hot water over the tea bag while contemplating the ethics and risks of eating a breakfast burrito left on her door.

The ethics? She didn't know who it belonged to and it would be wasteful to throw it away. She could ask the other tenants if they were missing a breakfast burrito, but her neighbor Winston perpetually had the munchies and would claim it whether his or not.

The risks? What if some crazy person had left a poisoned burrito? Having consumed a poisoned breakfast burrito, she'd die happy, but still, was it worth it?

Her phone pinged with an incoming text.

Hotshot: *Jules, thanks for stitching up my hip. I don't let just anyone do that. The crew at the station made breakfast burritos this morning so I had them deliver one to you. I'll be home all alone. Come visit me.*

Having met his mom, Antonia, who had a cool shop on Main Street, and with a girlfriend, Juliette doubted he'd be home alone. But thank you, hotshot, the amazing burrito was hers.

She put the food on a plate and sat at her miniscule dining table. Unfolding the flour tortilla to dump on the salsa, she wrapped it up again and bit into the delicious blend of flavors. Oh good heavens, it was good. Chewing with her eyes closed, she decided firefighters had the right idea about cooking meals as part of their work life.

Swallowing, she propped up her phone.

Juliette: *Thank you for the delicious breakfast burrito. I'm eating it now. It's exactly the right food at exactly the right time. I was starving. Stitching your ass is all part of the job, but as it's a nice ass, it wasn't a chore. Sorry I can't visit. I'm going to try for a few hours' sleep.*

Okay, it was a little flirty, but what the heck. Three little dots appeared on the screen.

Hotshot: *I need sleep too. I really do like you, Juliette, and want to see you.*

That made her pause because he sounded serious. Hard to tell in a text, but still. She shook her head and replied.

Juliette: *Sleep well, hotshot.*

She hated thinking he was doing anything more than flirting since he had a girlfriend who worked at the clinic. She'd been at the job only for a couple of months so there was still staff she didn't know, but she couldn't think of anyone Mateo had paid special attention to.

Only able to consume half of the burrito, she wrapped the remainder in the foil and put it in the refrigerator for later. In her bedroom, she pulled down the blackout shades and shuffled to the bathroom to brush her teeth.

Turning off the light, she crawled under the covers and was instantly asleep.

CHAPTER THREE

Mateo cut through the parking lot behind Easy Money. Cyndi Lomeli spotted him and met him at the back door, which had been outlined with a multicolored string of lights.

"Oh Mateo, I heard you were injured on the job. And on your ass too."

He'd given up correcting people. "Ass is fine."

"I'd say mighty fine." Cyndi gave him a flirtatious wink.

Some people dismissed Cyndi as a dumb blonde, and she had a reputation for being open and free with her affections. She also had a huge heart and a sweet friendliness that drew men like bees to clover.

Not that Mateo had ever been one of those men. They might flirt, but he thought neither one of them wanted to risk their amicable friendship over a hookup.

He opened the door and the sound of live music spilled out.

"Just listen to that music. It sounds like Owen booked a good band tonight." Cyndi took Mateo's arm as they walked the short hall past the restrooms and into the bar area.

"Oh my gosh, look how pretty Owen decorated everything. It's so festive." Cyndi sighed happily.

With Thanksgiving behind them, folks around town had gone nuts with the holiday spirit. Main Street was lit up with strings of lights, and shop owners had set up displays along the boardwalk. There were Santas with reindeer, baby Jesus in the manger, menorahs with blinking stars of David, and the red, black, and green of Kwanzaa.

One shop with a Mother Nature vibe displayed decorations made of acorns and pine cones. The people of Sisters had the biggest hearts, and everyone had a place.

Inside Easy Money, holiday lights twinkled and glittery snowflakes and globes hung from the ceiling. Boughs of greenery sparkled behind the bar. Even the windows had been decorated. "I think this is Keeley's influence. Before they got together, Owen would put up a string of lights and call it good."

"You're probably right. Schoolteachers are good at this kind of thing. It makes the holidays special, you know?"

They hung their coats on a rack and when he turned, he spotted Juliette Kirk sitting at the bar. Their gazes locked. Bam. His heart gave a hard lurch.

It was the same every time he saw her. Her gaze shifted to Cyndi and back to his and he could see her adding two plus two and reaching five. Gage Landry sat next to her, his body turned toward hers.

Hell no, that wasn't happening.

"I love this song, Matty. Dance with me?"

Distracted, he brought his attention back to Cyndi who turned eyes thick with mascara on him.

He shook his head. "The beat is too fast in my current condition. Stitches in the ass, remember?"

In the past couple days, the pain from the injury had diminished greatly, enough that he'd stopped taking pain meds. He thought he could go back to work, but still had another week off duty.

Cyndi pretend-pouted. Carter Benoit, a burly rancher from the next town over, approached. Mateo had an inkling Carter had a thing for Cyndi so he greeted the man with a handshake and gladly stepped aside so he could lead Cyndi to the dance floor.

Behind the bar, Owen filled orders, his attention returning frequently to the woman ensconced in the back corner booth, papers and a laptop spread in front of her.

Keeley Montaigne taught at the local high school and liked to find a spot in her fiancé's bar to grade papers or whatever else teachers did.

Mateo guessed it was one way to spend time together. He'd already received an invitation to their spring wedding. He wanted Juliette to be his plus one, but was waiting to ask until he had a better idea she'd say yes. Her giving him that kiss at the ER made him hopeful.

Mateo wanted to join her at the bar, but had a stop to make first. He made his way across the room, waving when people called out to him. He approached a booth where the mix of voices and laughter made him smile.

Four women sat with frosty margaritas in front of them and a giant plate of loaded nachos in the middle of the table. Damn those looked good. "You ladies behaving over here?"

"Behaving is for the birds. What we're doing is having fun." The woman who spoke rose to her feet and took his cheeks in her hands before giving him a smacking kiss. "How's your butt, my handsome boy?"

"Butt's fine, Mom." Antonia Reynoso wore a long flowing skirt paired with cowgirl boots and dangly earrings. "Thanks for bringing a vat of pozole. As always, it's the best."

"It's your favorite so that's what I brought."

He chatted with her friends until Antonia returned to her seat, waving him away. "We can't talk about you if you're standing here. Go have fun with people your own age."

He turned to do just that. His butt wouldn't tolerate sitting on a barstool, and since Juliette was at the end of the bar, he moved to a spot beside her and leaned against the wall. He gave Gage a steady look that held a hint of warning.

Gage, being the intuitive guy he was, raised a brow and smirked.

Juliette looked at Mateo from under her eyelashes. After much internal debate, he'd finally determined her eyes were gray, a mysterious smoky gray without a hint of blue. They'd caught him the first time he'd seen her.

The other thing that caught him? The mass of curling red hair she was constantly trying to tame into a ponytail or bun. His current sex fantasy involved Juliette naked and lying in his bed, wild springy curls on her head matched by wild springy curls farther down.

Tonight, she'd not only caught her hair in a ponytail, but had it pinned back at the sides. He tugged on a curl that had come loose.

"How you doin', doc?"

"I'm not a doctor, and I'm doing fine." There was that tone again. She batted his hand away. "How are you healing?"

"Good. It doesn't hurt anymore." That was mostly true.

"Is that why you're not sitting?"

He shrugged. "Stitches pull when I sit too much so I try to stand." His gaze caught hers. "I want to be by you, so this is where I am."

"You and Cyndi make a cute couple."

He grinned, glad he could set her straight. "We're friends, but not a couple. We ran into each other in the parking lot. I think Carter is finally making his move. He's had his eye on her for a while."

The music changed and Owen moved around the end of the bar, and crossed the room. He took Keeley's hand, drawing her to her feet to lead her to the dance floor. Keeley's face shone as Owen pulled her into his arms.

Juliette tilted her head as she watched them. "Aw. They're so good together."

"Yeah, they are." Mateo leaned forward so only she could hear him. "The band's playing a slow song. I can manage slow with my stitches. Dance with me?"

He caught her hesitation, but she pushed her empty glass aside and slid off the stool. He took her hand and felt something dark inside him light up when he pulled her close. With one hand holding hers and the other on her shoulder, her body swaying with his, they danced to the old classic "Stand By Me."

When the music transitioned to something faster paced, he continued to hold her close, not willing to give up the moment. "You ever had Easy Money's loaded nachos?"

She shook her head.

He raised his brows in mock amazement, continuing to sway with her despite the faster tempo. "You've lived here five months and haven't had Easy Money's loaded nachos?"

"I confess, it's true."

"Let's get a booth and we can share an order. After, we can follow it up with the famous cheesecake. Or, if you prefer, we can go to the restaurant side and get something fancier."

"I told you I won't date you, Mateo." She said the words but those smoky eyes of hers were locked on his lips, and suddenly all he could think about was kissing her.

Clearing his throat, he said, "I'd like to know why since I like you a lot. But this isn't a date. It's two friends running into each other at a neighborhood bar and deciding to share a meal."

She smiled up at him and said, "Okay, friend, I'd like that."

In that moment, he felt like the luckiest guy on the planet.

They left the dance floor as a group came through the hall, the roundly pregnant women the community had started calling the Triad, with their husbands. Delaney and Walker, Emery and Shane, Cam and Sawyer—he was friends with all of them, some since elementary school.

Juliette seemed to know them as well so they were absorbed into the group and when everyone had decided to push tables together, he saw his plan of having Juliette to himself evaporating under the onslaught of friendship.

Gage sat at the opposite end of the table, which was fine with Mateo.

Delaney sank into a chair with a groan. She pushed against the mound in her belly. "For the last month, this kid didn't let me breathe. Now that she's dropped, I can breathe, but have zero bladder capacity."

Mateo draped his arm on the back of Juliette's chair, leaning slightly toward her. When she narrowed her eyes, he gave her an innocent look. "Sitting this way helps ease my painful stitches."

She laughed. "Poor baby."

"Exactly." He shifted his attention to the group. "You all look ready to pop."

"I feel ready to pop." Cameron shifted in her seat. "There is no position I can sit or sleep in that's comfortable." She narrowed her eyes at her husband. "But the lieutenant here sleeps like the dead. Not fair."

Sawyer brought her hand to his lips for a kiss. "I'm banking sleep so I'm ready for when the little guy is up all night."

"It's nice you're all having an evening out before the babies are born," Keeley said. She sat at the end of the joined tables. Owen stood behind her chair, hands on her shoulders as she leaned back against him.

"Have you seen how much baby stuff we have?" Walker looked shell-shocked. "We're still unpackaging things from the baby shower. The baby's room is full. Our room is full. How does a tiny human require so much stuff?"

"That's one of the mysteries of the modern world," Shane remarked.

"We had the best triple baby shower ever, but yeah, there's a lot."

"I think half the town turned out," Cam said. "It's nice to get support from so many people in the community." She turned to Mateo. "The fire department was awesome to get us all car seats."

"We're all invested in the well-being of every one of you. We're happy to do it." Despite what he'd told Juliette, the stitches bothered him, and he shifted to ease the pull.

Sawyer tipped his head at Mateo. "Thanks, man."

Jen, Owen's assistant manager, arrived with a platter overflowing with the loaded nachos. "Make room, folks, there's two more of these coming out." Owen went to the kitchen and brought out the other two platters while Jen returned with baskets of chips.

"This baby better move her butt to give my stomach room. If I can't have a margarita, I'm having my fill of ooey-gooey loaded nachos." Delaney passed out the plates, and in minutes conversation quieted as they all chowed down.

Draining his beer, Sawyer set his bottle on the table. He eyed Mateo. "I got your text earlier."

At the questioning look from the others, Mateo addressed the group. "There's a long-range model from the National Weather Service that's showing the potential for a significant rain event late next week. Y'all will be popping out babies about then so we need to keep an eye on how the forecast evolves."

"What are you worried about? That we'd be driving to the clinic in a storm?" asked Emery, expression worried.

Owen pulled up a chair beside Keeley, who scooped guacamole onto a chip and offered it to him.

Mateo didn't want to alarm anyone, but being forewarned meant being prepared. "If it's a significant rainmaker, we're concerned about flooding, roads being washed out, and power outages. We'll be monitoring the forecast and sending alerts to those who have the app." He paused. "You all follow Sisters FD on social media?"

Heads nodded and he went on, "The storm track could move north or south of us, but making a plan is a good idea in case it comes our way."

"What kind of plan?" Delaney asked.

"The fire department advises anyone with health concerns, and that includes expectant mothers, to have a plan in place for emergency situations, including if they're stranded and need to deliver at home."

Nervous looks zipped around the table.

"Like I said, it's early days and this storm might never materialize. I don't want to freak anyone out, but we also don't want to be caught by surprise."

CHAPTER FOUR

Juliette walked out of the bar with Mateo. It'd been fun to be included and spend the evening with the friend group. She glanced around the parking lot. "Where's your truck?" Mateo's fire-engine red truck was hard to miss.

"At home. I only live a few blocks away so I walked."

"Come to think of it, I never see your truck here."

He shrugged. "My brother-in-law was killed by a drunk driver when I was a teenager. He and my sister had twin boys and overnight she became a single mom. It had an impact. If I'm having a drink, I don't drive."

"Oh, that's horrible. I'm so sorry for your family. How's your sister now?"

"Good. She's remarried, and Greg is a good man. The boys graduate high school this year."

He stopped her in the glow of a light post.

The night was cold and their breath frosted the air.

He had a way of looking at her that made her feel like she was all he saw. The warning voice in her head telling her she didn't want to be part of the Mateo Reynoso harem was getting dimmer because she simply wasn't seeing it.

Maybe she'd misjudged him. He was friendly, but like with Cyndi, it seemed he kept things casual. That said, she'd distinctly heard reference to a girlfriend when he'd been brought to the ER, and cheaters were the worst.

Frustrated with herself, she asked, "Do you want a ride home? Is your butt okay if you sit in a car?"

"I'm fine. Thank god the stitches are coming out tomorrow. But yeah, I'd like a ride."

They crossed to her Subaru, and she used the fob to unlock the doors. Pulling out of the parking lot, he directed her to turn off Main and onto a quiet street with older ranch-style homes. When she parked in his driveway, they sat quietly.

"Tell me why you don't like to be called doc."

She gave him a startled look. "Because I'm not a doctor." The light from his stoop shone in his eyes.

"Understood, but there's something more there."

She bit off a sigh. "It's a thing in my family. My parents, my brother, they're not only doctors, they're highly successful and at the top of their fields. My brother, Oliver, is a brilliant surgeon and recently took a position at Stanford, where he'll teach as well as practice medicine."

She gazed out the windshield. "We're from San Diego and my father has been chief of surgery and my mom's been head of oncology at a medical center there for the past decade. Recently, they've been lured to the East Coast where, like Oliver, they'll have academic as well as medical posts."

"Impressive, but I don't see that being the direction you wanted."

"No, and no matter how hard they push me, I still don't want it. For Conrad and Barbara Kirk, having a daughter who's a lowly PA is embarrassing. They say I'm undervaluing myself and not reaching my full potential.

"Mom called this afternoon with the goal of persuading me to move east with them. She assured me with her and Dad's status, they can get me into the med school where they'll be teaching. I'd have to take the MCAT, but I'll be accepted. Nepotism at its finest."

"What does your brother say."

"Fuck 'em."

Mateo gave a bark of laughter. "He's on your side."

"A hundred percent. He pursued medicine to the level he has because it's all he ever wanted. He knows I love being a PA and wants me to be happy. He helps run interference with our parents."

"That's good. I'm glad you have an ally. I'll stop calling you 'doc.'"

His understanding, as much as his thumb rubbing over her palm, made her feel warm inside. She liked sitting in the shadowed light and talking with him.

"Why Sisters?"

She studied him. "Why all the questions?"

"I want to know you before I convince you to get naked with me."

She laughed. "That's direct."

"Why Sisters?" he repeated.

"I went to Camp Tioga. It's not far from here. I went every summer from age ten and became a counselor when I was in college. Some of my best friends are from there. I fell in love with the Sierras, so when a position came available at the clinic, I applied."

Something in her expression must've given her away because his hand tightened around hers and he said, "There's more."

She sighed. "I guess I was also looking for community. I want to live someplace where people care about each other. Sisters feels like that to me."

"Sisters has its problems like all places, but at its core are amazing people who look out for one another."

"I'm glad I ended up here."

"I'm glad too." He laced their fingers together.

"Did you go to camp?"

"Yeah, in San Diego."

"Really? What kind of camp?"

"A camp for Fire Explorers. You know, kids who want to be firefighters. We stayed in dorms at a university and learned CPR and first aid and basic firefighting techniques. All cool enough, but the best part was surfing lessons and snorkeling. It was pretty great."

He raised a hand and tugged her hairpins free, then pulled off the band of her ponytail.

"You've got a thing for my hair."

"Got that right."

She could *feel* her hair spring out in corkscrews around her head. "Now you've gone and set the beast free."

"I love your hair."

"You're not the one who has to deal with it. I've been thinking about getting a Brazilian blowout."

"A Brazilian what?"

Not sure how they got on the topic of hair treatment, she replied anyway, "It's a way of smoothing out the curls that's not as harsh as having it chemically straightened."

"Good god, why would you do that? Why is it women with straight hair want to curl it, and women with curly hair want it straightened? I guess that applies to dudes too, but your hair is beautiful as it is." In the dim light she could barely make out his crooked grin. "I'm kind of obsessed with it."

His expression turned serious. Suddenly the inside of the car felt overly warm and she thought she should roll down a window.

He raised his gaze to hers and the heat ratcheted up higher, and she wondered if she could be burned alive with just a look.

With a hand cupped lightly behind her neck, he brought his head closer. He paused and she knew he was giving her a chance to back away. Suddenly she was tired of being cautious, tired of not knowing if he kissed as well as she thought he would. Tired of wondering if the spark she felt between them would burn hot or fizzle out and die.

Leaning in to him, she kissed him. The sizzle of electric shock had her jerking back, eyes wide. "What was that?"

His grin flashed. "That, sweetheart, was chemistry."

Then his mouth was on hers and she had the same buzzing reaction, but this time she didn't let go.

His lips moved over hers, his hand moving inside her coat to stroke along her rib cage, the other spearing into the curls he liked so much.

Their tongues tangled, and she absorbed the taste of the whiskey he'd drunk earlier in the evening. She wanted more whiskey flavor, more chemistry, more Mateo.

She grabbed the front of his coat and yanked him closer.

He gave a shaky laugh.

"I could develop an addiction to your mouth. Don't stop kissing me," she growled.

He obliged, his mouth moving over hers with focused intensity. Fireworks sparkled behind her eyelids. When they finally broke apart, he leaned back against the car door, breathing heavily.

The spark between them fizzling out and dying was no longer a worry.

He scrubbed a hand over his face. "I feel like a teenager making out in the car. I'd ask you to come in, but as much as I'd like that, I think we both need to process."

She stared out the windshield. "Okay."

"Hey, look at me." When she did, he went on. "I don't want a casual hookup. Not with you. I want more than that, and I don't want to mess it up. I'll call you in the morning."

Would he say that if he had a girlfriend? Suddenly tired of it, she opened her mouth to ask him, but he was already out of the car. Circling the hood, he tapped on her window.

When she lowered the glass, he leaned in and caught her lips in another kiss that forced all other thoughts from her mind.

She was in deep trouble, and wasn't even sure she wanted to be rescued.

***

Glad to be working days, Juliette climbed the stairs to her apartment, weighted down by grocery bags she'd been determined to carry in one trip. The front Mateo had warned could bring heavy rain was on track to hit their part of the Sierras head on. Storms typically dumped their rain on the western slopes where Sisters was located and, because of the rain shadow effect, left the eastern side of the mountains much drier.

The wind coming ahead of the front whipped her hair, today contained by a wide headband. Pine needles rained down from a giant tree towering over the building's two stories.

Recently, she'd been weighing whether to find somewhere else to live. Maybe she should make the leap and buy a house, something small with a yard. She'd like to get a dog.

With her door locked behind her, she turned on the oven and put away the groceries in her tiny kitchen. A gust of wind shook the windows.

The small apartment complex was right on Main Street, and her unit was on the street side so traffic noise was an issue. She shared a wall with Winston, which wouldn't be a problem except that during the summer he habitually smoked weed on his side of their adjoining balconies, which meant if she wanted to use her balcony, she could expect the overpowering skunky smell.

Cooler temperatures had forced Winston inside, and now the odor came through the vents.

With the oven up to temp she slipped in a spinach and feta quiche she'd picked up at the store. She'd have enough time to take a shower while her dinner warmed.

One good thing about the apartment: she never ran out of hot water.

Lathering her hair while steam billowed, she reviewed the back-to-back-to-back appointments she'd had with the Triad. Emery'd experienced no more bleeding, so Juliette felt she was safe there. Delaney had some serious contractions going on, but they were Braxton Hicks, and thus unproductive.

Juliette rinsed the shampoo and applied conditioner.

Cam's pregnancy had been easygoing. She'd managed to avoid the nausea the others had contended with, and nothing unusual had come up.

Due dates were stacked up for the week ahead, Monday, Wednesday, and Friday. A schedule the babies weren't likely to abide by. The only thing Juliette had concerns about was the weather causing problems. As long as all the team members were on hand, everything would be okay. But Doctor Tran lived down the mountain in Sacramento, and Anayah lived a half-hour drive away in Grass Valley.

A loud cracking sound came from outside. The wind had grown even more ferocious, and she was a little worried it could peel the roof off the apartment building.

She'd stepped out of the shower with a towel wrapped around her torso, and bent forward to wrap another towel around her hair.

The creaking sounded louder. She stood straight, clutching the towel, the hairs on her neck prickling.

Then a tremendous crash shook the building and she pitched backward. The entire wall of her shower disappeared as a giant tree branch ripped the wall open.

The curtain rod, tile, and debris from the tree went flying. Juliette felt herself falling and her head smashing into something solid.

With a groan she dropped into darkness.

CHAPTER FIVE

The call came over the radio and Mateo immediately hit the lights and sirens. He knew that address. A tree branch had broken through the roof and wall of an apartment building. Status of the occupants was unknown.

The rescue squad tires squealed as they took the turn onto Main.

"Taking it a little fast there, Matty." Davey was riding shotgun, with two crew members in the backseat.

"That's Juliette's apartment."

"Oh shit. Do what you need to do."

They pulled into the apartment parking lot, first on scene. Swinging out of the cab, he heard the siren and deep horn of the aerial ladder truck still blocks away.

Mateo pulled on his turnout gear while assessing the situation. A branch as big around as he was had sheared off a pine tree and ripped through the back corner of the end unit.

He pulled on his helmet and grabbed a Halligan bar. "Get the gas shut off," he told the others. "I'm going up."

"Wait, man. What about protocol?" This came from Marco, a rookie who got nervous whenever he had to think outside the box.

"I'm going up." Mateo raced to the stairs, taking them two at a time.

Using the bar, he forced open the door. He'd never been in her apartment, but he knew it was Juliette's. He'd looked it up when he'd asked Davey to deliver the breakfast burrito, and had driven by because he'd wanted to know where she lived.

"Juliette!" When that got him nothing, he called again. "Juliette!"

He didn't smell gas, which was a good sign as he made his way to the back corner where the tree branch had hit.

He pushed open a door and his heart stopped cold in his chest. Juliette lay on the floor, a towel loose around her head and another beneath her. Pale, pale skin and her absolute stillness had panic clutching at his throat.

She was only feet from the shower enclosure where the tree limb had torn open the wall like a can opener.

He dropped to his knees and forced himself to conduct a thorough assessment as he'd been trained.

With his fingers on her carotid, he felt her pulse, strong and steady. Her chest rose and fell as she breathed. Relief threatened to overwhelm him, but he had to pull it together.

He lifted an eyelid and used a penlight on one eye, then the other. Equal and responsive. He moved his hands over her body to locate injuries, and found a lump at the back of her head. Judging from her location, she likely hit it on the sink.

He radioed that he'd found one occupant in need of medical care.

Juliette stirred, opening her eyes and blinking at him. His heart rate leveled down enough that it no longer felt like he was on the verge of a heart attack.

"Mateo?" She clutched his hand.

"Yeah, baby. I got you." He brushed her hair back from her forehead, his hand not entirely steady. "Can you sit up?"

She nodded and winced as he helped her to a sitting position. That's when she realized she was naked, and tried to pull up the towel. She shivered as a gust of wind blew through the opening in the wall.

He heard his team inside the unit and whipped off the outer shell of his turnout gear and wrapped it around her.

He spoke into his radio. "Bring in an emergency blanket." Then he said to Juliette, "You've got a lump on the back of your head. The skin's not broken. You hurt anywhere else?"

She frowned, then shook her head and winced again. "I don't think so."

"Let's get you standing then we'll see about getting out of here."

Davey appeared in the door, shaking the folds out of the mylar blanket.

"Eyes averted, pal," Mateo growled.

"I need my clothes. Or my robe. It's hanging on the back of the door."

Once she was on her feet, he held her arm to keep her steady. Grabbing her robe, he helped her arms through the sleeves. With the belt tied, he wrapped the emergency blanket around her again. Shaking debris out of a hand towel, he used it to squeeze the excess moisture from her dripping hair.

"Let's go."

He pulled on his turnout coat and took her down the hall. She still seemed shaky, so he motioned for the stretcher.

"I don't need a stretcher."

"Yeah, you do."

"I'm fine. It's only a bump on my head."

"Sweetheart, you're going to let me do my job. We're taking you down the stairs on a stretcher because that's the safest way to get you out of here. The ambulance will take you to the clinic, where you'll get a concussion assessment. If they want to keep you overnight, that's what'll happen."

When she opened her mouth to argue, he pressed his finger to her lips. "You're a PA. You know how this goes. I saw your backpack upstairs. I'll grab that. Anything else you want? Your place is going to be red tagged."

She closed her eyes and sighed. "Of course it is." Her shoulders slumped. "I have a really nice quiche in the oven."

"I'll take care of it. How about this, the guys and I will grab whatever we can: clothes, electronics, personal items. The rest will have to wait until the building inspector deems it safe. The damage doesn't look structural and I don't see a danger of collapse, so you'll likely be able to get the rest of your things later."

"There's a plastic box with my important papers on my bookshelf. Can you get that?"

"Sure thing. Once I have your stuff, I'll catch up with you at the clinic."

The team got her on the stretcher and fastened the safety straps while he turned off the oven. He grabbed a handhold and helped carry her out, Juliette looking pale and vulnerable wrapped in the shiny blanket.

They reached the bottom of the stairs as the ambulance turned into the parking lot.

Scott and Nicole brought up the gurney.

Scott elbowed him. "Hey, man, it's your girl."

"It is. Concussion is likely. Bruise on the back of the head. Take good care of her."

They transferred her to the gurney, replacing the mylar with a drape. He bent over her and pressed a kiss to her forehead. "I'll be there as soon as I can. You're safe now, sweetheart."

***

Juliette sat on the exam table and fidgeted. Her head hurt and she'd been diagnosed with a mild concussion, which she knew how to manage. She wanted to be discharged, but where would she go? She no longer had an apartment.

Anayah had run through the assessment. Yes, Juliette knew her name, the date, who was president. She knew she was at the clinic.

Where she was fuzzy was the details of how she'd ended up on the floor of her bathroom with part of her wall gone.

Putting away her groceries and sliding the quiche into the oven was crystal clear, as was enjoying a hot shower. But what happened after that was a blank until Mateo was leaning over her and she was lying on the floor.

Naked.

Damn.

Any idea of the first time Mateo seeing her naked involving sexy lingerie and flattering lighting evaporated under the reality that she'd been unconscious with wet hair.

Then there was the little detail that the branch had come down where her shower had been. Even with the memory lapse, she realized she'd been in that shower only minutes before. She could've been killed.

The thought was sobering.

She stared at the ceiling. Should she call her parents? No, it would be better to call Oliver and have him tell their parents. But she didn't have her phone.

Where was she going to live? Where was she going to store her possessions until she found a place? She couldn't quiet the thoughts even knowing she needed to stay calm to help her brain heal.

But Scott's words to Mateo echoed in her sore head: "Hey, man, it's your girl."

***

Juliette was ready to check herself out by the time Anayah returned.

"Hey, girlfriend, Doc Hanson says as long as you observe concussion protocols you don't need to stay overnight. Listen, with the storm coming, the town council is paying for motel rooms for clinic staff and first responders who aren't local. I already have a room. You and I can share, and that way I can keep an eye on you."

"Thanks, Anayah, but I got her." Mateo entered the room, Juliette's backpack slung over his shoulder and a plastic bag hanging from his hand. He set them next to her on the bed. His gaze traveled over Juliette like he was absorbing every detail, which made her heart flutter.

Anayah put her hands on her hips. "I think I'll need the particulars before I give over my good friend with a concussion into the hands of a firefighter, capable though he may be."

"Gotcha." Mateo smiled easily, but Juliette was getting better at reading him. This was important to him, and he wasn't above using charm to get his way.

He gripped Juliette's knee, his thumb stroking her leg through the blanket. "If she's willing, Juliette will come home with me. I'm off tonight. Mom's already at my place stocking the refrigerator and changing sheets in the guest bedroom. They were clean, but she seems to think not clean enough.

"The rescue squad helped get everything they could out of Juliette's apartment. Her things are in bins and being stored in my garage." His gaze found Juliette's. "Your keys were in your backpack, so Davey drove your car to my house. I know it's a presumption that you'd want our help, sweetheart, but we didn't have much time. The department is preparing for this storm and there's another structure damaged by a fallen tree, so we've been busy."

"Was anyone hurt?" she asked.

"Luckily, no."

With brows raised, Anayah turned to Juliette. "Are you okay going with Mateo?"

Juliette didn't know if she felt dazed from being hit on the head, or from Mateo taking charge. She rubbed a thumb on her forehead to ease the ache the Tylenol had yet to touch. "Are you sure, Mateo? You're busy and I can stay at the motel."

He turned to Anayah. "Would you mind if I have a private word with our friend Juliette to convince her she should let me take care of her?"

Anayah grinned. "Sure thing. Call if you need me." She left the room, closing the door behind her.

"Mateo, I—"

He held up his hand, shaking his head. "A minute, Jules. I need a damn minute." He bent over her, a hand brushing the side of her face. "You scared the shit out of me, and I have to convince myself you're really okay." He pressed his lips to her forehead. "You're going to be fine." He muttered the words like he was trying to convince himself.

Straightening, he reached for the plastic bag and withdrew two paper plates covered with aluminum foil. He handed her one with a plastic fork. "Coke, water, or Sprite?"

"Water."

"Back in a minute."

She lifted the foil to reveal a large wedge of the spinach and feta quiche she'd had warming in her oven. He came back with two chilled water bottles and set one on the rolling bed tray.

She swallowed against the emotion tightening her throat.

"Thank you, Mateo. Thank you for everything."

He arranged the plates on the tray between them and sat on the bed next to her legs.

"At some point, Juliette, you'll realize I'll do anything for you." While she was processing that statement, he pointed his fork. "Eat."

Suddenly ravenous, she took a bite of quiche. It was barely warm and the crust was soft, but it tasted delicious.

Mateo had been thoughtful and she was having a hard time keeping her perspective.

When someone said they'd do anything for you and acted on it in the best way possible when you needed them the most? It felt impossible to guard her heart.

She'd thought she'd been in love before, or at least in deep like, only to find the man who'd asked her to marry him wasn't what she thought he was. Wasn't what he pretended to be. Her feelings for Mateo were both richer and more complicated.

Mateo's gaze snagged hers. She took a bracing breath and asked the question that could no longer go unanswered. "Who's your girl, Mateo?"

CHAPTER SIX

Mateo paused, water bottle at his lips. Then slowly, he set it down. His eyes glinted with a hint of vulnerability. "You are."

She coughed, thumping her chest before recovering.

"You okay?"

"Um, fine. When Scott wheeled you into the ER and covered your butt, he'd said your girl wouldn't see anything. He was referring to me?"

"Yeah. He knew I have a thing for you, but it's not like I assumed anything. It was his way of messing with me."

"I thought you had a girlfriend." At his dumbfounded look, she forged ahead. "Here at the clinic. I was trying to figure out who your girlfriend was, but I couldn't remember seeing you talking to anyone in particular."

"Except you."

"Yeah, except me. I'm only now realizing that."

He took her hand. "I've been crushing on you since we first met. But you staying at my house? Don't think I'm maneuvering you. If you're more comfortable with Anayah, that's fine. I want you with me, but you feeling safe and comfortable is more important."

"Mateo, I'd like to stay with you."

His smile beamed like the sun. "Good. That's damn good."

***

Thunder rolled overhead and Juliette leaned against Mateo. They were lounging on the couch in his living room, the lights were off as part of concussion care, and a fire in the gas fireplace made the room cozy. She'd called Oliver, who'd insisted on talking with Mateo before he'd been satisfied she was in good hands.

Fairy lights twinkled from greenery on the mantel, and a small potted evergreen in the corner had a star on top and small ornaments hanging from its branches. A couple of wrapped presents sat below it.

"I like your decorations. It's hard to believe Christmas is less than a week away." She tilted her head to study his profile. "How do you celebrate the holidays?"

She felt him shrug. "I'm not religious. To me the holidays are about tradition and celebrating family and friends, and letting them know you love and value them."

"I like that."

"How does your family celebrate?"

"When Oliver and I were kids, it seemed more about family, but in the past few years my parents seem more interested in hosting and attending parties. They spend time with people I don't even know."

She lifted a shoulder. "Oliver and I make time to see each other. He's got a new girlfriend. I think he really likes her, and her family invited him to spend Christmas with them. They invited me too, which is kind of them, but I'm staying in Sisters. I'll be spending my time looking for a place to live."

She thought he was about to say something, but he seemed to change his mind; instead, he pressed a kiss to her temple.

With the living room curtains open, they watched lightning fork across the sky followed by thunder echoing off the mountains. Rain started with a few fat drops hitting the roof and within minutes became a torrent.

"Wow. Mountain weather is intense," she murmured.

"I'm glad you're here with me." His arms tightened and she snuggled against him, reveling in the feeling of being right where she was supposed to be.

***

The sound of rain beating on the roof, along with the howling wind, brought Mateo out of sleep. He lay quietly studying Juliette's profile in the half light of early morning. Everything in him yearned for her and for the future he could see for them together. She stirred and stretched, then shifted to gaze at him with sleepy eyes and wild curls framing her face.

"I can't believe we slept together without making love."

He traced a finger across her cheekbones. "We will. But you have a concussion, so it's not now."

His finger dipped to her collarbone. "I was engaged once." He hadn't intended to say the words. They simply spilled out of his mouth.

"Yeah? Me too. What happened?"

He turned onto his back. "Her name was Naomi. I loved her. Or maybe I convinced myself I loved her. She said she loved me, but in the end, she didn't. Not enough anyway." He shrugged. "She backed out two days before the wedding."

"Oh Mateo. That had to be devastating."

"It was. At the time. Now I know I dodged a bullet so I can't really be mad about it. Better then than three years later."

"Kinda makes it hard to trust someone though. At least that's been my experience."

He laughed. "Pair that with my prom date sleeping with another dude the night after the dance, and you could be right. It's taken me a while to put that aside." He paused, then asked, "What happened with you?"

She took his hand, outlining it with the tip of her finger. "My parents had a yearly holiday party at our house for the surgical residents at the hospital. Brady was one of them. I was in my last year of college. I had finals the next day and didn't want to attend, but my parents insisted.

"Brady made a beeline for me when I came down the stairs. He wooed me, I guess you'd call it. It was a whirlwind romance, and before I knew it, he'd asked my father for my hand in marriage. The next day he was down on one knee with the most stunning diamond ring I'd ever seen."

"Did you love him?"

"No, but I liked him a lot and thought I could love him. Eventually."

"You said yes."

"I did. People don't think about the pressure when someone is down on their knee in front of a crowd. My parents were thrilled, and I was so tired of always being a disappointment to them so I went along with it."

"They thought you were a disappointment?" He couldn't keep the incredulity out of his voice. Whatever had happened in his life, he'd always known his parents loved him unconditionally. "What did Oliver say?"

"He took me down to the beach so we'd be out of earshot of Brady and our parents and grilled me. He could see I wasn't head over heels. When I said I was sticking with it, he made me promise to have a long engagement."

"Ha. Smart guy."

"Yeah. It was a long enough engagement for me to catch Brady doing it against the wall with the pool guy."

She said it offhandedly, but Mateo was pissed. "Fucking asshole."

"To say the least. In fact, that's what I called Brady while he was pulling up his Tommy John boxers. Brady was yelling that I didn't understand the pressure he was under.

"Oliver came running and risked damaging his surgeon's hands by plowing a fist into Brady's face."

"Good for him."

"I think my parents were more disappointed with the breakup than I was."

"You had to be hurt."

"No permanent scars other than a low tolerance for cheaters and liars."

"Yet you fell for me."

"I fell, all right, but I never thought you were a cheater or a liar. You never promised me anything. Anayah and I figured you were a player."

He snorted. "You thought I was a man-whore, you mean. I've never slept around, and once I laid eyes on you, Juliette, you were all I could see."

The kiss started sweet, then heated fast.

He was struggling to remind himself she'd been diagnosed with a concussion only the night before when his phone rang.

He sat up, phone to his ear.

"Reynoso." He listened. "Okay, I'll be there. Thanks."

He turned to Juliette. "That was dispatch. The storm is causing flooding. I need to go in." A thought occurred and he picked up his phone again. "I'm calling Sawyer and Walker. If Mill Creek floods, they won't be able to get the women off the farm."

"Oh god, you're right." She got out of bed, pulling on her robe before heading to the bathroom.

Mateo called Sawyer and, after a tense conversation, hung up the phone. Juliette came in as Mateo was grabbing his clothes for the shower.

"Cam's water broke. She and Sawyer are on their way to the clinic. Delaney was having regular contractions, so she and Walker are already there.

"Sawyer got a call from Shane. He and Emery are on their way into town because he didn't want to get cut off if Mill Creek floods."

"Wow. Okay. I need to get to the clinic."

He took her shoulders, giving her a searching look. "How's your head?"

"Sore where the bruise is. Otherwise, fine. No headache. I need to get to the clinic. We could have three women in labor at the same time. I hope Doctor Tran stayed in town."

CHAPTER SEVEN

Mateo insisted on driving Juliette to the clinic, arguing she'd be safer in his four-wheel-drive lifted truck. She was glad he'd insisted as rain and wind buffeted the vehicle, and Mateo steered around debris in the road.

At the clinic he parked next to the ambulance bay. He reached behind the seat and brought out an SFD hat he placed on her head. With a poncho draped over both of them, they ran for cover under the overhang.

Entering the clinic through the sliding doors, they stood on the mat dripping. Anayah spotted them. "Thank the good lord you're here, girlfriend. We've got two in labor."

Juliette found a towel. "I'll be there in a minute."

She offered the towel and Mateo dried his face and draped the poncho over himself. She took the hat from her head and placed it on his. They stood with gazes locked on each other.

"I've got to go."

"Me too."

Neither of them moved.

"Be careful, Mateo."

"I will." He kissed her hard and fast and was out the door, chased by a gust of wind.

Juliette stopped at the nurse's station in the ER. Tupu, wearing a bracelet made of traditional Samoan red beads, handed her a granola bar.

"What's this for?"

"For you, my redheaded friend, who will need the nourishment. Labor and Delivery has now admitted the third member of the Triad."

"All three are in labor?"

"Indeed. We're light in the ER because the fine people of Sisters are heeding the storm warnings and staying home."

"Don't say that in front of Anayah. She's superstitious like that. I'll put my things in my locker, and I'll be ready in a minute."

Backpack stashed, she donned her lab coat and crossed to L&D. Anayah bustled out of a room and spotted Juliette.

"I'm assigned to L&D with you, at least for now. Doctor Tran is on her way. Doc Hanson is ill, but available for phone consults. We can call physicians from other departments if we need them, but none has performed a c-section."

"Then we'll hope Doctor Tran is here if we need one. Let's get started."

L&D had three rooms and the Triad occupied them all.

Juliette stepped into Room One where Delaney had a death grip on Walker's hand as she rode through a contraction. Juliette washed her hands and donned gloves. "Hey, Delaney. You and your sisters all coordinated on a delivery date, I see."

"Yeah, since we found out we were sisters, we do everything together." Delaney breathed deep as the contraction eased.

"When did contractions start?"

"Around ten p.m.," Walker responded. Even wearing hospital scrubs, he still had the bad boy vibe. Delaney sat up and he rubbed her shoulders. "They started to get regular around four. That's when we came in."

Juliette checked the whiteboard on the wall that showed dilation at five centimeters an hour before. She studied the monitor. "Your contractions are strong and the last one lasted a good fifty seconds. Let's take a peek and check the cervix."

Minutes later she removed her gloves. "You're moving along at seven centimeters so you're entering the transition phase. The epidural will help you get through the contractions."

Delaney lay back. "All good. Let's get going. I want to meet this little girl."

"How are you holding up, Walker?" Juliette asked. "You look a little pale."

"I never knew what women went through." He stared at his wife. "You're incredible, Laney."

"Back at you, babe."

"Keep up the good work," Juliette said, "I'm heading to door number two to check on my next patient."

She entered the next room to find the bed empty and Sawyer pacing. It never failed to touch her to see the toughest men, including the cop in front of her, struggling to hold themselves together and be strong for their wives during labor. She checked Cam's chart.

Sawyer stopped pacing and jammed his fingers through his hair. "Cam's using the bathroom. She says she wants to go for a walk. A freaking walk when she's having a baby. That doesn't sound safe."

Cam returned to the room and took her husband's hand.

"I understand your concern, but walking is good, Sawyer." Juliette was matter-of-fact. "It can help shorten labor and make contractions stronger. You two are still in early labor so you likely have hours yet. Taking walks will help pass the time. Cam's chosen not to get an epidural so she can move around safely for a while yet."

Sawyer gave her an assessing look like he was deciding whether to believe her, then nodded. "Okay."

"How are my sisters?" Cam asked.

"Delaney's progressing to transition. Walker looks more stressed than she does. Emery is my next stop."

Cam grinned. "I can't believe we're having our babies on the same day." She tugged Sawyer to the door. "Let's take that walk, big guy. We can stop and check on the others."

Juliette entered the next room to hear Emery laughing. Shane was looking over her shoulder at a tablet propped on her knees for a video call. Emery caught sight of Juliette and addressed the screen. "My friend and PA Juliette is here so I need to go, guys."

"Mom says she wants to say hi to the PA. Call back when you've got our niece."

Shane spoke to Juliette. "Em's family is checking in. Those two are her twin brothers."

Emery waved Juliette over as a middle-aged woman's face filled the screen. "Mom, this is Juliette. Juliette, this is my mom, Delilah."

"Hello, sweetie. I know my daughter wants an epidural, but I'm wondering if you've explained to her the benefits of natural childbirth."

"Nice to meet you, Delilah, and I'm glad we have a minute to chat." Juliette set about reassuring the worried mom. "Emery and I have spoken extensively about her options, and the choice is hers. Rest assured that an epidural doesn't make the birth any less natural."

Emery helped end the conversation and handed Shane the tablet. "Sorry to put you on the spot like that. Mom had strong opinions."

"I'm glad I could talk with her, and hopefully help her feel more comfortable with your choices."

"If it wasn't for the storm, I think my mom, stepdad, and brothers would all be here. I love them to death, but they can be a lot. Now," she smiled, "when can I get that epidural?"

"Let's see how you're doing first." Since a nurse had broken Emery's water, contractions had increased in frequency. Checking her, Juliette found her cervix dilated to three. "Let's wait on the epidural because that can sometimes slow labor. You're still in early labor and have a ways to go yet."

Juliette, who felt relief the sisters were doing well with no complications, went to the nurse's station where Shawna sat munching on cashews.

Anayah came through the double doors, followed by Owen and Keeley carrying large, insulated bags.

"Tell me that's food." Juliette's stomach rumbled. She and Mateo had downed quick bowls of cereal and she was keeping the granola bar from Tupu for an emergency. The day was going to be a long one, and could possibly extend into the night.

"It's lunch," Keeley announced. "Easy Money is closed today because of the storm. When we heard today was B-Day we thought we'd do our part to support the team. There are sandwiches for staff and the dads-to-be. We left half the spread in the ER break room."

The doors swung open again, Juliette's heart giving a hard thump when Mateo walked in. He headed right to her and cupped her shoulders while giving her a narrow-eyed assessment. "How's the head?"

"Good. I have a slight headache, but took some ibuprofen."

He stroked her cheek. "You take a break when you need it. I'm serious, Jules."

A whoop sounded from the hall and Cam waddled toward them, Sawyer telling her to slow down.

"Are you two officially together?" she asked.

Mateo's gaze snagged Juliette's as warmth flooded her cheeks. "Are we?" he asked quietly.

"I'd like to be."

"Me too." He pulled her into a hug while someone whistled. "You make me happy," he whispered. Loosening his hold, he spoke louder. "That's the good news."

Juliette's stomach dropped. "What's the bad news?"

"The highway into town is washed out. Two lanes have collapsed. The two that remain are unstable and have been closed."

"Shit. We're cut off." Sawyer frowned.

"Pretty much. The highway going east is open, but conditions are rough," Mateo informed them. "Repairs can't start until the storm has passed. It could be weeks before it reopens."

Keeley looked at Owen. "We won't get our food delivery."

"We'll be fine for a couple days with a modified menu." Owen tilted his head, his gaze speculative. "What do you say we take a vacation?"

"A vacation?"

"Yeah, princess, a vacation. You're on school break for a couple weeks. Food delivery is going to be expensive if it's coming over the mountains. Closing the bar isn't a bad idea. We can fly out of Reno. You and I can find an island in the Caribbean and sit in the sun."

"You better not be teasing me, Owen Hardesty, because I'm so in."

Owen grinned and turned to the group. "We'll set up the food and check in with the Triad. Then the princess and I have a vacation to plan."

Keeley beamed. "Enjoy the food and call us when we have babies."

"I am so, so jealous," Juliette muttered as Owen and Keeley disappeared into the break room with their bags.

"You and me both, girlfriend," Anayah agreed.

Mateo ate with them before rejoining his squad. Staff had received the news that Doctor Tran had been on the highway traveling up the mountain to Sisters before being turned back by the highway closure. The clinic would continue to be without an obstetrician with three women in labor.

Luckily, the day progressed with the normal rhythm of labor and delivery. At mid-afternoon, Delaney gave a mighty push and dark-haired Harper Jane was born.

Shawna quickly dried the squalling infant before placing her on her mother's chest with a blanket draped over both. Standing behind Delaney, Walker reached over her shoulder and gently stroked his daughter's head.

"She's beautiful," he whispered.

"Do you want to cut the umbilical cord, Dad?"

Walker looked startled, then grinned. "I'm a dad now." He kissed Delaney, then said, "Yeah, I'll cut it."

Two hours later, Juliette sat on her swivel chair in front of the patient while Shane coached Emery through another contraction. They were coming stronger and faster. Anayah had been called to the ER, but another nurse had been brought into L&D. Shawna prepped the bassinet for the newborn.

Emery rested between contractions. "How are my sisters?"

"Delaney and little Harper are perfect. Cam's labor is slow, but she's holding strong."

"They went with Harper? Oh, that's sweet." Her face contorted. "Another contraction is coming. I can do this."

"I want a good strong push, Emery."

Emery pushed through that one, then the ones following.

"You're doing great," Juliette murmured. "She's crowning."

"Is that her head? Is that our baby's head?" Shane looked dazed.

"That's her. Rest a second, Mama, until the next contraction."

When the contraction came, Emery pushed and her little girl was born.

"My god, darlin', you did it. That's our girl."

Juliette suctioned the baby's nose and mouth, gave her a vigorous rub when drying her, and was rewarded by a strong cry. With her daughter skin to skin, Emery cuddled her close. "Hello, Violet, welcome to the world. Say hi to your daddy."

Love simply glowed from the exhausted and relieved parents.

Once the placenta was delivered intact, Juliette left Shawna attending to mother and daughter, and took a minute to sit.

Two healthy babies, two sets of parents ready for their next stage in life.

She chewed on her granola bar as she sat tilted back in the chair, and closed her eyes. She smiled when strong fingers rubbed her temples. "Mm, that feels good."

"You didn't even see me. How do you know I'm not some random dude?"

"Because it's you." She opened her eyes to see her hotshot firefighter leaning over her from behind.

"I heard you're the boss delivering babies like there's nothing to it."

"The Triad is doing awesome. You want to meet a couple of adorable baby girls?"

"Hell yeah, I do, but in a few." He shifted to kneading the back of her neck. "How are you feeling?"

"I'm fine."

"No bullshitting, Jules. This is me."

"Okay. I have a headache. I'm dead tired. But mostly, I'm fine. Better now under your magic fingers."

"You should be home. I'll take you. You've had a concussion and need to rest."

"No, Mateo. I'll go home after Cam delivers."

It struck her that they were both referring to Mateo's house as home. Clearing her throat, she said, "Tell me how it is out there. Is it still raining?"

"Yeah, it's still raining. We've got flooded intersections and trees down. With the exception of the twenty-two-year-old I brought in who'd decided to take out his kayak in Mill Creek, which is ripping by the way, people have mostly stayed home and out of trouble. I think the new app the chief rolled out has worked well to communicate with citizens."

"What happened to the kayaker?"

"He got himself wedged between debris and support columns on a bridge. Davey and I rappelled down to get him. He's getting x-rayed for a crushed hand."

"You do dangerous work." She rose to her feet and turned to him. Tugging his head down, she kissed him. He pulled her flush against his body and took the kiss deeper.

"You two lovebirds need to break it up." Shawna's voice had them jolting apart. "Sister number three is getting close."

Mateo kissed her forehead. "I talked to my captain. He's calling in the rookie as a replacement for me. As soon as Cam delivers, I'm taking you home."

"But you're needed out there."

"You also need someone to take care of you. That's me. Marco wants the experience, and I'm on call if anything serious goes down. I've got a couple hours, then I'll be back." With another kiss, he was gone.

Two hours later, Cam was still pushing and nearing exhaustion. Sawyer was steady and supportive, but Juliette could see the tension in the lines of his face.

Anayah rubbed her lower back. "I think the baby is sunny side up."

"I think you're right."

"What's sunny side up?" Sawyer demanded.

"It means the baby is facing the mother's front instead of her back which is the optimal position for delivery."

"Do you want to try to rotate him?"

Juliette considered Anayah's suggestion. "Let's give her a couple more pushes and see how he does." She checked the monitor. "Another one's coming. You ready for this, Cam?"

"I can do it."

Sawyer dropped his head to his wife's, eyes closed. Then he straightened and gripped her hand, murmuring words of encouragement as she pushed.

"Good job, Cam. That was productive. Let's try again."

The next contraction came hard and fast. Cam bore down through that one, then the next.

"Baby's crowning. You can do this, Cam."

Then there he was, sunny side up. He immediately began crying.

Repeating the process for the third time that day, Juliette quickly dried the baby and placed him across his mother's chest. His father wrapped an arm around his wife and cupped his son's tiny body with his hand.

"What's his name?"

Voice rough with emotion, Sawyer replied, "James Theodore."

56

Running a finger over the baby boy's downy head, Cam murmured, "James is for Sawyer's grandfather, Theodore for his uncle."

"Aw, that's nice. Congratulations to you both."

***

Later, when Mateo came to walk her out, Juliette laid a hand on his arm. "Wait."

Three tall men stood together in the hall, each holding a swaddled infant in his arms, holiday lights twinkling above their heads.

She took out her phone and snapped a picture. The image spoke of love, friendship, and family, the perfect embodiment of the holiday spirit.

CHAPTER EIGHT

Juliette leaned back against Mateo, this time in his luxurious bathtub. The man had made good choices when he'd fixed up his house. "I love your bathtub."

"Yeah?"

"It's got these hot water jets and temperature controls. Very nice," she assured him.

He dripped bubbles across her breasts. "I'll have you know the adjustable jets and aerators are hydrotherapy features, all designed for relaxation."

"I approve of hydrotherapy features. I'm so relaxed I could fall asleep."

"We can't have that," he whispered as his hands dipped underwater. Circling, rubbing, stroking, he moved them over her breasts, then lower to her belly, then lower still.

It'd been twenty-four hours since they'd arrived home from the clinic, and both fallen exhausted into bed.

But waking up in Mateo's bed that morning had been a much different experience than the first time. He'd made love to her. Slowly, thoroughly, and with attention to her pleasure. While the storm moved east and away from Sisters, they spent the day mostly cuddled together on the couch, talking.

Mateo was adamant that she rest her brain, so no reading, no scrolling, no TV.

She couldn't even look at listings for rentals.

Lucky for them, making love wasn't on the list of banned activities in the concussion protocols.

She sighed as they moved together in the tub, reaching climax with bubbles swirling around them, then again in bed.

After, they lay cocooned in warm flannel sheets. Juliette had never felt more replete or cherished.

Mateo shifted to lean back against the headboard, drawing her up with him. With the recessed lights on low, his skin gleamed.

"Owen gave us cheesecake. An entire lemon meringue cheesecake." Juliette sighed. "Cheesecake sounds really good right now."

"Owen gave us cheesecake because he and Keeley needed to get to Reno to catch a plane. They didn't want it to go bad. We're supposed to share with the Triad."

"I guess it would be selfish not to share."

"It would. We'll have cheesecake in a bit." He ran a curl between his fingers, brows drawn over his eyes.

"You have ridiculously long eyelashes," she murmured.

"Move in with me."

She gave an involuntary jolt. "I'll find someplace to live. I haven't even had a chance to look. I'm even considering buying a house, but I'll need to talk with a lender to see if I can swing that."

"I'm not asking you because you don't have a place to live. I'm asking because I love you. I want you to move in with me."

Everything in her stilled, then lit from within with a golden flame.

"We're moving fast, and I get that. You can stay in the guest room if you'd feel more comfortable. I won't like it, but you can. But you'd be here, I'd be here, and maybe with time you could love me too."

She pressed her fingers to his mouth, then bent forward and replaced them with her lips. "I. Love. You." She interspersed each word with a kiss.

He caught her wrists, his eyes blazing. "You love me?"

"Yes, Mateo, I love you. I've been falling a little bit every time I saw you. Once I knew you liked me and only me, I couldn't stop myself from falling all the way."

Juliette absorbed the warmth of his embrace. "This is a place to build a life. We have three perfect new babies, our community came together during a big storm, and we found each other."

"And we have cheesecake." He tipped his forehead to hers. "I love you. These are going to be the best holidays ever."

BRIGHTON HOLIDAYS

M. TASIA

AUTHOR'S NOTE

Welcome back, my friends. I'm happy you've decided to join me for a trip back to Brighton, Texas, where it all began. I've missed the amazing characters I created over eight years ago, and this little visit is long overdue.

In this story, we will celebrate the holidays with Lee and Frank, whom we met briefly in *Gabe*, Book One in my Boys of Brighton series. Lee is a firefighter and friends with Gabe and Johnny, and Lee and his partner Frank welcomed their first child via surrogate in Gabe's book.

Let's visit Brighton and catch up with its colorful cast of characters. This small town has a big heart, and its residents celebrate the holidays in distinct ways.

I want to wish each of you a Happy Holiday in whatever form that is yours.

As Lee and Frank discover, you can spend your time running ragged, trying to satisfy others, or you can take the time to discover what the season means to you and the ones you love. I hope you experience all the love and joy the season offers and carry it into the new year.

Love, Michelle XO

CHAPTER ONE

Brighton, Texas – Eight years after Book 1, *Gabe*

Lee

"The hot spots are finally out," Captain Gabe Mason announced. "Let's get these hoses packed up."

"On it," Lee said as he removed his helmet and wiped the sweat and soot from his forehead.

His turnout gear was covered in black streaks due to a combination of water, soot, and the char that surrounded him. It'd been a long night fighting the barn fire, the third in as many months, and he was eager to get home to his husband, Frank, and son, Jacob.

Jacob's first day of third grade was today, and he didn't want to miss drop-off. Of course, he knew Frank would be there to take him, but Lee had never missed a first day of school since Jacob began kindergarten, and he didn't plan on starting now.

The weather was warm, and he found it hard to believe that summer vacation was over. The days were moving fast, and he longed for a way to slow everything down. It felt like only yesterday they'd brought Jacob home from the hospital, and now he was a busy eight-year-old with friends, after-school activities, and what felt like an abundant social life compared to either of his boring fathers.

Lee was exhausted. Much the same as every person on the crew, but no one would rest until every last charred timber and scorched bale of straw was checked and rechecked for hot spots. Thankfully, none of the cattle were harmed, and they'd even managed to rescue a family of barn cats from the flames, keeping the tragedy to physical damage with no loss of life.

"The fire marshal's on his way," Gabe stated after disconnecting his call.

"I hope your dad can figure this shit out before someone gets hurt," Lee said as he loaded the relay hose into the side tool compartment of the fire truck.

Chief Roger Mason had taken over as fire marshal for Brighton and surrounding areas almost three years prior, and Gabe was promoted to chief. Lee had thrown a party for his best friend to celebrate the achievement and mark the occasion. He and Frank had rented out the main room at the Haven Center to accommodate the large crowd, which included most of the citizens of Brighton. Haven, Jesse and Royce's ever-growing project, which started in Brighton and became a model for similar havens across the country, was a safe space for LGBTQ+ young people to find peace and community away from abuse, street life, hostile families, and situations out of their control.

"Agreed. This firebug needs to be stopped," Gabe stated. "It's only a matter of time before someone gets caught in one of these fires."

"This shit is getting out of hand," Ben said as he joined them. "The asshole setting these is getting on my last nerve."

Ben Mason, war veteran, Gabe's cousin, and a fellow firefighter, looked as pissed off as he sounded. His husband, Grady, worked as a police officer in Brighton. Since their jobs often overlapped, they had to've been discussing who might be the culprit, and how to stop him.

"We'll catch whoever is setting these fires and lock their ass up so they can't harm anyone else," Gabe said as the fire marshal's truck pulled up and Roger Mason stepped out shaking his head, bag in hand.

The entire town was on alert. Dante and his Sentinels, a team of former military personnel who lived outside town and ran an investigative protection company, were tracking down leads in order to stop this maniac from setting any more fires.

Suspicions were running wild, and Lee was beginning to worry that a mob would form if things continued on this path. Brighton was a friendly, welcoming small town, but if someone messed with its community, that someone would pay a price higher than they bargained for.

"What do we have?" Roger asked as he joined them.

"Another suspicious fire using accelerant on the far east corner of the barn. Once the old timbers caught, the flames moved straight up to the hay loft, and at that point, it was a matter of getting the livestock out in time. The building couldn't be saved," Gabe reported.

"Anything left behind?" Roger asked.

"Nothing. At least nothing noticeable at this time. Perhaps we'll find something after the scene is completely cooled. I hope it's not a repeat of the first two where we found nothing," Gabe answered.

Sometimes they got lucky and found triggers they could trace, and sometimes arsonists left things behind. A calling card of sorts for the authorities to find. Their egos needed to be stroked by taunting the authorities by leaving clues. Some even stuck around to watch the show.

Shadow, Vincent, and Spider, Sentinel members, were in the surrounding bush and fields in case the arsonist stayed behind to watch the destruction. The Sentinels were attempting to hone in on the arsonist, and Lee hoped they, or the PD, would catch him soon.

"Spider has not reported in yet," Gabe stated.

"Okay, I'll take over the site and look around."

"Let's get this packed up," Gabe ordered, and the team went to work wrapping things up and preparing to leave.

With any luck, Lee would return home before Frank and Jacob left for school.

***

Frank

"Grab your backpack, buddy, we have to get going," Frank told Jacob, who was looking expectantly out the front window.

"We can't go. Dad isn't here yet."

"We can't wait any longer or we'll be late for school."

"It's the first day. Dad always comes to school with us on the first day."

"I know, Jacob, but your dad's at a fire. He can't leave. It's his duty to put it out to protect the town."

"Can't we wait a few more minutes?"

"I'm sorry, buddy, but we've already waited as long as possible."

Jacob huffed as he walked away from the window, grabbed his backpack, and headed for the garage. Frank felt like the bad guy, but what choice did he have? He couldn't let Jacob be late for his first day of third grade, no matter how much he also wanted to wait for Lee. They were the firefighter's family and knew how unpredictable his hours were. For the most part, Jacob understood, but when Lee missed special occasions, such as today, all the understanding in the world didn't make up for an eight-year-old's disappointment.

The drive to the elementary school took only five minutes, and soon they were standing on the sidewalk outside with other kids who were laughing and playing as parents kissed and hugged them good-bye. It felt like a joyous social occasion until Frank looked down at his son.

He could easily read the look on Jacob's face, and the dejected slump of his shoulders said it all. Their boy was upset that both his fathers weren't here with him, as they'd been every year since he'd started school.

Frank placed his hand on Jacob's shoulder. "Jacob, I'm sor—"

Sirens blared and could be heard coming from down the street. Everyone turned to watch as a fire truck pulled in and stopped in the back of the school's parking lot. Firefighters poured out from the open doors.

They were covered in soot and looked like they'd been through the wringer, but Frank had never been so happy to see his smiling partner running in their direction. His relieved expression matched several other parents as they saw their spouses and partners arrive. Johnny and Lucy cheered as Gabe hopped out of the truck's driver's seat to join the other parents and partners.

"You made it," Jacob yelled.

"Of course I did." Lee grinned. "Wouldn't miss this for the world."

Jacob ran into Lee's open arms.

"Careful, kid, you'll mess up your clean clothes. I'm covered in grime," Lee said but made no effort to back away, holding on tight to Jacob as he smiled wide.

"I don't care," Jacob said, and Frank struggled to control his emotions. This was his family, and as he did every day, he asked himself how had he gotten so lucky.

Their lives had changed in so many ways since Jacob, and both Frank and Lee constantly talked about how they didn't know there was that much love in their bodies for the little guy who brightened their world.

Many gay couples never got this opportunity, and Frank and Lee never took a single moment of their full lives for granted. It was hard to believe Jacob was beginning grade three when it felt like only yesterday they were bringing him home from the hospital. Life never slowed down, and nowadays, things seemed to be moving at light speed.

The school bell rang.

"Okay, get in there and do us proud," Lee said. "Love you, kid."

"And have fun," Frank called out.

With a final hug for both of them, Jacob grabbed his backpack with renewed vigor and followed the rest of the children into the school. Just before he passed the threshold, he turned and waved. A huge smile had replaced his previous hangdog look, and the sun shone a little brighter.

"Will you ever stop being the hero?" Frank asked as he leaned into Lee's side.

Lee pulled him into his arms. "Never, baby," he said before kissing him.

Frank couldn't help but laugh at his live-life-out-loud husband. After over twenty years of being together, the excitement never faded, and somehow grew even stronger.

"Let's go home," he said.

"Lead the way."

CHAPTER TWO

Lee

Now was as good a time as any to bring up what he'd been considering over the past several days. Jacob was in school, and they didn't have to censor their conversation, as all parents did to some extent when discussing family matters.

"I would like to stay home for the holiday season this year," he said told Frank. He'd planned on being a bit more eloquent about it, but having the subtlety of a bulldozer meant he jumped first and asked questions later.

Frank stopped loading the dishwasher and turned to look at him.

"Hear me out," Lee said, raising his hand before his husband could speak. "Jacob is growing up so fast it feels like we're running out of time before he would rather do anything other than hang out with us. I know we typically spend Christmas Eve through to the twenty-sixth with my parents in California. Then we fly out to New York to spend New Year's with your family, and while that has always been fun, honestly, I'm over it. I want us to stay here in Brighton in our home. No packing, unpacking, washing clothes, repacking, flying, or driving. Just us. We could always visit the family over the summer holidays to make up for missing the winter holidays."

Frank seemed to be thinking it through, which could go either way. Lee couldn't tell.

"I agree," Frank said.

Lee waited for a moment, but Frank remained silent.

"You do?" He expected more pushback. They'd been doing the same routine for the past seven holiday seasons.

"Don't sound so shocked." Frank chuckled. "It's a reasonable suggestion."

"I worried since you and your parents are close."

"We are, but this is about us and our little family. I agree that time feels like it's slipping away faster and faster every year. Jacob's in third grade. Next, he'll be in middle school, and then he'll be a teenager. Not much longer before he thinks we're boring and old."

"Speak for yourself. I'm not old."

"Sorry, lover, but facts are facts. Besides, you look hot with that touch of silver in your sideburns."

"Silver?" Lee gasped while running his fingers through his hair, knowing full well that he'd been going gray for years. "Where?"

"Don't worry, you're a silver fox."

"Damn right."

Frank chuckled and threw the dishcloth at Lee's head. He caught it and set it on the kitchen table. They'd been together since high school, and there wasn't a day that went by when Lee wasn't reminded of how lucky he was to have Frank.

"How do you think we should break it to our parents now?" Frank asked.

"The sooner the better. That way, they can get used to the idea over the next few months, and they won't feel blindsided if we don't tell them until November."

"You think they'll be pissed?" Frank was always concerned with everyone else's feelings, and it wasn't that Lee didn't care, but he was less likely to bend to other people's desires.

"We're adults with our own family. How long did they think we'd be zigzagging across the country every December? They'll understand," Lee assured.

"Famous last words if I've ever heard any," Frank said. "At least with my family being Jewish, Hanukkah is a moving target. We don't have to show up at the same time each year as we do with your family."

"True. And let's not forget how my parents go nuts with the tree and decorations. Those blow-up lawn ornaments and lights all over their house can be seen from space. It's like being with the Griswolds."

"I don't know. It was kind of nice seeing the opposite side of the spectrum from my family. Hanukkah is more low-key. We light the menorah, eat amazing food, and Jacob gets a gift for each of the eight nights, but there's no razzle-dazzle."

"Sometimes less is more," Lee stated. "After a while, it all becomes too much noise."

"Funny how we view the other's holiday traditions. Considering I never had the big commercial Santa Christmas hoopla, I see it as a fun novelty, but you see it as an overblown spectacle. It's not as if we are actively practicing any belief or adhering to traditions outside of when we visit our families."

Neither he nor Frank were strict about religion or traditions. Even though Lee had been raised Catholic, he didn't attend church, and figured as long as you were a good person, were kind and understanding, and did your best, you embraced the goodness and love religion was supposed to espouse. Frank felt the same way, and had stopped adhering to Shabbos or being kosher many years ago. But both of them brought the best of what made them who they were, and that's what they passed down to their son, who enjoyed both ends of the holiday spectrum.

"True. I see you and your family lighting the menorah, saying ancient prayers to celebrate the Festival of Lights as a refreshing and spiritual departure from what I was raised with. Don't get me wrong, we had a nativity scene, but it was outnumbered by the Santas by three to one."

"Here's a question for you. Since we're considering not going to our parents, who continue to hold on to both versions of their traditions, how do we celebrate the holidays here? Before Jacob, we usually traveled somewhere with a beach, and we've never had to make a decision about how we'd celebrate. After Jacob, we've always been away over the holidays with family, who shared their traditions."

"Huh. Good question. I don't have an answer right now, but we're intelligent men who want the best for Jacob. I'm sure we can find a happy medium. Really, how hard could it be?"

"You think it'll be that easy?" Frank asked.

"I'm sure we'll come up with something."

"Yeah, I can't wait to remind you that you said that." Frank chuckled before returning to loading the dishwasher.

Lee sat back in his chair at the kitchen table and took a sip of his coffee. It wouldn't be too hard to combine the two holidays. He'd spent his adult life getting up close and personal with raging fires. The holidays should be a breeze.

***

Frank

"It's not that we don't want to see you, Mom. This is about us. We want to spend time here at home this year," Frank tried again to reason with his mother. "We'll visit over the summer holidays. It'll be fun. We'll go to Long Beach and Coney Island. Maybe we'll rent a place for a couple of weeks out in the Hamptons."

"Why are you doing this? Is it Lee? Does he feel uncomfortable with us?"

"Mom. Really? He loves you, and you know it. No need for melodrama. We're not going to his parents either. This has nothing to do with not wanting to see the family. It concerns our family and our desire to slow things down while Jacob is still young enough to want to spend time with us. He's growing so fast. We want to savor our time with him."

"Okay. That I understand. And you're right. Time moves so fast. Before you know it, your children have grown up and moved away." He could hear the melancholy in her voice.

"I promise we'll come in the summer and have a great time. We can video call on Hanukkah and New Year's so you can see Jacob. It won't be so bad. I promise. Please understand."

"Okay, if you're sure."

"We are. We need this time together while we can take it."

"I'll let your father know, and we'll talk soon."

"Thanks, Mom, I love you."

"Love you too. Say hello to everyone for us."

"I will. Bye."

"Bye."

He felt like an insensitive heel. He let his mother down and was being selfish. What was he thinking? Maybe they should go.

"I know that look," Lee said as he entered the living room. "No, you aren't an awful person. No, you're not being self-centered and selfish. Yes, you're an amazing son, husband, and father, and you are not responsible for the world's happiness."

"You know me well," he deadpanned. "What gave me away?"

"I should know you. But that vein in the center of your forehead is always a good indicator when you're stressed," Lee said as he walked behind Frank and wrapped his strong arms around him. "You're an amazing person."

"The counselor needs counseling," Frank stated.

"You're human. You can't be expected to handle everything alone or always know what is best for everyone. You're so damned concerned about everyone around you that sometimes you forget to take care of yourself and what you want and need."

"That's why I have you," Frank said, and he meant it.

Lee was his sounding board. His checks and balances. He kept Frank from hyper-fixating on any number of things, and lived life firmly rooted in facts and not what-ifs. As with all professions, he could help others sort out their hang-ups but was clueless about dealing with his own. Like a gardener having a messy front yard.

"And you always will, baby."

"How did your parents take the news?" Frank asked, wanting to get off the subject of his parents.

"About the same as yours. Not happy, but ultimately understanding. They'll be fine, and so will yours. What matters is how we want to spend our time together. Not breaking our backs arranging flights and travel itineraries, carting luggage across the country, and feeling like we never have a moment to slow down and enjoy the holidays."

"At least Jacob is excited about staying home this year," Frank said and was truly thankful for that. "He can't wait to decorate and attend all the festivities in and around Brighton."

Of course, they'd decorated for the holidays before, but never to the extent of spending the season at home. It had always been a race to the airport as soon as Jacob's school holidays began so that they had time to make it to California, spend time there, and then load up again, fly to New York, and do it all over again before rushing back to Brighton to recuperate for a few days before school was back in session.

Every year, Brighton held festivals, and their friends had parties to celebrate the season, but they'd missed much of it, having to race between two coasts. This year would be different. This year would be spent at a slower pace without the need to schedule every moment of every day during the holidays.

The old saying that they'd needed a holiday from their holiday was spot-on in their case since Jacob came along. It would be a welcomed change, slowing it all down.

"Should we get a real tree this year?" Lee asked. "We'd be around to care for it."

"Why not? It'd be the perfect time," Frank agreed. "Jacob would have fun picking one out. Come to think of it, I'm not sure what decorations we have."

"Let's go take a look in the attic. We can get an idea of what we have and what we need to pick up."

"The man with a plan," Frank said as he stood with renewed purpose.

"Better than sitting around worrying about it."

"True. Once we take steps forward, it'll help solidify the change in my mind and calm my concerns. Usually, I'm the one telling clients this stuff. I need to listen to my own advice."

"Yep, you do. Grab the notepad off the fridge, and we'll take notes," Lee suggested.

They were doing the right thing. They had to cherish every moment while they had the chance. Sometimes, life got so crazy that they'd rush from one thing to another and never enjoy the moments in between. That had to change, and this year it would.

The attic wasn't as spacious as it used to be. Boxes lined the walls, and furniture sat under sheets to keep the dust off them.

"Did we always have this many boxes up here?" Lee asked as he lifted another cardboard box out of his way.

"Over the last eight years, we've collected quite a bit. I guess I've never realized how much there truly is."

They'd moved into this house a little before Jacob was born. Before that, they lived in a one-bedroom apartment above the bakery in downtown Brighton. With a baby on the way, they knew they needed more room, and a yard for their son to play in, so they found this four-bedroom home on a quiet cul-de-sac not far from Gabe's house. It had worked out perfectly, and fit their family and their needs.

"I found the Halloween decorations," Lee announced while holding a fuzzy, two-foot spider.

"Good, leave it out. We'll take it down with us."

"We still have a week before October."

"Yeah, but it'll save me looking for it later."

"Good point."

Frank removed the lid from the plastic tub beside him and couldn't help but smile. He pulled out the first onesie and held it high. "Was he ever this small?" he asked, filled with nostalgia.

Lee looked up and smiled. "It's hard to believe Jacob fit into that."

Frank pulled out a small stack of bibs and a pair of tiny socks. Holy shit, how had time flown by so quickly? He distinctly remembered the afternoon they'd brought Jacob home, his first smile, first tooth, first word, and first step. He felt Lee's arms wrap around him and leaned back into his husband as memories flooded him.

"You are one hundred percent right," he said.

"Of course I am," Lee joked. "But for argument purposes, what was I right about?"

Frank couldn't help but laugh.

"About time slipping by and having to slow down and enjoy the moments together. I—" Frank was cut off by Lee's ringing phone. He looked hesitant to answer, but it could be important. "Go ahead and answer it."

"I'm sorry," Lee said before pulling his phone out of his pocket and reading the screen. "Shit."

"What's wrong?"

"Another fire. It's a big one. They're calling in all off-duty firefighters still in town to help."

"Go. They need you."

"I'll be back as soon as possible," Lee said, kissing Frank before standing.

"Please, be careful."

"I always am, baby. I have you and Jacob to come home to." Then he was gone.

Life with a firefighter was unpredictable at best, and terrifying at worst. It was the life he'd signed up for and part of the man he loved. It was a double-edged sword, preparing for the future while fighting not to think of the possibilities each fire call presented. Life held no guarantees. His mother used to say you could be hit by a bus tomorrow. Morbid but true. He'd learned to make the best out of what he had right in front of him here and now, and going forward, that was exactly what he intended to do.

CHAPTER THREE

Lee

This shit had to stop. Four-foot flames shot out from the third of three nearby barns as they tried to clear the second barn and ensure all the horses got out. They didn't worry about haltering them. They opened their stalls and chased them toward the entrance. Better to have to round them up after the fire was out than having to dig their graves.

Between dodging the hooves of frightened horses, falling timbers, and the rising flames, Lee and the rest of the crew had to move two tractors full of fuel far enough away so they didn't explode and send missiles of torn metal out into the surrounding area.

Thankfully, one of the two had keys in the ignition, but the second had to be towed away by chains attached to one of the pumpers, which took valuable time and manpower.

Of course, the farmer and his family were helping, and more and more people from Brighton were showing up to help, but now that the third barn had caught fire, they were running out of time and had to shift their thinking to securing and protecting the rest of the farm from the growing flames.

Frightened and screaming, horses barreled down the aisle between stalls straight toward them.

"Watch out," Lee yelled. "Incoming."

The two other firefighters with him quickly dove into empty stalls, allowing the animals to run by, and out the open doors.

"That's all of them," Ben hollered as he pulled the hose into the barn.

Lee quickly joined him, grabbed the hose, and let the water flow. It typically took a few of them to hold a hose in place as the amount and speed of water flowing out of it could knock them on their asses. Their forces were split between the three barns and the rest of the property, but with the help of the townsfolk and the Sentinels, they were putting up one hell of a fight.

The smoke made it almost impossible to see more than a foot in front of them, and if it weren't for their masks, they'd be unable to breathe.

The sky was dark, but it was the middle of the day. The fire roared its anger as it ate through the timbers and flowed across the ceiling in waves. The water hissed and sputtered as it came into contact with the flames, but after hours of fighting, Lee could finally see a tangible difference as the area still in flames grew smaller.

Their bodies were exhausted, but they'd never stop fighting. This wasn't simply a job. It was a calling. A mission to protect people and their property, and none took that duty lightly. No one in their right mind willingly ran into a burning building unless something deep inside of them compelled them forward. The need and drive to make a difference, to save a life, to save a structure someone had spent their entire lives creating. The reason didn't matter. All that mattered was the drive to do it.

"First building's fire is out," Gabe announced over the coms.

Finally, all they needed to do was douse this second barn. The third had already been brought under control thanks to the teams' ability to get on the fire early and quickly.

"Moving forward," Lee announced, and began walking the hose deeper into the barn as the flames sizzled and fought back, but eventually, they were extinguished.

They couldn't stop now, or the fire would erupt anew. Pushing harder while they had the upper hand would bring this fire down sooner. Another crew was working on the other end of the building, leaving the flames with nowhere to go. In a highly coordinated operation, the teams converged on the last of the flames and ended the destruction.

Night had fallen when Lee emerged from the shell of the horse barn, and the moon was high in the sky. So much for seeing Jacob after school. He'd already be in bed. Lee would call Frank as soon as he could so he wouldn't continue to worry.

Lee looked around at the damage. The first barn was burned to the ground, the second was a shell of burnt timbers, and the third had only minor damage to the east end.

Horses were corralled in temporary pens in the distance while in the foreground, hoses snaked from a myriad of fire trucks, and water haulers had come to help. The flashing lights from emergency vehicles reflected off the puddles of muddy water dotted across the area. It resembled a war zone, especially when the Sentinels Spider, Vincent, Shadow, Coop, Shannon, and Dante marched through the mud in their tactical gear, covered in soot, heading toward Gabe and his father, the fire marshal.

Lee went to join them, hoping one of them might have a lead on the source of this fire and the three prior fires. On his way over, Lee noticed a horse lying on the ground beyond the temporary ring that had been constructed. It wasn't moving and was covered by a blanket. Shit. Their streak of no casualties had sadly ended.

"Do you think you'll be able to track them?" Gabe asked Dante as Lee stepped up beside him.

"Yeah. Whether it leads to the person responsible is yet to be seen," Dante said. "Either way, we'll keep you updated."

"Thank you to you and your team for your help today," Gabe said. "We needed all hands on deck with this one."

"Always here to help. We'll catch this bastard and bury him in a cell so deep he'll never see sunlight again," Spider growled.

"Amen, brother," Lee agreed, soliciting a nod from everyone present.

There wasn't a soul in Brighton who didn't want to catch this crazy lunatic and shut him down for good.

***

Frank

"Trick or treat," Jacob said as Ellen Mason opened her front door.

Gabe's mother smiled wide and asked, "Are you a zombie doctor?"

"Yes, ma'am," Jacob said while eagerly holding out his bag.

Frank couldn't help but laugh. "He couldn't decide whether to be a doctor or a zombie. So Lee suggested he combine the two."

"It was the perfect solution," Lee said from where he stood on the sidewalk.

"You look great, Jacob," Ellen stated before dropping some miniature chocolate bars into his bag.

"Thank you, Mrs. Mason," Jacob said with a big smile.

"You're welcome, sweetheart."

Jacob ran back to the sidewalk to Lee while Frank thanked Ellen once more and joined his family waiting for him.

"Can I go to the next house on my own? I'm old enough and promise to thank them," Jacob asked.

Lee looked over at Frank. "I'm good with that if you are."

"Okay, but remember to use your manners, and we'll be right here on the sidewalk waiting for you."

"Really? Thanks," Jacob cheered and ran to the next house, joining the masses of children who were laughing and running up and down the sidewalks of Brighton.

"Look at him go," Lee said.

"All grown up," Frank said. "At least he thinks so."

"Kids want to be adults, and adults want to be carefree kids. Ah, the circle of life," Lee joked.

"So true. Oh, there's Rick, Bear, and Joshua."

The big biker, Clem "Bear" Mitchell, and his husband, Rick, had adopted Joshua after his sister had passed away, leaving her precious son behind. The little guy was two at the time and was now Jacob's age and were in the third grade together.

The moment Joshua saw Jacob, he ran to his friend and began showing him all the candy he'd collected in his plastic pumpkin. As the two compared their candy hauls, Rick and Bear visited with Frank and Lee.

"Happy Halloween, guys," Rick said.

"Happy Halloween," Lee responded. "How's your night going so far?"

"Good." Bear nodded. "Even if we're the third wheel."

"Third wheel?" Frank asked.

"Yeah. Josh thinks he's old enough to go trick or treating on his own," Rick said, shaking his head. "They grow up so fast."

"That seems to be a theme this year," Lee remarked.

"Frank said you guys were going to be home this year for the holidays," Rick said.

"Yep. For the first time in eight years, we've decided to slow things down and stay home."

"That's great. Since you'll be around, the three of you gotta come to our annual Christmas party. Typically, we have it the weekend before Christmas," Bear explained.

"That sounds great," Lee said while looking at Frank, who nodded in agreement. "We'll be there."

Frank allowed himself to enjoy the feeling of planning to attend holiday parties without letting the guilt of not traveling to his parents get in the way.

Things might work out after all.

CHAPTER FOUR

Frank

"It's normal to miss your family, especially at this time of the year," Frank told Oliver, a Haven resident. "However, I hope you know you've gained a family here in Brighton who will willingly choose to share the holidays with you."

"I know, and I appreciate it, but sometimes I think back to before my parents kicked me out when the house was decorated, and *Frosty the Snowman* was playing on the television. Everyone was happy, and my sister circled all the toys she wanted Santa to bring her in all her catalogues. It was perfect."

"Nostalgia is a strong emotion that gets even stronger around the holidays. Looking back, we sometimes romanticize the scenes that play out in our minds."

Oliver sat quietly, and Frank appreciated that the young man was contemplating what he'd said. The holidays could bring out extreme emotions, good and bad, and his hope was to relieve some of the pain that typically came with the holiday season.

"I understand what you're saying. If I sit back and look at the scene critically, I notice my parents arguing in the kitchen. Usually, it was about me. My problem."

"Problem?"

"My gayness. My feminine energy. My constantly embarrassing my father and my mother attempting to calm him down."

"That had to be difficult for you."

"He always acted like I was doing it on purpose. He used to ask me if I hated them like this was some sort of revenge. Why I couldn't be normal."

"You are perfect the way you are," Frank said, hoping Oliver believed him. "It hurts when someone who is supposed to love you no matter what can't accept your authentic self. That being gay was some sort of payback for a wrong."

"How can I miss people like that?"

"No matter what, they're your family, and a part of you will always long for that connection."

"Even if I don't want to?"

"Yes. Even if you don't want to. We form connections with the people with whom we spend the most time. Good and bad. All we can do is accept them for what they are and forge new connections. Healthier connections provide us with what we need and with people who value us for the person we are. It's not easy, but every step you take in that direction brings you closer to your own happiness."

"Do you think that one day it won't hurt to think about them?" Oliver asked.

"Truthfully, the memories will always cause you some pain, but the severity will decrease until you get to the point where it's only a passing thought. Your life will have grown to include people who cherish you, Oliver, just as you are."

Frank wished he could tell him that someday he'd think about his parents and not be affected, but that would've been a lie. The one thing he swore he'd never do to his clients, no matter how much it would make things easier or give them temporary relief, was to lie or exaggerate. It wasn't fair to set them up for disappointment. Too many people in their lives had already done that.

"Thanks for never lying to me, Mr. Rogers," Oliver said. "I'll see you next week."

"You're welcome. Have a good week."

After the young man left, Frank couldn't help but think about what it would have been like if his parents had cast him out for being gay. It wasn't the first time he'd considered the repercussions of not having the support he'd received growing up.

When his thoughts inevitably turned to Jacob, it was unimaginable to think of turning his back on his son, no matter what. However, that happened daily to numerous kids worldwide. No matter how enlightened the human race became, the lack of tolerance and understanding would continue until the end of time.

***

Lee

"He's going to love it," Gabe said as Lee opened the box to show him what had recently been delivered.

"We have one, of course, but it's pretty basic for when we were in college and then living in the apartment, but this year feels special, a turning point in how we'll spend the season going forward. We were usually at his parents' house during that period, so the one we had was collecting dust. I wanted to make it a combination of traditions."

"When are you giving it to him?"

"Tonight, when I get home from work. Jacob helped me with the design for Travis to create."

Travis was Police Chief Bo Mason's partner, and one hell of an artist in many different mediums. He could paint, carve, sculpt, chisel, you name it, and the guy could create a masterpiece out of it.

"That little shop Travis has in town has been extremely popular since it opened. Johnny has had a few things made by Travis."

"You only have to give the guy a rough idea of what you want, and it's like he reads your mind or something. I never dreamed it would come out so well," Lee said. "Hey, have you heard more from Dante about the arsonist?"

It had been three weeks since the last intentionally set fire, and everyone was on the lookout for the arsonist's next target. Of course, the firehouse had had other calls for service, but all of them had been accidental or weather-related.

"Yeah. At the scene of the last fire, the fire marshal determined that the accelerant used matched the previous fires. While typically fuel wouldn't be so helpful, this time it is because it's jet fuel, not plain gasoline, which you can get at any filling station. There are only so many places where you can find jet fuel in a two-hundred-mile radius of Brighton, and most have security cameras."

"Finally, we caught a break. So your father and the Sentinels are closing in on this crazy bastard." That was a relief to hear.

"It's only a matter of time," Gabe assured.

"That's great news. Hopefully, they catch him before Christmas. I still can't believe next week is December first. I'm still full from Thanksgiving. Where has the time gone?"

"I feel ya. Johnny went straight into Christmas mode the day after Thanksgiving. Lucy's already made her letter to Santa because she doesn't want it to get lost in the mail."

Lee noticed Gabe couldn't help but smile when talking about his family.

"The White Hair Crew loves replying to all the kids' letters. Grandma Rose would be proud that the tradition continued after she and Grandma Graham passed. Between the three remaining ladies, your mom and aunts, no kid will go without a reply from Santa and a gift at the annual festival."

Gabe smiled even wider, and Lee figured it was because of the thoughts of Grandma Rose. The lady was one of a kind, had been loved fiercely, and took people under her wing regularly. She held the heart of Brighton for ninety-four years and was irreplaceable. She'd passed away in her sleep, not slowing a single day beforehand, and her funeral brought in not only the entire town, but people from far and wide whose lives she'd touched. Johnny's brother, Saint, had flown in from Los Angeles along with former community members who had moved away.

"I'm sure she's looking down on us, keeping an eye on everybody, making sure everything keeps ticking along," Gabe said.

"I wouldn't doubt it," Lee agreed. "Okay, I better get home for dinner. I'll see you tomorrow."

"Have a good night," Gabe said before turning and heading toward his truck.

It took him less than fifteen minutes to drive home, even after stopping at the grocery store for milk and bread. The smell of garlic and onions greeted him and made his mouth water when he walked through the front door.

"Spaghetti night," Lee cheered. He loved spaghetti night.

"You, sir, are correct," Frank joked as Lee entered the kitchen.

Frank was standing at the stove and Jacob was doing his homework at the kitchen island. Lee set the groceries on the counter and the box containing his surprise on the kitchen island before walking up behind Frank and kissing his neck.

"Hey, baby. How was your day?" he asked.

"Good. You?"

"Nothing exciting happened, which is great. How about you, kid, how was school?"

"Good, but I've got so much homework. What's in the box?" Jacob asked.

"It's that special something we made for your Pop," Lee said, eliciting a wide smile from their son.

"Pop, open it. It's a surprise."

Frank turned from the stove with a questioning look. "For me? What did you guys get me?"

"You're going to have to open the box to find out," Lee said, and Jacob bounced up and down in his chair.

"Open it," Jacob shouted.

Frank wiped his hands on the dishcloth he'd thrown over his shoulder and opened the top of the box. Lee hoped the shocked expression on his face was a good sign or the night was going downhill fast.

"We had it made for you, Pop. Do you like it?"

Frank reached in and lifted the hand-carved Hanukkah menorah from its nest of bubble wrap. The nine intricately carved branches of the candlesticks. Eight for the eight nights of Hanukkah, and the elevated ninth to hold the candle that lights all the other candles on each evening of Hanukkah. It marks the significance of the miracle of oil that kept the fire burning in Jerusalem's Holy Temple for eight nights.

"It's stunning," Frank said, and Lee could see the tears welling in his eyes. "You two had this made for me?"

Jacob jumped down from his chair and ran over to hug his Pop before saying, "It's for our family traditions."

Each stem of the candelabra twisted like a rope upward and into the small carved bowl that held each of the nine candles. The base was wide and sturdy, like a tree holding out its branches, and each of their names was engraved on the base.

"It's to symbolize the branches of our strong family. We wanted you to have something made especially for you and our family. I respect your Jewish ancestry and want it to flourish in this home. Hanukkah is a celebration of a miracle, and you two are my miracle."

Frank couldn't hold back any longer as he set the Hanukkah menorah on the table and gathered Jacob and Lee into his arms.

"It's perfect, exactly like my family. Thank you. I will prize this for the rest of my life."

CHAPTER FIVE
Frank

Frank set his gift in a place of honor in the center of the bay window at the front of their house. He'd purchase the candles in the coming week as Hanukkah wouldn't be celebrated until the twenty-fifth of December this year when they lit the first candle.

"You've always been the owner of my heart, Lee, but you've outdone yourself this time," Frank said as he joined his husband on the couch.

It was late, and Jacob had already been in bed for over an hour. They'd celebrated with a delicious spaghetti dinner. Lee and Jacob loved it when he made their favorite meal, and it happened to work out that he'd decided to cook it the evening he received his gift.

"That's good. I promise to take good care of it," Lee assured him.

"You always do. Travis must've been working on that piece for months."

"Jacob and I went to see him shortly after we decided to stay home for the holidays."

"I can't believe Jacob was able to keep a secret from me for so long."

"He knew how important this surprise was. He played a big part in deciding on the final design. I'm so proud of how hard he worked and took this responsibility seriously," Lee said as he set his cup on the coffee table.

"It means a lot that the two of you worked so hard to give me something so special. Typically, we're at my family's house for most of Hanukkah, so it never crossed my mind that perhaps we'd need something a bit more special than my old college one."

Lee pulled him closer, and Frank curled into his husband's arms. From the beginning of their relationship, they'd often lie in this position while watching TV. It was comfortable, soothing, and familiar.

"You're worth it, baby. We love you. You're the heart of this family."

"I am?" He'd never viewed himself that way.

"Of course you are," Lee said, leaning forward slightly to look in his eyes. "You keep our family going. Without you, it all falls apart. I thought you knew that."

"I guess I've never thought of it. I've always viewed you as the foundation."

"Okay, well, that makes sense. If we look at our family as a home, I'd be the structure while you'd be everything inside. I'm not sure if this is coming out right," Lee chuckled, "but that's how I see it."

"I understand what you're saying. It's like each of us holds a special position that creates a whole home when combined."

"Right. You get it."

"When do you want to start decorating the house?" Frank asked. "Jacob's ready to go."

"Let's wait until we get the tree this weekend," Lee said. "I don't want to go crazy like my parents do every year."

"You mean we can't have twenty blow-up figures in the front yard?" Frank joked, knowing how much Lee cringed whenever he saw his father's collection.

"No, please. I beg you. One is fine. Two at the maximum. I couldn't take it if we went nuts like my father. You can't see the grass, and when they're deflated, it feels like there's been some sort of massacre. It's damn depressing in the daytime."

"Okay, got it. Keep it to a sane level, no mass deflating." Frank chuckled. "Anything else?"

"I'd like to put up lights on the house."

"We usually do that."

"Yeah, but I want to really up our game this year."

"Right. No blow-up carnival but twinkle lights a plenty."

Lee's hands slid down to Frank's sides moments before his fingers dug in, and the tickling began.

"Are you making fun of me, mister?" Lee laughed.

Frank couldn't help but laugh and squirm. Lee knew how ticklish he was and used it to his advantage.

"No, no. I'd never do that." Frank laughed.

Lee stopped tickling him and held him close.

"I didn't think so. Ready for bed?" Lee wiggled his eyebrows.

"Definitely. Lead the way."

***

Lee

Two weeks before Christmas, and he'd been on duty for the past forty-eight hours at the firehouse. Roughly thirty hours in, he'd received a call from Frank about what could only be considered shocking news. Their parents had randomly shown up on their doorstep, both sets. They'd decided to surprise them by coming to Brighton to spend the holidays.

Surprise wasn't the word Lee would use. Shocked, confused, terrified, astonished that they thought to show up without calling. Without a hint of warning. His mother had reached out to Frank's mother and together they'd decided if we couldn't go to them, they'd come to us.

Holy shit.

Frank wasn't able to talk for long, and Lee imagined the parents were taking over their house as he spoke. Jacob was thrilled that his grandparents, Safta and Saba in Hebrew, were there and everyone would be together over the holidays. Thankfully, they had two spare bedrooms, but the house wasn't large enough to hold three families comfortably or sanely.

Lee wasn't sure if this was a nightmare coming true, but imagined this was as close as it got. It wasn't that he didn't love his family because he did, but shoving them all under one roof could prove to be disastrous.

It was close to seven in the evening when he pulled his truck onto his street and realized too late that the glow ahead was coming from his house. As he got closer, the lights got brighter, and that's when it hit him. People were standing on the sidewalk in front of his house.

His fear quickly turned to exasperation as he pulled into the driveway.

"Why me?" he asked the empty truck.

The singular snowman inflatable that Jacob had chosen and they'd set up in the yard was now joined by his many inflatable friends. There was a Santa, and, of course, his reindeer, a nativity scene, five-foot blow-up ornaments, a flashing North Pole sign, and a whole friggin' sleigh. His father hadn't wasted any time.

When he got out of the truck, his neighbors waved and commented on how they'd gone all out this year. Children stood smiling with their parents, watching the spectacle of inflatables and flashing lights. Lee thought he'd escaped the insanity this year. He was wrong. It followed him to Texas.

Lee waved back and smiled before reluctantly heading for the front door. He took a deep breath, reached for the handle, and prepared himself for the chaos within. However, when he pushed the door open, he was met with silence. Shocked, he took a few steps forward and looked around the living room. Empty. Where was everybody?

"In the kitchen," Frank's voice echoed down the hallway.

He followed his husband's voice and found him sitting at the kitchen table with a bottle of beer in front of him. Yep, he'd had a rough day.

"Where is everyone?"

"Taking a tour around Brighton with Jacob."

"How are you?"

"That's a tricky question."

Lee set his duffle down on the floor and sat in the chair next to Frank. "Start at the beginning."

Frank picked up his beer and took a deep gulp.

"Jacob and I were sitting down for lunch when there was a knock on the front door. I open it to find my mom and yours standing on the front steps and our fathers unloading bags from an Uber they'd taken from the airport."

"No warning."

"None. Jacob shouted with the kind of glee only an eight-year-old would have the moment he saw them. They were laughing and hugging like it was some great miracle."

"Miracle."

"Yep. Then it began," Frank said.

"What began?"

"The takeover."

"Ah, yes. I noticed the front yard."

"It's not only your parents and the front yard," Frank groused as he pointed to the kitchen counter where a new toaster oven sat beside their microwave. "And there's a bar fridge in the dining room."

"Why?" Lee asked, confused. "We have large appliances."

"My parents are kosher."

"Yeah, they are," Lee said, remembering that just now. There'd been a lot going on.

Lee hadn't thought of it because Frank wasn't kosher. But when they went to New York, it wasn't unusual to find double appliances in Jewish households.

"Couldn't we have properly divided the dairy and meat in one fridge?" Lee asked. He respected their kosher adherence, and never wanted to offend them. As Frank wasn't kosher, Lee wasn't sure of all the rules.

Many aspects of being kosher must be observed. One was never to mix dairy and meat. And the one Lee knew for sure was no pork.

"Sure, with proper precautions, but my parents arranged for quite a bit of kosher meat to be delivered today to last them until the New Year, which is in the new bar fridge."

"Um, okay. That makes sense. Wait a minute, new year? How long is everyone staying?"

"Exactly, New Year. Over three weeks. A box with new pots and pans is on the dining room table. Honestly, I didn't see this coming. It wasn't on my radar or bingo card." He shook his head. "Also, your dad had a delivery from Home Depot. They used a lift truck to set the over-sized pallet on the driveway."

"The Christmas decorations?"

"Yep. I've never seen that many extension cords hooked up at one time. Can you please make sure to have a look at it so that it isn't a fire hazard, or that we don't overload the entire town of Brighton and cause a blackout?"

"On it."

"Thanks. While you're at it, you might also want to look at your dad's attempt to hang a Santa from the roof."

"Shit, there's a Santa on our roof. I didn't look up."

"Yep. He's dangling up there with a couple of elves. It looks like dear old Santa chucked the pointy-eared buggers right off the roof."

"Shit. Okay. Save the elves, got it. Um, do I want to know why a twenty-five-pound bag of flour is on the counter?'

"Baking. Lots and lots of baking and cooking. The grandmothers plan on baking. Tons. I've officially been extricated from my kitchen for the foreseeable future."

"Oh." Lee couldn't think of anything else to say.

"On the bright side, Jacob's having the time of his life," Frank commented with his first smile since Lee arrived.

"I imagine he is having a ball."

This would be great fun for an eight-year-old. What kid wouldn't like to be fawned over by their grandparents, have their house lit up like a Christmas carnival, and their grandmothers baking up a storm just for him? Right now, life for their son was perfect.

"Mazel tov," Frank said as he raised his beer and took another drink.

"Okay, I think you've manned this ship long enough. How about you go to our master bath and have a nice long soak in the tub? I'll take over from here."

Frank looked at him in what could only be described as massive relief.

"You mean it."

"Yeah. Go. Relax."

Frank stood so fast that the chair almost tipped over onto the floor. He was halfway out the kitchen entrance when he turned. "Come get me if you need help."

"You don't mean that." Lee laughed.

"You're right, I don't. Good luck. I love you." Then he was gone.

Now, where was the ladder?

CHAPTER SIX

Lee

"So I hear your family's in town," Gabe said as Lee restocked the first aid kits they carried in each fire truck.

"Yep. They've effectively moved in," Lee said, but he wasn't far off.

Between the deliveries, decorations, cooking, and any number of other changes, Lee wasn't sure if it was still his and Frank's home or their parents' house. It'd never crossed his mind that this was a possibility. Their quiet home for the holidays had been replaced and turned into a three-ring circus, and as his father's display grew ever larger, so did the nightly crowds that gathered to watch the display, making his father search for more ways to wow the people of Brighton. Their mothers started serving hot chocolate and cookies to their nightly visitors. It'd turned into a nightly party, and Jacob couldn't be prouder that his house was the gathering place.

Frank had decided to use the opportunity to do some good and set out a donation bin, with the proceeds going to the Haven Center. They'd already collected over two hundred dollars in cash donations and bags of donated nonperishable food.

"You don't sound particularly happy about it," Gabe remarked, that damn smirk of his wide and snide.

"They've hijacked our entire holiday plans."

"Is it really so bad?"

"I woke up this morning to Barbara Streisand belting out Yuletide favorites as my mother was bandaging up my father's hand for the third time after I tried to reason with him that we didn't need to put lights around the rose bushes. He can't be stopped."

"From what I hear, the town's loving the light display."

"So is the electric company."

Gabe laughed. "You've never been a Scrooge. Tell me the truth, what's going on?"

Lee sucked in a deep breath. He knew Gabe was trying to help, but how did he explain how he felt without looking like a complete asshole?

"It's stupid, really."

"If it's bugging you, it's not stupid. I remember when I was fixated on helping Johnny recover from the injuries to his hands left by the fire. You sat my ass down and knocked some sense into me. You told me that I was being an overbearing asshole and that I had to back off and let Johnny find his feet."

"And he did."

"Yes, he did. Now start talking."

"Okay. As crazy as this sounds, for once, I wanted to be the Christmas hero this year."

"The hero? You're a firefighter. You are a hero."

"Yeah, I get that, but that's in my work life. I want to be the same as a dad."

"Jacob loves you."

"I know. That's why I think this feeling doesn't make sense, but it's there and it sucks."

"Why don't you explain it to me?"

"Growing up, my father was my hero. Never more than during the holidays when he'd go all out and decorate our house. People would travel to see it, and all my friends would tell me how much they wished their house looked like ours."

"But I thought you hated all the blow-up madness?"

"I do now, but as a kid, it was magical. I thought this year would be my chance with Jacob."

"I get it. You feel as though you're being overshadowed by your father every year because you believe Jacob looks at him the same way you used to when you were a kid."

"Facts are facts. Jacob is having a great time with his grandparents here, and our house has become spectacular. I can't believe I'm forty-two and jealous of my father. How messed up is that?"

"Not so messed up as you think."

"No?"

"Nope. When I was a trainee, everyone looked up to my dad, the fire chief. It felt like I'd never have the same respect people had for him. He was the hero in my life and everyone else's. I was fighting an uphill battle with no way of ever catching up in the eyes of my teammates."

"You do have the respect of everyone. No one ever questioned your abilities."

"Exactly. That uphill battle was in my own head, not reality. You're already the hero in your son's life by being the dad you are. You're competing with yourself."

Lee felt the truth of what Gabe said wash over him. Was he competing with himself? Was it all in his head?

"No matter what you do, you will always be the hero in your son's life. He loves you, and so does Frank. You can't ask for more than that," Gabe said as he slapped Lee's back.

"No, I can't."

He already had what most men only dreamed of. What the hell was he worried about?

***

Frank

He could tell there was a difference in the way his husband was acting. Lee looked happier and more carefree than he had in days.

The holiday festival was in full swing, and Brighton's Main Street had been transformed into Santa's winter wonderland, only with fake snow. They were in South Texas, after all.

Jacob ran ahead with Lucy and Joshua as the grandmothers helped the Mason Aunts set up the bakery table, and the grandfathers discussed the latest advances in LED lighting while surveying the various decorations. The grandparents had hit it off nicely for four people who hadn't spent much time together before this.

The residents were out in full force, and booths were giving out hot cider, hot chocolate, cookies, and all sorts of treats. Christmas carols were being sung, and all the children eagerly awaited Santa's arrival.

"Are you going to tell me what's gotten into you?" Frank asked Lee as they walked down the sidewalk hand in hand.

"What do you mean?"

"You're acting like you don't have a care in the world."

"I'm enjoying our first Brighton Holiday Festival as a family," Lee said with a wink.

"Okay, you keep it to yourself, but I've gotta say I like this new attitude."

"Let's just say I've readjusted my thinking. How are you doing through all this chaos?"

"I'm actually beginning to like the constant movement and cozy feeling of having a full house."

"Even though you've been kicked out of your kitchen?"

"Yeah, I could do with a break from cooking occasionally."

"Words I never thought I'd hear coming from your mouth," Lee joked, pulling Frank closer. "I say we roll with it, baby, and enjoy the time while we have it."

"Besides, Jacob is having the best of both worlds. He's got his grandparents and can do all the fun things at home."

"Dad, Pop, hurry up," Jacob hollered as he ran back to them. "They're about to hand out presents." The boy grabbed their hands, and pulled them forward.

"Okay, okay, we're coming, kid." Lee chuckled, and they followed their son up to the grass square, which was set up like Santa's workshop with a large red velvet chair set in the middle for the big guy himself.

Children started cheering, and bells began jingling. Frank almost choked on his hot chocolate when he turned to check out who was playing Santa this year. Bear Mitchell, a local diner owner and a tough-as-nails biker, had his typically black beard painted white along with his bushy eyebrows. He was a giant man, but it looked like they'd added a bit of padding around his middle. The red velvet suit with white fluffy trim was in such contrast to the jeans- and leather-wearing biker that he'd never expected to see him playing the main man.

"Is that Bear?" Lee asked in what sounded like disbelief.

"Oh yeah."

"That's a look I never expected on him."

"Me either," Frank said, trying to hide his laughter.

Rick, his partner, and their nephew Joshua were wearing elf hats and were helping Bear hand out the gifts.

"Look, Joshua's uncle is playing Santa Claus," Jacob said in awe. "Hey, Dad, could you play Santa some year?"

Jacob looked up at Lee, waiting for an answer.

Without missing a beat, he answered. "If you want me to, son."

"Yesss," Jacob cheered before running up to get in line with the other children.

"I can't wait to see you in that red suit." Frank chuckled.

"I'll give you your present when we get home," Lee said suggestively.

"Well, I've been a really good boy this year."

"Yes, you have."

CHAPTER SEVEN

Lee

Three days before Christmas, and they were fighting another intentionally set fire. Lee had hoped these days were behind them as the authorities closed in on the arsonist. At least this time, the fire was contained in an abandoned three-story building on the outskirts of Brighton.

They pulled up to find the third story fully engulfed in flames, and as they began rolling out the hoses, he caught sight of Shadow and Spider emerging from the surrounding woods carrying a man who looked to be hog-tied. Dante, Coop, and Vincent walked out behind them as Shannon pulled up with an SUV.

"They got the bastard," Gabe said to their group. "He stuck around to watch the show."

"Finally. This is finally over," Lee said as he shrugged on his gear and air tank, grabbed the end of the hose, and headed in with the rest of the team. Some carried axes, others held Halligan bars, which were crucial for cutting, prying, and chopping wood walls and doors, punching ventilation holes in buildings, or pulling down walls.

With any luck, they could put this out without the fire spreading too far. When they reached the second floor, it was already heavy with smoke, and by the time they rounded the stairwell on the third floor, the flames were already licking around the door frames and along the ceiling.

The team spread out and went to work. The flames forced them back down the stairs at one point, but they regrouped and fought their way back up. The heat washed over them as Lee used his bar to tear down the wall to his left. Ben had taken over the lead with the first hose as a second was brought up the staircase.

The idea was to remove anything burnable from the approaching flames, giving it no fuel to continue burning as it got down to the concrete and metal beams. They were making headway and pushing the flames back when Lee heard the crack above the roar of the fire. He spun around in time to see the ceiling begin to give way above the hose team.

In a flash, he took two steps in their direction and threw himself forward, using his momentum to clear the distance. He shoved the two men holding the hose back against a nearby wall as the ceiling collapsed around him. The last thing he remembered was a sharp pain radiating up his right leg, then nothing.

***

Frank

Frank walked into the emergency room of Brighton General Hospital to find the room filled with people. Firefighters, police officers, Sentinel team members, and EMS stood when Frank entered through the sliding doors. Lee's father and mother were with him, and Jacob stayed home with Frank's parents, waiting for word. He didn't want to make their son feel any worse by seeing all the worried people and medical staff. He'd call when he had word on Lee's condition.

"How is he?" Frank asked as Gabe met them at the desk.

"He's in surgery."

Frank could feel the blood drain from his face and was thankful for the hands on his shoulders keeping him upright. His worst nightmare was coming true.

"How bad is it?" he asked. No one would tell him over the phone.

Before Gabe could speak, the ER doctor came out from the back treatment area.

"Mr. Rogers?" he asked.

"Yeah, that's me."

"Your husband is in surgery. We were lucky to have an orthopedic surgeon on staff, so we didn't have to wait."

"How is he?"

"His right leg is broken in two places. He suffered a concussion and two broken ribs. The rest are superficial cuts and scrapes, none concerning or requiring intervention."

"Will he be okay?"

The doctor smiled wide, which Frank found odd given the situation.

"Before they took him into surgery, your husband wanted me to tell you that it would take a whole lot more than this to get rid of him."

Frank felt the tears roll down his cheeks even as he chuckled at his husband's words.

The doctor placed his hand on Frank's shoulder. "He's banged up and bruised, but he'll heal just fine."

"Thank you. Thank you so much."

***

Lee

"Here you go," Frank said, handing Lee a cup of coffee.

"Thanks."

The day was drawing to a close as he surveyed the mounds of wrapping paper and boxes scattered across their living room floor. It'd been the perfect Christmas surrounded by family. Presents had been handed out, and even though Frank's parents didn't celebrate Christmas in the Santa Claus kind of way, they oo'ed and ah'ed with every gift Jacob opened. Their bellies were full from the traditional kosher meal they'd prepared, and their spirits high.

"It's time to light the menorah," Frank said.

Lee's father pushed his wheelchair to the bay window where their new menorah sat. Hanukkah began on the twenty-fifth of this year at sunset, and it felt like the perfect time to combine their two families and beliefs.

"This is for you, Jacob," Frank's mother said as she handed him a package.

Excitedly, he tore it open, revealing a bag of gelt—silver foil-wrapped chocolate coins— a book, and a new dreidel, which would be a lot of fun playing this evening. Under the book was an envelope, and when Jacob opened it, Lee could see the cash inside.

"That is for your savings, Jacob," Frank reminded him.

"I know, for college," he replied with a smile. "I'm going to be a doctor, like the ones who helped my dad. Thank you, Safta and Saba."

Lee could feel his heart beating faster at his son's announcement. He'd never indicated what he'd like to be when he grew up.

"That is an honorable and selfless profession. Good choice," Saba said.

Everyone gathered in front of their Menorah as Frank placed a candle in the first right branch of the holder. In the center sat the shamash, the candle used to light all the other candles from left to right. Considering it was the first night of Hanukkah, there was only one candle to be lit by the shamash.

Frank removed the center candle and recited the ancient prayers with his son, his father, and mother. "*Baruch atah Adonai Eloheinu Melech ha-olam, asher kid'shanu b-mitzvotav, v-tzivanu l'hadlik ner shel Hanukkah.* Blessed are you, Our God, Ruler of the Universe, who makes us holy through Your commandments, and commands us to light the Hanukkah lights."

Then Frank lit the shamash and handed it to Jacob. "You can light the candles this year, son," Frank said as he wrapped his arm around Lee's shoulders.

"Really?" Jacob asked.

"Yeah."

Jacob took the shamash and lit the first candle of Hanukkah before placing it back in the center.

"*Baruch atah, Adonai Eloheinu, Melech haolam, she-asah nisim laavoteinu v'imoteinu bayamim hahaeim baz'man hazeh.*" Saba recited the after-candle-lighting blessing in Hebrew.

"Blessed are You, Adonai our God, Sovereign of all, who performed wonderous deeds for our ancestors in days of old at this season."

In the light of the Hanukkah candle with the flashing of Christmas lights in the background, three families, three generations, and two traditions came together in one glorious celebration of life, love, and family.

Lee hugged Frank and Jacob close, as did their parents. His entire world could be summed up in this moment with one word.

Home.

Happy Holidays, Everyone. Lots of Love, Michelle XO

GREY

L.P. MAXA

This is so niche, but to all the girls who chug sparkling water.

Love is messy, because we're all a little messed up.

—Pretty Poetry

CHAPTER ONE

Grey

"Where do you think you went wrong?" I woke to the sound of my mom's exasperated voice. I could picture her peering at me from the foot of my bed, arms crossed and hip cocked. I knew that tone like the back of my hand.

"*Me*? You're the one who let him go gallivanting off to Europe when he was seventeen." Now my dad.

Great. I kept my eyes closed and my breathing even, hoping they'd eventually get bored of whatever performance they were putting on and leave me the hell alone. Was the sun even up? I refused to pry open my peepers to check.

"I sent him on an educational school-sponsored field trip with multiple chaperones." My mom came from a wealthy family and traveled her entire childhood. She'd been happy to send me to another country for some culture and diversity.

My dad snorted out a laugh. "Yeah well, he got an education all right. That nudist beach they finally found him on will never be the same."

My mom gasped. "Maybe the nudists wouldn't have been so *friendly* if you hadn't let him pierce his pecker for his sixteenth birthday." I cringed. I didn't love my mom talking about my dick, or calling it a pecker like I was a toddler.

"Oh, c'mon. It was a little baby bar through his shaft. It's the boring kind of dick piercing."

Wake me up at the crack of dawn? Fine. Insult my dick piercing? Absolutely not. I plucked the pillow from under my cheek, using it to cover my ears as I groaned, "You're *both* atrocious parents. Now please go away."

"I'll take credit for his remarkable vocabulary."

"You would." I could all but hear my dad's eyeroll in his voice.

"Go. The. Frick. Away." I might have been a twenty-one-year-old world traveler with a pierced dick, but I was still residing under my parents' roof. And as cool as they were, I would've gotten popped on the back of the head for cussing in front of my mom.

My mom shook my shoulders. "It's time to get up."

Someone tore the blanket from my body. Cold. It was December in north Texas and it was cold in my room. "What? Why?" My money was on my dad stealing my covers. My mom was probably too scared I was sleeping naked.

"If you think you're spending winter break sleeping 'til noon and having your mommy do your laundry, you have another thing coming, my dude." My dad ruffled my hair, then yanked it a little.

My mom grabbed my face, pinching my cheeks together. "Yep, it's take your son to work day for all the days in your foreseeable future."

"Dad's shop doesn't even open until noon." I reached down around my ankles, trying to find my covers without actually opening my eyes. I'd made a mental stand and I refused to budge.

"Oh, you silly boy. You're not going with your father." My mom tsked. "You got in trouble, *big* trouble. Real trouble. That requires real *big* punishment."

"And my shop is nothing more than an all you can eat buffet for your pierced and tattoo'd little ass." I could hear the smirk and slight admiration in my dad's voice. "Literally."

"I think I might vomit." My mom gagged, and then her shoes padded across the floor to the other side of my room. I heard my closet open. My eyes were still closed because at this point it was a game I was playing with myself. How long could I pretend that I was going to be allowed to go back to sleep. "You will be working with me, at the art gallery."

"Noooooooooooooooooo." I flopped around on my mattress, throwing an actual tantrum like an angry child. My mom's gallery, while esteemed, was boring as hell. Tattoo artists were a blast, the pretentious artists my mom tended to work with? Not so much. They took themselves way too seriously and didn't get my humor. Hell, they probably didn't understand satire in its entirety.

"We had to pick you up from *jail*. We had to beg the university not to place you on suspension." The hangers in my closet scrapped across the wooden rod holding up my clothes, which meant my mom was looking for something suitable for me to wear. "You're lucky we aren't shipping you off to some sort of hard-core scare 'em straight military school."

I knew I was lucky. I also knew that my mom's parents, *Babs* and *Pop-Pop*, made a donation to the new art center on campus to help smooth things over. I was their only grandchild. They worshipped me. I could do no wrong in their eyes. Too bad my own parents weren't of the same mind set.

I gave in and sat up, wrists hanging over my knees, eyes peeking open to greet the shitastic day. "You throw one little rave—"

"You threw it in the dean's building. You gave his daughter MDMA." It was rare for my dad to be in for a punishment, he was more of the *live and let learn* mindset. I'd really pissed them off this time if he was standing shoulder to shoulder with my mom and reading me the riot act.

I started ticking off points on my fingers, once again pleading my case. "Uh, numero uno, the dean's building is the only place on campus with a rooftop terrace. I wanted my guests to be able to see the meteor shower. It was basically a science elective. I should've been awarded extra credit. Dos: I didn't *give* her molly. The invite clearly stated, BYOD. D being drugs. I'm not an idiot, and I'm not a dealer. She found her *own* molly and was rolling when she got there. And number uh, tres? Honestly, it's a miracle the dean didn't show up three minutes earlier because if he had he would have caught me railing her tight ass across his de—"

"Nope." My mom cut me off, coming out of my closet with a button-down shirt I didn't even know I owned. "If I've told you once, I've told you a thousand times, I don't need details."

"But the details are what prove that not all of the 'incident' was my fault. So really, my punishment should be sterilization tech and front office bitch for dad." I shrugged, almost feeling the tattoos on my shoulders dancing with the movement. "The dean's daughter's daddy issues are not my bad." I glanced up at my father, checking to see if I was getting anywhere.

His lips were pinched together into a hard line. He was trying to look stern. His eyes always gave him away though. I could tell he found my argument at least mildly compelling and somewhat amusing. I waggled my eyebrows, but he gave a slight shake of his head. I sighed, dropping my gaze in resignation. I'd lost before I even started. If dad was too afraid to crack a smile, mom must be really upset.

"Fine." I climbed out of bed, grabbing the stiff shirt from my mom. "I'll put on boring clothes and go hang out with the holier than thou artists and suffer through my winter break. Merry Christmas to me." I understood I needed to be punished. I knew I'd crossed a new line with jail time. But still. This sucked.

"Apologize to your mother." My dad narrowed his brilliant blue eyes, obviously not appreciating my take on the art gallery vibe. "Now." Damn. I could count on one hand the number of times I'd heard my dad use that tone, and it was never with me.

I stepped forward and wrapped my mom in a hug. "I'm sorry you had to pick me up from jail, and I'm sorry I threw a rave." It was a tiny rave, a baby rave. Really, it was little more than good lighting and a few speakers. I admit the location could've been more inconspicuous, but I was trying to think out of the box and help people trip under the stars. I was a visionary, and we as a people are rarely understood.

She squeezed me tight. "And?"

I pulled away, lips pursed. "And what?" Her eyebrows disappeared into her red hairline. "I'm not apologizing for fucking the dean's daughter."

My mom popped me on the back of my head, saving my dad the trouble.

CHAPTER TWO

Grey

My mom's art gallery was a passion project and not always as bad as my whining would suggest. The converted warehouse's open floor plan wasn't stuffy or pretentious. Actually, it was the perfect blend of understated opulence. Unless you were there when it was being poured, you wouldn't know that the custom polished concrete cost more than marble. Maykin Miles Salinger was a talented artist and an even better curator. She knew talent when she saw it and she preferred her gallery to house the undiscovered over the uninspired.

My temporary punishment/job was basically grunt labor. I had to move art around into different spaces and streams of light until my mother was satisfied with its placement. Not a huge deal right? Wrong. My mother changed her mind like prostitutes changed wigs. Plus, she'd made me dress like a stuffy art dealer for added penance.

I'd moved the same abstract brush fire four times, my mom humming to herself with each placement. If she didn't pick a spot soon, the next place I intended to hang the massive canvas would be the dumpster out back. At least then I'd get some cool air on my face.

"Mom. It's hot as hell in here. If I'm going to be moving art around all day can I at least ditch the shirt and tie?" December in Texas this year was colder than in years past, and my mom had the heat cranked up. I was beginning to wonder if that was part of my punishment too: to make this place feel like actual hell.

She hummed again, ignoring me entirely. I knew she wouldn't stay mad forever. All I had to do was wait her out. She'd been dealing with my shenanigans for twenty years.

I had fantastic parents, and understood how lucky I was. For the most part, they let me be me. I got to pierce and tattoo myself before most kids would. I got to dye my hair and dress how I wanted. I went through an extreme sports phase and ended up with three broken bones and one concussion. I thought I wanted to be a musician for a bit, and they put up with the large drum set in my bedroom. They rolled with the punches. But. Apparently jail and the threat of being kicked out of the only university I'd applied to was where they drew the line. Good to know. Boundaries are healthy.

"I like it *there*."

I fought the urge to roll my eyes. *There* was the first placement we'd tried. "Fantastic."

I hung the piece and then stepped back, admiring my work and shaking out my sore and tired arms. "Am I done?" I'd been at this glorified moving gig for hours now.

"No" My mom turned her back and headed toward the front of the gallery. I followed along, smiling when I saw we were wearing coordinating black converse. Hers platform, of course.

High price goth was definitely the dress code around here both when the gallery was open to the public and when she had meetings. At home? Ripped up jeans with t-shirts. Always. "I have a new artist who should be arriving any moment. All their work is being brought with them and needs to be in place before we can be done for the day."

An entire collection that needed to be hung before I could leave? I take back all the nice thoughts I had about this place three minutes ago. Fuck this gallery. I drained a bottle of water and pulled out my cell to see what my friends were up to. Had to be better than my day.

The double doors at the front of the warehouse opened and a large crate was pushed inside on a stainless-steel furniture dolly.

"Kasen, I'm so glad you made it." My mom wore a huge smile on her face like she was greeting an old friend. She hugged the man standing near the door. He looked vaguely familiar, but I was having trouble placing him. His name... Oh duh.

Kasen and Emmie were related to my parents' best friends, Nicky and Evie. Evie and my mom went to college together and my dad took over Revival Ink when Uncle Nicky moved to Austin to run the Revival Ink location there. Evie and Emmie were sisters, from a huge extended family of super fucking famous people. "Grey, get over here and say hi to Kasen."

I held my hand out. "Hey man, how's it going?" We saw Uncle Nicky and Aunt Evie all the time, but it had been ages since we'd seen the whole crew. There were literally too many of them. The RiffRaff and Devil's Share family would fill the entire gallery. "I didn't realize you were an artist. Weren't you like a male model or something back in your hay-day?"

He laughed lightly, dipping his head like he was almost embarrassed. "Yeah, once upon a time I was a model. I do photography mostly now, but I'm not the artist. It's my daughter, Luca."

I glanced past him as the warehouse doors opened once again. The sun streamed in, blinding me momentarily. Then an angel descended from the heavens, clouds parted, and birds began to sing.

Leggy like a ballerina, a beautiful blonde glided in. She was wearing a skirt and sweater set. Like an actual matching set, with a headband. Jesus. It was all in black, which made it only slightly less precious.

"Luca, it's so nice to finally have you here. I've been looking forward to this for months." My mom embraced the girl, kissing her cheek like she was from Europe and not Highland Park.

Luca. Cool name. She smiled warmly at my mom. "I'm excited. I really am. Thank you for having me." Her eyes cut to me, curiosity in her gaze. Usually, the tattoos made people who eyed me for the first time do one of two things: express distaste or desire. But Luca, she was intrigued, like she had questions, and I didn't hate that she did.

"Grey. Grunt labor and her son." I stepped forward holding out my hand, unprompted, trying to earn points with my mom with polite manners. And with this girl, in case I decided I wanted to ask if I could put my hand up her skirt.

"Nice to meet you." Her palm was small and soft in mine, pale skin against my olive complexion. Hers a blank canvas, mine a doodle pad for my budding abilities.

She was beautiful. But most likely too repressed to be any sort of fun. This girl, this innocent looking human was an *artist*? I doubted her work was anything I'd like.

I liked messy, emotional. She appeared to be the type of person that didn't like to get her hands dirty.

And art?

Art was the best when it was filthy.

CHAPTER THREE

Grey

I lost the tie and I went into the back and turned off the heat. If my mom wanted me here for another couple of hours, that was fine. But I wasn't about to suffer any more than was absolutely necessary. Luckily my mom already outlined where she wanted all of Luca's work to go, so this time I wasn't subjected to her whims and the sun's exact fucking beams. They were back in Mom's office going over contracts and creating a price sheet, so I was left to get this project done on my own.

I hadn't really taken a moment to check out her work while I was hanging it. I'd wanted to finish my task and go do something more interesting. Maybe I'd stop by my dad's shop on the way home, bring him a peppermint mocha and make sure he'd forgiven me. My dad's anger dissipated much quicker than my mom's. It probably had something to do with his A.D.D.

I took a step back after hanging the last piece. Yep. Exactly what I'd expected from little miss put together. Light colors, pastels and shades of beige. Huge canvases covered in clouds or flowers or pretty landscapes. Beautiful. But boring. Like Luca. Art imitating life. Maybe my mom owed Aunt Evie a favor or something because this collection was not what her gallery usually housed.

I went to escape out the front door, but stopped short when something caught my eye in one of Luca's paintings. Was that a woman on her knees? No. There was no way. Was there? Hidden in the background of the picturesque field of wildflowers, there appeared to be someone getting head. Was I crazy?

I moved to another piece, searching it for hidden brushstrokes. *There.* Words, hidden, almost the same shade as the clouds. I knew that song. *I like the way you still say please while you're looking up at me.* Damn. I kept studying each piece, seeking the treasure locked inside.

I chuckled, whispering to myself. "Is that a man snorting a line of coke?"

"Is that what you see?"

I jumped a foot in the air, not realizing that Luca had come to stand behind me. I swallowed, cocking my head to the side, going for unaffected. "Yeah. Art's subjective though, right?"

"It is." She stepped up beside me, moving her head to match mine, like she wanted to see her work the exact way I was viewing it. "However, not everyone can so quickly see what I'm hiding in these paintings. If they did, my dad would probably shit a brick."

I turned to her, a sly smile on my face. "You're hiding actual sex, drugs, and rock and roll in your pieces?"

"I am."

"Because you don't want your daddy to see?"

"It's a little more complex than that, but sure." She moved to the next canvas, glancing behind her before she used her finger to show me the word spelled out in flower petals.

Fuck. Beautiful, and anything but boring. Her *and* her work. I was intrigued, I was fascinated. I studied her, like this was the first time I was seeing her, like she was the art.

Searching for what I'd so quickly dismissed.

Her long blonde hair, soft and shiny. Her tiny nose turned up slightly like she was born unimpressed. Blue eyes, dark though, like a storm. Her sweater hid too much, but her skirt hugged her tight ass.

She was here for a few days, and I had time to kill.

I turned to face her, giving her my full attention. "If you ever need to work out those daddy issues of yours, I'm your guy." I shrugged. "It's sort of my specialty."

She smiled, biting at her lip as her lashes fanned her high cheekbones. "It's comical that you think I want to work through my issues." She gestured to her art. "If I was well adjusted, how would I ever find the space to create." She winked and then turned on her actual ballerina flats, calling over her shoulder, "See you around, Grey."

***

I walked into Revival Ink, high fiving the chick manning the front counter. She was our piercer, fantastic at her job, and gorgeous to boot. She wasn't into dicks though, the appendage or the personality. "Mal, how's it going?"

"Busy. We could've used your help over break. Way to fuck us all over with your bullshit." She pulled me in for a warm hug, because really who could stay mad at me? No one, if you hadn't caught that yet.

"Believe me, I'm learning consequences. Jail would've been easier." My arms were aching. I worked out, I stayed active. But holding giant paint-filled canvases over my head all day was brutal. I knew I would barely be able to hold my toothbrush tomorrow morning.

"Bleu is finishing up with his last client of the day." She jerked her head toward the back of the building. "I made cookies, go have a snack and wait for your daddy."

I let her comment slide, there were cookies to be eaten. Mal made the yummiest desserts. She could open her own bakery if she didn't enjoy shoving needles into peoples' bodies so damn much. She'd been at Revival Ink since I was in high school, she pierced my dick. Baby boring piercing, my ass. It'd hurt, and taken a long time to heal. My dad could fuck off with his piercing hierarchy.

I munched on a cookie and took out my cell, typing Luca Maxwell into the search bar. Nothing about her art came up. Not a website, not a LinkedIn, no social media. Nada. Maybe she was one of *those* artists that was above promotion, like it was beneath her to dabble her wears on the internet.

"Try Luca James." My dad popped his head over my shoulder. "She uses her middle name for her art."

"Wear a bell, old man." That was the second time today someone had decided to try to give me a mini heart attack. I also hated the fact he'd caught me creeping. I switched my search and the page loaded dozens of articles and websites. "Here I got you this, peace offering."

He chuckled and took the coffee out of my hand. "How did it go today at the gallery?"

"Fine." I slipped my phone back into my pocket, not about to scour Google images in front of my father. "Your wife is a master at penance. It's the little things really: the tie, cranking up the heat in the building, making me move pieces around only for them to end in their original location."

"Well kiddo, we learned early on with you that subtle pisses you off more." He leaned against the door frame, a smug smile on his face. "Changing the password to the wifi, taking all your device chargers and locking them in my closet, only buying pea milk for two weeks."

My parents were inventive, I'll give them that. "Did you know that sweet little Luca James was hiding dick pics in her art."

"Among other things." He grabbed another cookie, handing it to me. "You think your mom signed on to fill her gallery with flowers and pretty pictures? You know her better than that."

"And her dad doesn't know?" Kasen didn't strike me as stupid, or blind.

My dad shrugged. "He knows, he simply doesn't comment on it. Kasen has spent his entire life around artistic people. The good, the bad, and the ugly. He and Emmie know why their daughter's art sells. But they also know why she creates, and that matters more."

"She crazy?" I had to ask. I'd also spent my entire life around artistic people. Some were talented, some were haunted, and some were plan insane.

"No." He scoffed, then narrowed his eyes like he was trying to peer inside my pretty skull. "She's also not *for* you."

Not for me? Nonsense. Every hidden hot mess was for me. "Because?"

He straightened. "We're close with her parents."

"Puhleeeese. Those Devil's Spawn's kids are all over each other, and I'm not convinced some of them aren't actually blood related. I mean how do they even keep track? The family tree is starting to look a little wonky if you ask me." He was going to have to do better than that if he wanted me to keep my hands off Luca.

"Okay." He took a step closer to me, trying on his best authoritative parent glare. "She's signed with your mother's gallery, where you currently work. It's a conflict of interest."

I faked a dramatic yawn. "I'm seasonal help, at best."

He snorted, trying to hide a laugh. "How about…liability?" He nodded, like he was proud of himself. "It's a liability to have you get involved with one of your mother's artists."

"Liability? In what way?" It's not like I was going to take her bungie jumping off the nearest bridge, or play that stabby knife through the fingers game before I fucked her.

"You have a terrible track record with the ladies. Tears scatter behind you like a trail of breadcrumbs marking your path through this world." He mimed spreading crumbs. And I stifled an eye roll. "You'll break her heart. And *that*, my dude, is a liability."

I didn't agree. I'd met Luca once, briefly, but she didn't strike me as the kind of girl who would let her heart enter into the equation when it came to me. She'd handed me my ass and then strutted away with a wink. I was pretty sure I'd met my match. "I think you're wrong about her, I think—"

"*I* think that doing *anything* to further upset your mother after she had to bail you out of jail a few nights ago is ill advised."

Dammit. He had me there. Mom seemed super fucking irritated with me. The last thing I wanted to do was make things harder on her than they already were.

I sighed, hanging my head in concession. "Fine. You win this round, old man." I grabbed the container of cookies off the table. "I'm taking my shit, and I'm going home." He chuckled, shoving me playfully out the door.

CHAPTER FOUR
Luca

Maykin Miles Salinger's gallery was a big get for me. She wasn't doing me a favor either, I'd made sure of it. I'd come for a visit on my own, borrowed my mom's SUV and brought a few paintings with me. No one knew I was coming. I lied and said I was visiting SMU for the weekend. My parents were so thrilled that I was showing interest in college that they happily let me leave.

I'd known Maykin my entire life, but it wasn't like we vacationed together or anything. She was my Aunt Evie's best friend. She and her husband were around occasionally. Birthday parties and barbeques, things like that. I never remembered meeting Grey though. And he would've been hard to miss. Tall and skater boy handsome like his dad, but vibrant and alluring like his mom. He was the perfect melding of two pretty awesome people.

I hadn't seen him since the day we got into town and I refused to ask anyone where he was. I refused to be intrigued by him and his devilish smirk. I was here to work. This was my job. My career. I wouldn't be distracted by hypnotizing eyes and intriguing tattoos. If the show went well, then my path was set, and even my overbearing parents couldn't try to change my mind.

School was never for me. I didn't excel in academics like my little brother. Liam was an actual genius. Four years younger than me and already being scouted by schools like MIT.

When I was little, I tried to dance like my mom. She had a studio where she was a ballet instructor. It wasn't for me either. The one thing, the only thing that had ever brought me real joy was my art. Painting.

I'd been at my Aunt Evie's house one day when I must've been five. There was an easel in the corner with a canvas, and an entire set up of brushes and paints. She saw me staring and told me to go for it, to make a mess, to have fun. Later I'd learned that Maykin had sent the supplies to my cousin London as a Christmas gift, and she hadn't been interested.

My life had come full circle. Maykin Miles Salinger had inadvertently introduced me to my passion, and now almost twenty Christmases later, I had a show opening at her prestigious downtown gallery.

"You ready for tonight, kiddo?" My dad patted my knee, a warm smile on his face.

I complained about the future my parents wanted for me, but I knew it was all out of love and concern. They wanted me to be happy, but they were scared. Musicians, dancers, artists, creators were basically all they knew. They'd both grown up inside a proverbial snow globe of talent and notoriety. Chaos. They wanted calm for Liam and me. Peace. Stability and safety.

"As ready as I'll ever be." I turned my gaze back to the window. The sun was starting to set, the glittering lights of the city coming to life. I was a far cry away from the small town where I'd grown up a Devil's Spawn's Progeny. Third generation, respectively. "Thank you for coming with me, for staying while we got everything finalized and set up."

Grey assumed I was hiding things inside my art because of my parents. That wasn't it though, not entirely. My family saw my art, they really saw it. They saw me, and they loved me. No matter what kink I hid in a field of wildflowers.

"Where else would I be? I'm your number one fan." He gave my leg a shake. "Your mom and Liam are meeting us at the gallery, and Granny and Gramps are already there waiting." My dad was listing family members off on his fingers, and we both knew he would run out of digits before he ran out of people. "Smitty and Grand Dil won't be here until tomorrow, the old guys couldn't get out of that reunion gig. They tried though. But we're meeting them for breakfast and they have Maykin opening the gallery for a private showing."

The Devil's Share, my grandpa's band had decided to play a slew of reunion shows this year. Smitty said they were all getting fat and their fingers would stop working any day now, so they might as well make some retirement padding while they still could. They didn't need the money. They owned the majority share of RiffRaff Records, which was thriving.

And contrary to the ribbing they received from their kids, they certainly hadn't let themselves go. Uncle Jacks still had a six pack for fuck's sake. Just ask him, he'd show you.

I assumed they were bored. Aunt Lexi said they were horny for their glory days. It was sweet and very like them to demand Maykin open the gallery for a special showing. Uncle Dash probably offered her an ungodly amount of money to get his way. He once paid Uncle Talon and his band a hundred grand to change the order of the songs on their record so that the first letters of each title would spell out BIGDDASH.

Speaking of retired rock stars tossing money around like confetti… "I don't want the family to buy all my art. You told them that right?" If I had my way, they wouldn't have even known about the damn show. I wanted to see if my art sold, *really* sold, to people I wasn't related to in any way shape or form. "If they come in there and purch—"

"I told them." He nodded his head, lips pursed. "They all swore they wouldn't buy one single piece of art. They believe in you kiddo, you know that. We all do. This show is going to a huge success."

I was confident in my talent, I was. But I was also getting more and more nervous the closer we got to the gallery.

This was it. I was putting myself and my art out there for the world to judge.

I hoped they liked what they saw.
I hoped my art spoke to them.
I hoped it appealed to their eyes and whispered to their desires.
I hoped tonight was the first night of the rest of my life.

CHAPTER FIVE

Grey

I'd been working at the tattoo shop during the day and the gallery in the evenings. I was pulling double time because my dad needed someone to help with the front desk and scheduling. Their main chick was out sick as a dog. I didn't mind doing two jobs at once. I ended up going to the gallery so late in the day that my mom wasn't making me wear the damn button up and tie anymore.

Plus, grunt labor carrying large canvases and crates meant I was getting a workout in at the same time. I thought I would feel more put out, not hanging with my friends over the winter break. Turns out, I didn't miss any of them all that much. The only person I had an urge to see was Luca. I'd been missing her at the gallery, and part of me wondered if that was my dad's doing. He really hadn't wanted me to hook up with her. And he knew if I wanted to, I would.

"Mom, you here?" It was Luca's show opening, and my dad and I had both come to support the gallery. My dad came to all these big nights. He loved my mom more than anything, and never missed any of her shining star moments. He was so damn proud of everything she'd accomplished here. And vice versa. Mom told anyone and everyone about Revival Ink and how talented my dad was. They were sweet. They were goals. Not that I was racing in that direction or anything. Obviously. "Mom? Mother? Momma? Mom? Maykin? M—"

"I'm here, I'm here." My mom came up behind me, tickling my ribs and making me squirm. "Chill." She released me and moved further into her office, picking up the glass of champagne that was sitting on her desk. "Thanks for coming, G."

I fluttered my eyelashes playfully. "Of course. Tonight will be great, I can appreciate a good piece of….art." I knew how my dad felt about me and Luca, but maybe by some miracle my mom would be cool with it.

She narrowed her eyes over the rim of her flute. "You better be here to admin the art, and the art only." She shook her head. "Luca isn't—"

"For me." I nodded, letting out a long sigh. "So I've been told." I hated it when she and my dad teamed up like this. If they agreed on a course of action, I was screwed. Or not screwed in this instance. "Welp, let's get on with it then." I needed to show my face, congratulate Luca and then get out of here. "I have plans."

If I couldn't have her, I wanted to go find someone I could have. It'd been over a week since that roof party. Texas never had particularly brutal winters, but there was a chance of snow starting tomorrow and the bars would be considerably less packed with the threat of flurries. We didn't know how to exist or drive in a white Christmas.

"Oh that's funny. I didn't realize you had plans other than being here with your mommy and daddy." She handed me the last swallow of her drink. "Because you're still grounded."

I tossed it back, fighting the urge to stomp my foot like a small child. "I'm still grounded? I've been working my ass off for a week. That doesn't earn me a little yard time, warden?"

She shook her head, not even bothering to turn around and look at me. "Nope. No time off for good behavior. When you get arrested, you serve the full sentence."

"You got arrested?" Luca's sweet voice carried a hint of amusement.

I hadn't realized she was waiting right outside my mom's office. She looked beautiful, wearing a tight black cropped shirt, and black trousers below which were Gothic inspired Prada loafers. She had this tortured artist meets old money vibe tonight. It was a heady combination and a far cry from the sweater set she'd be in the first time I met her. I found I enjoyed each version of Luca I'd gotten to see.

"Luca, sweetheart, you look fantastic. Love the shoes." My mom brought her in for a hug, kissing one of her cheeks like she had the first time.

"Thanks. They were a good luck gift from my Aunt Lexi." She tucked a strand of hair behind her ear, glancing down at her feet and laughing lightly. "I'm so nervous. I didn't think I'd be this nervous." Her words were spoken softly, almost like she was speaking only to herself.

My mom snatched a flute of champagne from a passing waiter and handed it to Luca. "Here, one glass before everyone arrives, it'll help drown those nerves." Luca took a small sip. "You hang back here, I'll come get you when it's time, okay?"

Luca nodded, taking another larger sip of her drink. Her hand was shaking.

"I can stay with her." I gave my mom my most innocent smile, letting her know that I would be a good boy. Luca looked like she was going to pass out, it would have been wrong to leave her alone and inside her own head.

My mom waited until Luca turned toward the office and then she grabbed my ear, dragging it down so she could speak directly into it. Which, yeah, hurt like a son of a bitch. "You better behave, do you hear me?" I nodded and she released me.

"Jesus mom, chill." Did I find Luca hot? Yes. Did I want to bend her over my mom's sturdy desk and take her for a spin? Also yes. Would I? No. Most of her family was outside and the other guests would be arriving any minute. I was reckless, not stupid.

"Don't touch that girl." One final warning and then she plastered a smile on her face and went into gallery owner mode.

"What were you arrested for?" Luca was perched prettily on the edge of the desk, like she knew all about the fantasies living inside my head.

I shut the door, drowning out the increasing hum of voices and music. "I threw a rave on the roof of the Dean's building."

She nodded, lips pursed like she was impressed. "Nice. Drugs?"

"I wasn't high, and I didn't supply. But there were drugs present, yes." I sat in front of her in one of the two available chairs. Slouching down, I man spread my legs. We were close, but not touching. I wasn't breaking any rules. I'd wanted to see how she reacted to me being in her space. She'd simply raised an unimpressed eyebrow.

"Were you the only one who got caught?"

I doubted my mom would want me sitting here telling one of her artists about my indiscretion. But I had time to kill and this seemed like a good distraction for Luca. "The Dean caught us, not the cops. He allowed everyone else to leave, but made me stay."

"Why?"

Well, at least she didn't seem nervous anymore. Really, I was doing the gallery a favor by keeping her so thoroughly entertained. My mom wouldn't let me use my hands, so my words were all I had. It was her own fault really. "I was fucking his daughter, in his office. She was high. Again, not from drugs I provided. But. Yeah. He was pissed."

"You're dating the Dean's daughter and he had you arrested anyway?"

I couldn't help my soft laughter as I shook my head. "I didn't even know the Dean had a daughter until he told me to get my hands off her." I stood, putting me inches away from her. She had to tilt her head back to hold my gaze.

She smelled like amber and spice, and I wanted to press my nose to her slender neck and breathe her in so deep that I'd never forget how delicious her scent was. "Never met a girl I wanted to keep longer than a couple of hours, you understand."

There was a smile playing on her lips and a light in her eyes that was drawing me in like an adrenaline junkie to a twenty-foot half pipe made of ice and snow.

She wasn't put off, she wasn't disgusted.

She liked it.

CHAPTER SIX
Luca

He'd distracted me. He'd relaxed me. Between Grey and the champagne, I wasn't feeling nervous anymore. Now I was feeling turned on. His eyes, his voice, the way he spoke with no apologies for who he was and what he did. I was into it. I was into him. We were staring at each other, existing and breathing and connecting without sound. There was something here, something between us.

Grey was the first to break the silence. "You ready for this?"

I nodded. The show, him, to face all the people on the other side of the door. I was ready for it all. I didn't care which came first. I'd never felt this way before, no one had ever given me chills with their voice alone.

He leaned forward, his cheek brushing against mine and his chest pressing me back against the desk. I drew in a deep inhale, pushing us tighter together in the process. "Then let's go." He pulled back and handed me the champagne flute he'd been reaching for. There was another devilish smirk on his lips and a wink for added measure as he took a few steps back, away from me.

Seconds later the door opened, almost like Grey had sensed we were about to be interrupted. Maykin was standing there with her eyes closed and a wince on her face. Grey chuckled, "Mom. If you were that worried, why didn't you knock?"

She opened one eye, and then both. "I'm impressed, son."

"You told me to behave, so I did."

I bit my lips together, now understanding why he hadn't made a move when I was so clearly telling him he could.

"I was a perfect gentleman, right Luca?"

"Yes." I straightened, flute in hand. "He was very well behaved."

"Well, that's a first, but I'll take it." Maykin held the door open wider. "The gallery is at capacity, and you've already sold your first piece."

"Are you serious?" I was overjoyed, I also couldn't help but be skeptical. "Wait, did someone I'm related to purchase it?"

Maykin shook her head. "No sweetheart, this buyer is a collector from Houston. I've known him for a couple of years now, and he has no connection to RiffRaff, The Devil's Share, Clashing Swell, or Revival Ink. I promise."

Well, that covered all my family and friends. "Wait. Did he happen to be a huge "fan" of my dad's modeling career?" My dad was exceptionally popular back in the day. Like girls had cut outs of him in their lockers and men fan boy'd.

I was hesitant to think that this was real. That my work was outside, in Maykin's gallery and selling to people who didn't care that I was related to ultra-famous rockstars.

Maykin shrugged. "That one I can't say, but he is married to a wonderful woman and they have three grown children." She rubbed her hand on my back. "Make your rounds Luca. They love your work."

I glanced behind me, catching Grey's eye before I stepped outside the safety of the office. He winked and it was all the encouragement I needed.

***

The next four hours passed in a blur of introductions and praise, including lots of hugs and kisses and congratulations from my family. And sales. All the paintings sold. Every single one of them. I couldn't believe it. The entire night had been so surreal. Now it was late, the champagne was gone, as was the crowd. It was me, my parents, Maykin, Bleu, and Grey. We were polishing off the last of the hors'oeuvres and I was double checking the database to ensure no one I was related to had purchased any of my art.

"Adding up those totals? Going to go buy more Prada gothic wear?" Grey perched on the corner of Maykin's desk, legs out and arms crossed. His tattooed forearms caught my eye and I licked my lips to check for drool.

Grey Salinger did it for me, no doubt. He was gorgeous, but his playfully self-assured attitude is what really cinched it. It was hard to find that perfect balance between endearing and cocksure, but he walked it like a tight rope expert.

I forced my gaze away from him and back to the computer screen. "I'm making sure no one I know bought a painting. My great uncles love to spend money, and my family would buy every piece I created if they thought it would make me feel accomplished."

"Mmmm, well you're going to be pissed."

"Why?" I brought my face closer to the screen, scrolling to look for the culprit. I'd already researched five buyers and hadn't come up with anything suspicious. "Was it my grandpa? He isn't even coming to see the paintings until tomorrow." I stopped, seeing a name I never expected. "You bought one?" I sat back, looking up at Grey. "Really?"

I was flattered. He knew art. He had to. It was running through his veins in the form of tattoo ink and acrylics. His parents were art incarnate, both sides of the spectrum.

"Really." He shrugged. "I like your style. I like that unless you look closer, you're not really getting it. I like that you show the world a pretty picture in a sweater set. But your art is actually dark and fucking filthy."

Filthy was a stretch. But I'd take it. I hid the fun stuff behind the safety of a landscape or a still life. "I was so little when I started painting. It was always flowers and fields, and pretty pictures that would make my mom smile. I started hiding things in my paintings when I was fifteen. I used to put everything I didn't want to say out loud inside them. The things I couldn't tell my parents, the things I got away with. And it progressed from there. The older I got, the more bored I became."

"I know something about that." He wrinkled his nose. "I was so bored I threw a rave in the middle of campus. I knew I would get caught. Hell, I think I wanted to get caught."

"You wanted to go to jail?"

"No. *That* I didn't see coming." He cleared his throat. "I pushed it, and my parents, too far this time. I was craving excitement or something. Looking for the line, the boundary. So I could cross it." He held his finger and thumb up. "A few inches."

"Yeah." I nodded, smiling. "I think I'm always looking for the line too." I liked talking to Grey, I liked feeling like someone understood me, saw me. "It became fun, a game I was playing with myself."

He squatted down so we were eye level. He seemed to enjoy getting into my personal space, and I wasn't complaining. "I like your art." He put his knuckle under my chin. "I like your game."

I'd watched him, all night, even when I didn't want to. He drew my attention, and I'd found myself searching the gallery to see where he was, what he was doing. He didn't meet a stranger. He was so good at small talk and introductions, he put people at ease and he made them laugh. He was dressed in black, covered in tattoos and piercings. He should've come across hard and menacing, yet he was Zoloft in human form.

"I thought your mom told you not to touch me?"

He smiled. No, he smirked. "Just looking for that line to cross, baby."

I licked my lips again, and this time his eyes tracked the motion. There was something here, something between us. I could feel it, like water on a simmer begging to boil. "I leave tomorrow."

"All I need is one night."

"What about your parents?" I knew his mom had warned him away from me, but from the way his dad tracked him all night, I think he had as well. I understood where Maykin and Bleu came from. I understood the way they saw me, and why they were trying to save me. But I didn't want saving. I wanted Grey.

"Your show sold out, you're no longer my mom's artist." He stood, his hand slipping from my chin to grasp my throat. The fire in his gaze, the slight flex of his fingers against my flesh. I was powerless. "You're mine." The deep possession in his tone had my last thread of hesitation snaping and floating to the ground. Even if he didn't really mean it, even if I would never truly be his. I was more than okay with pretending.

"Okay." Acceptance slipped past my lips so easily, almost without thought. I'd accomplished what I set out to do. I created art I was proud of. I got a gallery showing all on my own, and then I'd sold every piece. I was making my own money. I was making my own path. I'd proven to myself and my family that I'd made the right choice.

I wanted to celebrate. I wanted to celebrate with Grey in the dark. Him and me and the stars. No one and nothing else. I wanted this for me. I wanted to be selfish and young.

"Tell your parents you want to go home, okay?" Grey used his hold on my throat to bring me to my feet and I swear I could feel my panties melting off my body. Everything he did was exactly right, like he had a road map of my desire. "Follow my lead?"

I nodded, biting my lower lip, not sure how else to answer him. I didn't trust my voice not to come out all affected and breathy.

I wanted to be cool like him.

Like this was a game we were now playing together and I could hold my own.

CHAPTER SEVEN

Grey

I left the office knowing that Luca would follow me. The way that girl reacted with my hand around her throat? She was mine. For as long as I decided to keep her. She'd turned me down with a wink the first day we met, but now that we'd had a chance to connect? No contest. All I had to do was get rid of the parents up our asses. "Mom, I'm heading out. You need anything before I go?"

"You're not coming for drinks? I didn't think you'd skip that." My dad crossed his arms over this chest, instantly suspicious that I was turning down the chance to drink on his tab at whatever fancy place the adults were headed to celebrate the success of Luca's show. "Where are you going?"

"Uh, home." My mom reminded me I was still grounded hours ago. I wasn't dumb enough to piss her off when I needed her to trust me.

"Home. Instead of a bar? On a Saturday night?" My dad's eyes moved between me and Luca, who was standing somewhat behind me. Was he on to us? They'd sent me in there to get her so they could leave. It's not like we shouldn't have come out of the office at the same time. And I was playing it so cool. I'd adjusted my hard on before I even turned the corner. I glanced behind me.

Was Luca the weak link? No. She looked fucking bored as hell and utterly uninterested in me or my plans.

I sighed, sticking my hands in my pockets. "Yeah, I'm going home. Do you need anything?"

My dad kept staring at me, trying to crawl into my brain again. Luckily my mom wasn't as focused on me at the moment. "No, we don't need anything." She smiled past me at Luca. "You ready to go? There is a beautiful bar down the street, they're still serving food if we hurry."

Luca's parents had sent their son back to the hotel with her grandparents and they were waiting by the door. "Actually, will you guys all hate me if I grab a lift back to the hotel? I talked to so many people tonight." She let her voice soften and drift off, like she was truly worried about hurting everyone's feelings. "I'm feeling a little overwhelmed to be honest."

Add the truth in while you lie, that was a fucking pro move if I'd ever seen one.

"Of course, kiddo. We can go with you, we—"

"No, you guys go and have fun. I'm really just beyond ready to be in bed."

Yeah, me too. In bed. In Luca. I kept my mask in place.

She stepped into her parents' arms, and let them hug her and shower her with more praise. They confirmed their breakfast plans, and then Luca earned her academy award for best supporting actress as she waved away their offers to drive her home. "The bar is within walking distance. I don't want you to have to take me all the way back to the hotel. I'll order a ride."

"Oh, maybe Grey can take you? Since he's headed home?" Luca's sweet oblivious mother had a beaming smile on her pretty face. Oh, Emmie. Poor, poor trusting Emmie.

"Uh, well, I um, I have a driver. You can take my driver." My mom stepped forward pulling out her cell phone and shaking it in the air like a crazy person. "Take my driver. Please, for the love of god, take my driver."

My dad was glaring at me, shaking his head as subtly as he could.

"If Grey doesn't mind, we'd much rather her be in the car with someone she knows." Luca's dad had his hand on his wife's back and his loving gaze on his precious daughter who apparently wasn't opposed to being choked. "You never know what could happen. Better safe than sorry."

"I don't mind, it's on my way." I shrugged like I couldn't give two shits when really I was biting the inside of my cheek to keep from grinning.

My parents were standing together, frozen, staring at me in horror. I couldn't help the snort that came out. They looked so stricken. They weren't stupid. Both Luca and I turning down their offer out of nowhere was suspicious as hell. But they couldn't very well tell Luca's parents that I was literally not to be trusted alone with their daughter. How would that make them look? I'd backed them into a corner and Luca had happily helped.

"Thank you for doing this, we really appreciate it." Kasen reached out and shook my hand and her mom kissed my cheek.

"Oh shoot." I slapped my palm on my forehead, my acting comically thick. "I bought one of Luca's paintings. I was going to take it to your studio for the framer to pick up." I turned to Luca, with a frown like I was afraid of putting her out. "Do you mind? It's already loaded in my car. The framer picks up from there and I want it to match a couple other pieces he's already done for me."

"You bought one of her paintings? Oh that's so wonderful to hear." Emmie was in love with me. No doubt about it. Was this the issue on that compound of theirs? Everyone trusted their kids too much? Was that why they were all hooking up all the time? *Jesus.*

"Leave it here, Grey." My dad stepped forward, his fists clenched. "Leave it here, and I'll take it myself tomorrow. Take her to the hotel, wait for her to get inside and then *go home.*"

I laughed away his clench jawed attempt to thwart me. "The weather isn't going to be great tomorrow, I don't want you driving around for no reason, that's silly. It'll be easy for me to drop on our way." I stepped past my parents, holding my hand out for Luca to join me. I laid my palm on her lower back and guided her out the door, throwing my parents a wink over my shoulder. "Y'all have fun."

I chuckled quietly once we hit the cool night air.
"I know we will."

CHAPTER EIGHT

Luca

Grey's poor, poor parents. They looked downright panicked. His softly spoken words out the door had been gasoline on the fire. They knew where we were going, they knew what was bound to happen the moment we were alone. I wondered if their fear was for my virtue, or for my parents finding out?

"Alright felon, where are you taking me?" I hid my smile as he linked our fingers together, pulling me down a dark alley. "Please don't murder me. I literally just made something of myself."

He squeezed my hand. "I think this is where I should make a joke about murdering your pussy, but it seems too on the nose. Don't you think?" I couldn't help but laugh, he was a breath of fresh air. He was unapologetically himself and I found it incredibly sexy. "I meant what I said to the 'rents. I do want to drop your painting off at my mom's old studio." We stopped beside an old International Harvester painted mat black. "It has a little apartment above it with the coolest views of downtown."

I climbed inside after he opened my door. The black interior was pristine, and the car smelled of clean leather. "Nice ride."

"Thanks. Actually, it belonged to your Uncle Nick." He rounded the car, leaving me to buckle myself in. "I was obsessed with this car my entire life and when I turned eighteen, my parents bought it from him."

"I thought it looked familiar." I rubbed my palms together, trying to warm up. Dallas was only a few hours north of the small town outside of Austin where I grew up, but that meant the winter storm would hit here first. "I think there's actually a picture of me sitting next to my cousin, Cohen, in this thing. I'm wearing Uncle Nicky's sunglasses and Cohen is in a diaper."

"Did you grow up on the compound with all the other little heathens or whatever y'all call yourself?" Grey revved the engine, whipping around to head away from the gallery.

I put my hands under my legs, trying to will the chill to leave my fingers. "Sort of, I guess. My mom and my Aunt Evie both decided that being close was enough. We lived in town, within a few minutes from each other. But it was a pretty short drive to the Devil's Share compound."

"It's you and your brother, right?" We got on the highway, the lights of downtown behind us. "I'm an only child and big families are so fucking interesting to me."

"It was Liam and me, and then of course Evie and Nick have Cohen and London who you know. The four of us are actually related by blood." I sighed, counting off all my proverbial cousins. "Then of course we have Jackson, Weston, and Walker. Those are Laundry and Brody's three boys who are related by marriage to Halen and Beau's girls, Lennon and Irelyn. Avory and Crue's girls, Lyla and Margot are related to Jett and Devin and Cash and Katie's kids, Bingham, Hayes, Mill, Charlie, and Cammie. Then Aunt Marley and Uncle Talon have Co and Miles."

"Damn. How many total?"

"Eighteen." I nodded when he sent me a shocked smile. "It's as chaotic and hilarious and disastrous as you're imagining it is." The heat finally started to pour out of the vents, so I rested my hands against them. "I wouldn't trade it for the world, but it's not anything I aspire to. I don't want a house full of kids, I don't want to eat every holiday meal at tables built for twenty."

"I never craved siblings. I never felt like I was missing out." We exited the highway, taking an immediate left down a quiet side street lined with older brick buildings. "I spent a lot of time with Cohen and London, and that was enough."

I knew that Grey's parents were close with my aunt and uncle, but I didn't have any memories of him. I was sure we'd crossed paths at one time or another, but we must've been too little to make any sort of lasting impression on each other.

Now though, I was ruined. He hadn't even kissed me and I knew I'd remember him and this night for the rest of my life. I could feel it in my bones. In my veins. Grey created this energy, this pull, and every cell in my body responded to him.

"Plus, I mean, you must be Mr. Popular, right? Throwing raves on campus." I was teasing, but honestly, I assumed Grey was the guy with a million friends. Everyone knew him, and everyone felt lucky for it. He was gorgeous, funny, and so easy to talk to. "Not to mention your roster must be pretty damn long."

He laughed. "My roster? Miss priss, what do you know about a roster? You were wearing a sweater set when we first met."

"Did you hear that cousin count? I'm surrounded by males on a daily basis. I know how a roster works." I tucked my cell into my bag as we pulled into a dark driveway. "And the sweater set is how I throw people off their game. I love to be underestimated."

Grey turned off his Scout, his wrist resting on the steering wheel as he turned to meet my gaze. "I did, you know. Underestimate you." He reached out, his knuckles trailing along the column of my throat. "You are so much more than I expected, and I'm an idiot for not seeing it from the moment you walked into the gallery."

"You don't need pretty words to get me inside Grey. I already said yes." I didn't want him to say things like that to me. I didn't want to miss him tomorrow.

"Well alright." He winked before hopping out of the car and coming to open my door. "Let's get your sexy little ass out of my car and into my bed then."

He picked me up, tossing me over his shoulder and taking me inside as the first snowflakes began to fall.

CHAPTER NINE

Grey

Luca slid down my body until her feet touched the floor. I kept my hand on her lower back, keeping her pressed against me. I wasn't ready to let her go, to create space between us. "This is the storage area, purgatory for the projects my mom deemed less than her best." I grabbed her chin when she made a move to step away. I knew she'd want to see, want to explore this graveyard of oil and canvas. "After." One word, it was all I needed to say. She nodded and let me lead her up the stairs.

Using this space to hook up with Luca hadn't necessarily been a conscious thought. I didn't start the night with a plan to bring her here. I didn't see this coming. My parents had made themselves clear, Luca was an artist under contract with my mom's gallery. A family friend, and completely off limits. I'd been a good boy all week. I'd stayed away from her.

Tonight though, sitting with her in the office, talking and learning more about who she really was? I'd been powerless. I'd needed more in a way that wasn't entirely sane.

More time, more words, more stolen touches. I watched her as she worked the room, as people gushed about her work. She was humble and kind, reserved and almost shy at times. But every few minutes, her body would still and her eyes would search the warehouse. Her attention would stop on me, and she'd smile.

She was seeking me out, making sure I hadn't disappeared. I'd been doing the same to her. There was something between us, something that mattered to me.

The main floor was pitch black, the heavy velvet curtains blocking all light from the street. I moved around the room, turning on lamps with mere muscle memory. "Welcome to my home away from home."

"So this is where you rotate the roster?" She walked around, checking out framed photos and little knickknacks, a timeline of my mom's life, and then mine.

My grandparents bought this studio for my mom when she was in college. She rarely came here anymore. She had a studio at home and she had her gallery. I used this little apartment more than she did. I didn't bring girls here though. "You're the first girl I've ever brought here to be honest." I shrugged, my hands in my pockets so I didn't reach out and haul her back to my side. "I'm more of a *let's meet at your place* kind of guy." Leaving was easier when I had to get home, or get to class, or get to my dad's shop.

"I've never done this before." Luca was standing in front of the bed now, tucked behind a brick half wall.

"Please tell me you're a virgin." I knew she wasn't, not with the way she rejected me with a wink the first day we met. Not with the way she laughed at my stupid dirty jokes, not with the way her eyes came alive with my hand around her throat. "I have zero reservations about taking it from you."

She snorted, finding no offense to my words. "Sorry jail bird, been there, done that." She crossed the small space to the kitchen, opening cabinets until she found a glass. "I've never gone home with someone I barely know to a random studio in the middle of a town I don't live in." She filled the glass with water before bringing it to her lips. "I've never attempted to star in my own Dateline Special."

I nodded. "Again with the murder?" She put the glass on the counter and turned to face me, humor in her gaze. "If you don't do the Dateline thing, what do you do? Monogamy?" I made a gagging face, to make her laugh. Honestly the thought of seeing Luca again and again, day in and day out, was almost appealing.

She rolled her eyes and moved back to perch on the end of the bed. "I told you, I have lots of cousins—"

"I knew all you kids hooked up. That many horny gorgeous people on one piece of land? It's too easy." I moved to stand in front of her, loving the way she was peering up at me.

"My cousins have a lot of friends, and go to a lot of parties." She ignored my teasing comment, which I found interesting. "I meet people."

Safety. She met people on her turf, surrounded by men who would no doubt kill for her. She was smart. Too smart to be here in this studio with the likes of me. She was too good, too pretty, too talented. I was lucky to be standing in front of her. I reached out, wrapping my hand around the slender column of her neck. "I won't hurt you, Luca."

"I know you won't." She scooted back on the bed, kicking her Prada loafers to the floor. "It doesn't make any sense, but I can feel it in my bones. You won't hurt me."

Her words were soft, spoken to me and the night. The low light of the lamps reflecting in her stormy eyes as she removed all her clothes, lying before me in black lacy lingerie that I hadn't predicted. Everything about her was like a pleasant mind-bending surprise. I wouldn't hurt her. My soul wouldn't let me, of that I was certain.

I peeled my shirt over my head, tossing it behind me as I toed off my boots. I crawled up the mattress, hovering over Luca. Her hair was a wild mess on my pillows and her chest was heaving. "Are you nervous?"

She shook her head. "No, it's not that." Her fingers danced up my side and until they wrapped around my arms. "We get one night, right? Let's make it count."

One night. I hadn't even been inside her yet and I was already positive that one night with this girl would never ever be enough. I emptied my pocket of the small box of condoms I'd had stashed in my glovebox, tearing one off. Her hands were steady as they unbuttoned my pants and shoved them down past my hips. Our movements were going from rushed to frantic and hurried. Ready. "I'll take my time later, okay? I swear. I just, I need—"

"Don't go slow, I want you inside me. Please."

This girl was going to be the death of me. I slid on the condom as she took off the small scrap of lace that had been covering her pussy. Fuck she was perfect, every damn inch of her was perfect. Smooth and soft and sweet. I wanted to taste her. I wanted to trace her skin with my fingers and my mouth. And I would. Later.

I pushed inside her, admiring the way her back arched off the bed and the small gasp that left her lips. "Oh my god." She moaned, wiggling her hips. "Is that a piercing?"

I chuckled, humming *mmhmm* against her neck. "Do you like it?"

"I don't know yet. Why don't you show me what it can do?"

I pulled back, smirking down at her beautiful face. I pulled all the way out before sliding back inside her, making sure to angle everything just right. I knew what my piercing was doing to her channel, I could feel her pulsing, gripping me impossibly tighter.

"Is that a *yes, I fucking love your pierced dick*?"

She nodded, her lips parted on a whimper. "More." I did it again, and again. All the way out and then sliding home, hitting the perfect spot deep inside her. I wasn't sure how much longer I could last. She felt too good, it was too perfect. Every nerve and sensation was on overload.

The sight of her losing her mind underneath me, the scent of her perfume, the feel of her pussy. I dipped down, needing to taste her. She was sweet, like the champagne she'd drank before we left the gallery. I caught her every moan, the two of us racing toward release, sharing the same space. The same air. I was consumed by her.

"Fuck, baby." I nipped at her flesh, where her neck met her shoulder. "I need you to come for me. I need to feel you."

I pounded into her harder, relentless, until she cried out my name as she came. Her nails sinking into my skin, her breaths in my ear, her pussy fluttering around my cock. It was all too much, it was everything.

Her pleasure triggered my own, dragging the orgasm from my body and her name from my lips.

CHAPTER TEN

Luca

We were in bed, still tangled in the sheets and each other. I felt like I was trying to come down from some sort of euphoric trip. It was the sex, but it was more than that. It was Grey.

Everything about him destroyed me. Being here, in his space with his attention on me, it was fun and light and heavy all at once.

I'd said one night, and he said that was all he needed. But the reality was, I wasn't ready to say goodbye. So I closed my eyes, breathing him in, allowing myself one small moment to acknowledge that I didn't want to leave, that I didn't want to go back to my empty hotel room and climb into cold lonely sheets. One small moment of sadness and regret, and longing. Then I sat up, refusing to be the girl who held on too tight after agreeing to let go.

I tapped my phone screen to check the time, shocked to see that I had missed calls and texts from both my mom and dad. "Uh, Grey? Did your parents call you? Mine have been blowing up my phone."

"My parents have been calling and texting since we left the gallery. I have death threats. And I think I'm out of their will." He trailed his fingertips up and down my spine, making chills dance along my skin. "Do you think yours know all the ways I completely defiled you? Maybe my parents ratted me out in a last-ditch effort to stop us."

I snorted. "I doubt your parents would do that. How would that conversation even go?" I ignored the voicemails and went into my texts. "It's the weather."

"The weather?" He leaned over the side of the bed, grabbing his cell from his pants pocket. "Shit." He launched himself off the mattress and opened the curtains covering the floor to ceiling window. "Luca, you've got to see this."

I wrapped the comforter around my still naked body, padding across the cold concrete floor to stand at his side. "Wow. I've never seen it snow like this." The street was blanketed in white, inches of pristine snow was covering every surface available. "Have you?"

"Occasionally we get snow, but this happened so fast. It must've looked like a snow globe out there." He pulled me into his arms, kissing the top of my head. "The view in here was pretty fucking spectacular, don't get me wrong. But I'm sort of bummed we missed that."

"Same." I rested my cheek against his skin, staring out the window. There was something about snow at night. It made the silence softer somehow. "Maybe we should check in with our parents. You know they have to be freaking out thinking we're on the road in this."

Call us over dramatic, but Texas infrastructure wasn't built for snow or ice. We were rarely prepared for any kind of wintery precipitation. Which meant roads closed down and everyone stayed put until it began to melt and temperatures reached above freezing.

"Mmmm. I'm pretty sure mine are freaking out that I've gotten you naked." He slipped his hands inside my blanket, cupping my ass to haul me into his arms. "Which, I have." He turned away from the window and laid me back down on the mattress, leaving the curtains wide open so we could enjoy the view. "Call yours first."

I raised my eyebrows. "You going to lie on top of me while I make this call?" He shook his head, and then started to kiss his way down my body before settling between my thighs. "Are you serious?"

He nipped at my skin in response. "I told you I would take my time after I fucked you senseless." His kisses turned downright sinful as he moved to my thighs. "You better hurry, because it's going to be super difficult to have a conversation once I really get going. Trust me."

I had every faith that he was telling the truth. Grey knew how to make me feel good. He'd proved that already. I dialed my mom, but it was my dad that answered on the first ring making my position much more awkward. "Please tell me you're safe at the hotel and slept through our calls, texts, and knocking on your door."

I winced, they'd already made it home and tried to check on me. I felt like a guilty kid, caught with their hand in the cookie jar. "Grey and I got stuck at the studio. We've been, um, looking through some of the art his mom has in storage and lost track of time. I'm sorry, I thought you guys would still be out on the town."

"Everything shut down, it's snowmegadon out there." My dad sighed, and I could picture him rubbing his forehead. He did that when one of his kids was stressing him out. "How did you two not notice?" He sounded mildly suspicious.

Grey's tongue darted out to flick my clit, making me jolt. His breath tickled me as he whispered, "She keeps the paintings on the bottom floor where there's no windows. It's like a basement."

"We've basically been in a basement the last hour. We checked our phones and saw all the missed calls." I bit my lip, trying to stay silent as Grey's tongue traced my center. "Are you guys okay? Everyone make it home?"

"We're back the hotel. Grey's parents are staying at the gallery. They didn't want to chance driving farther." He paused and I could hear my mom's muffled voice in the background. "Your mother wants to know if we need to come get you? Is it safe where you are? Do you have heat? Electricity?"

I snorted softly at their dramatics. "Yes. We're perfectly safe and warm here. I think I even saw a kitchen on the main level." I glanced passed Grey's head to the kitchenette where my water glass still sat. "Don't worry about us. You two stay at the hotel and I'm sure as soon as the sun comes up, the snow will melt enough for us to meet you at the gallery."

"Okay, let me know if anything changes. I love you."

Grey slipped one finger inside me, making my *bye* sound much more like a gasp. I tossed my phone to the side and reached down, grabbing his face and pulling him up to meet my eyes. "You need to call your parents."

He smirked. "I'd rather make you come on my tongue and fingers. Then my cock again."

"Same." I groaned as he stroked my inner walls. "But at least let them know we're okay, That we're safe."

"I think they know me well enough to know I had condoms stashed in my car." The car. I was wondering where that box had come from.

"Charming." He needed to be armed with a full box at all times? I wasn't sure how that made me feel, but I certainly didn't want to think too hard on it while part of his body was literally inside me. "This winter storm granted us one whole night alone in this bed. Call your parents, and then we don't need to do anymore talking until the sun comes up."

"I like the way your mind works, baby." He gestured with his head toward his cell resting beside me. "Would you mind? My hands are busy."

CHAPTER ELEVEN

Grey

Luca humored me, dialing my parents and putting them on speaker phone. My cell was resting on her stomach and I found the whole scene incredibly amusing. She got me, and that was such a turn on. "Grey."

Damn, I knew that tone. My dad was pissed. "Don't worry, we're alive and being safe."

"Being safe. You little fucker. You two are still together." It wasn't a question, and *little fucker* was basically a term of endearment in my family so I stayed silent. I was also busy torturing a squirming Luca. "You're at the studio. You were supposed to stop by there and then take Luca home. Please tell me what the hell went wrong."

"Well, we got here and Luca wanted to see mom's collection of misfit toys. One thing led to another and time got away from us. And now, you know, baby it's cold outside and all that." Luca laughed at my holiday references and I kissed her clit in appreciation. I loved how well she understood my humor.

"You never should've left with her in the first place. You are in so much trouble."

I glanced up, my eyes taking in Luca's sexed up hair and the bite mark I'd left on her shoulder. She was so fucking beautiful.

It was more than that though.

It was the way she was still naked, and she didn't care to cover up. It was in the way she was smirking at me, completely unphased and amused that my phone was balanced on her stomach while my fingers were stroking her pussy.

It was her art and her wit.

It was that she gave as good as she got.

It was her.

"This girl, dad? This night? Worth it, a hundred times over, worth it. Whatever imaginative punishment you two psychos are cooking up, I'll happily take it." I tossed my cell to the side, closer to her head and made my way back up her body. I suddenly had this urge to get closer. I needed more. I needed her surrounding me. Consuming me. I kissed her lips, my hand wrapping around her slender neck. She arched into me, her nails scratching down my back.

"You like her."

My dad's voice rang out, reminding me that he was still on the phone. "Okay. Well just wanted to let you know we're warm and safe and we'll be staying here tonight." I bit her bottom lip, making her squeal. "Bye now." I hit end and shoved my phone off the bed and onto the floor.

***

Luca was asleep on my chest, my fingertips running along her shoulder and back. The curtains were still open and there was more snow falling. The whole thing was so picturesque: the perfect girl, and the perfect night. I wanted to stay exactly as we were in this moment. I'd never felt this way before, this need to freeze time. *You like her.* I did. I really fucking did.

I knew the sun would be up soon and I was dreading the moment I'd need to take her back to the gallery. We'd both said one night, but why did it have to be that way? I was in school, sure, but she was an artist. And she could art anywhere.

Hell, maybe she could even art here. At my mom's studio. She could live here too. Shit. What was I doing? What was I thinking?

This wasn't me. This wasn't what I'd thought I wanted. One girl. But I'd never met a girl like Luca before. I didn't think they even existed.

"How are you still awake?" She groaned, pushing off the mattress and rolling her head like she was working some kinks out of her neck. "How do you have any energy left at this point?"

I pushed her hair off her shoulder, trailing my thumb down to swipe over her exposed nipple. "I can't sleep." I didn't want to tell her that it was because of her. That my mind was racing, trying to figure out if I could keep her. If I should even bring it up. "Since you're awake now too." I turned and grabbed her hips, guiding her body over mine until she was straddling me with her hair falling all around us. "Might as well make yourself useful."

She laughed, sitting up and tracing the skull tattoo on my chest. "You're crazy."

"About you." I sat up, grateful for the way she giggled at my lame-ass line. "One more time baby, you can do it." I dipped down, capturing her nipples, sucking one in my mouth while my fingers tweaked the other. She gasped, curving into me. It only took a minute of me playing with her, teasing her. "Trust me?" She nodded, her lips against mine. I pushed into her, completely turned on by her instantaneous faith in me and the fact that I wouldn't do anything to hurt her.

I threaded my fingers into her hair, pulling her head back and exposing her throat. I nipped at her flesh, one hand on her hip to help guide her movements. "That's it, baby, take what you need. Use me. Give me one more."

Our chests were pressed together, our legs tangled. We were so close. Being inside her like this, in a way I'd never experienced before. It was making me *feel* things I'd never expected. I cradled her face, bringing her lips to mine. "You feel fucking amazing."

She nodded, panting. "You're piercing like this, it's, oh god, it's good." I moved one hand down to her lower back, demanding she ride me harder.

"Just like that." I fisted her long blonde hair, I sucked at her sweet skin, making her whimper. "Give me one more and I'll let you rest, come for me, baby."

My words were her trigger, and I felt like a fucking king.

CHAPTER TWELVE

Grey

The sun was so bright, the white of the snow reflecting it in a way that made it almost too much to look at. We'd stayed in bed until the last possible moment, while our phones were both chiming every other minute with parents asking where we were and if we were okay. I hadn't wanted to leave the bubble of laughter and lust we'd created in that studio. It'd been like a dream, and waking up was proving to be a bitch.

I'd been worried things would be weird between us in the light of day. Especially since I had zero experience with the morning after.

I didn't allow sleepovers, until Luca. But there had been zero weirdness. I made her laugh, and then I made her coffee. She kissed me good morning and demanded I take a shower with her. I'd made her come on my fingers before she dropped to her knees to become better acquainted with my dick and it's piecing. Today had been as much fun as last night, and I was so fucking bummed it was coming to an end.

Which was why we were sitting inside my car, getting colder by the second, but still not making any move to get out. My hand was wrapped around her thigh and I wanted desperately to pull her into my lap. I didn't want our time together to end.

"Are we going inside at some point? Or have you decided to live in your car?" She turned to face me, causing my palm to slip even closer to her pussy.

"Careful, baby. I'll make you ride my hand until everyone inside can here you scream." I gave into my urge—shocker—pulling her into my lap. "Let's live in the car. It's roomy enough and we can order all our meals."

"That's actually pretty enticing." She kissed my neck, making me groan. "Except, I can feel your phone vibrating in your pocket, your poor parents are in there losing their minds. We should go in and put them out of their misery."

"Walking in there won't put their minds at ease." I slid my palms around her back, her skin was my fidget spinner and she didn't seem to mind. "They'll see my smirk and your thoroughly satisfied smile and they'll know that I made you come on repeat."

"Oh yeah?" Her arms wound around my neck. "Do I look thoroughly satisfied?"

I nodded, taking in her slightly swollen lips from my demanding kisses, and the semi-permanent blush on her cheeks from the stubble on my face. "Thoroughly."

She giggled, smacking a playful kiss on my lips before throwing open my car door. I helped her climb out when all I wanted to do was demand she stay. Beg for one more day inside that tiny studio apartment with her naked in my arms, in my bed.

Would one more day be enough? I knew the answer. I'd known it from the start.

I reached out grabbing her hand and pulling her to a stop.

No, one more day wouldn't be enough. I wanted all her days. I wanted to make her laugh in the morning, and make her come when the sun went down.

"Hey, so, I have a crazy idea." I used my hold on her to bring her closer, cradling her between my thighs. I wasn't going to let her go without telling her how I felt, what I wanted. Not telling her, it would haunt me forever.

She bit her bottom lip. "Crazier than that thing we tried around three o'clock this morning?"

I chuckled, leaning down to groan into her neck. "Way crazier." I pulled back, my eyes on hers. I wouldn't be a pussy about this. "What if we scrap the whole one night that? What if instead it was more like an every night thing? You and me, all the days, all the nights."

Her gaze narrowed, her fingers tightening in my shirt. "You want to see me again. And only me. Is that what you're saying?"

I nodded. "I think so, yes."

"You think so?" Her smile dimmed.

Shit. I didn't mean that to sound unsure. I wasn't unsure, I was the opposite of that. "I've never done this before. I've never wanted to do this." I rested my forehead against hers. "But the thought of never seeing you again, never kissing you, never talking to you. I don't know, it doesn't feel good. It feels, shitty."

"You like me." I nodded, not sure how to explain that I more than liked her. We'd just met, love seemed ridiculous. It was more than like though, it was obsession or infatuation. "I like you too."

I let out a breath, not even aware I'd been holding it. "So, you want to keep liking me and then like, not liking anyone else?" I wouldn't share her, I couldn't. The thought of her with anyone else sort of made me feel stabby.

"Are you asking me to be your girlfriend?"

"Don't say girlfriend." I licked along the seam of her lips. "I want to do not friendly things to you over and over until you can't remember your own name. Just my girl. Do you want to be mine?"

"Do you want to be mine?"

I whispered against her lips, "More than I ever thought I could ever want anything."

"I want to be yours too."

CHAPTER THIRTEEN

Grey

Well, I honestly didn't think falling for a girl and asking her to be mine was going to be on my holiday break bingo card, but here we were. Walking hand and hand into my mother's gallery, an hour late. Also, Luca had a hickey on her neck that I didn't notice until the sun hit it. This was either going to be a spectacular gift in my parents' eyes, or a complete cluster fuck. Either outcome was fine with me, because both still left me with Luca at my side.

"Are we hard launching?" Luca held up our joined hands.

"I'm definitely hard." I couldn't help it. I couldn't seem to get enough of her. And now, knowing that she was mine to touch and kiss and fuck? I was going to need IV fluids by the time New Year's Day rolled around. "Might as well rip the Band-Aid off though, don't you think? I'm not letting you leave Dallas until you're walking funny." Actually, I wasn't letting her leave Dallas at all, but that was a conversation for later, and preferably while I was also inside her.

She laughed, holding on tighter as I opened the door. Six heads swiveled our way. My parents, hers, and her grandparents. Smitty and Grand Dil. That's what she'd called them, and I was clenching my jaw to keep from cracking up. Smitty didn't look a day over fifty with tan skin and more muscles than I had. Grand Dil? She could be a total cougar if she felt so inclined. Not a wrinkle or pore in sight.

"There you are." Luca's mom came forward and dragged her into a hug. "I was starting to worry you two got lost." I was still holding her hand. To be fair, she wasn't trying to pull away either.

"Why are you touching my granddaughter?" Smitty could kick my ass for sure, but his tone wasn't angry, more curiosity with a hint of suspicion. "Bleu, why is your son holding my granddaughter's hand?"

"I'm Grey." I held out my other hand. "It's nice to meet you, sir. Luca has told me so much about you." That wasn't entirely true, but I was sure she would've talked more about her family if I'd let her come up for air.

He shook my hand, eyes narrowed and grip firm. "You're still fucking touching her." He squeezed my hand harder, making me wince.

"Smitty." Luca grabbed my wrist and jerked it from his hold before wrapping her arm around his neck and kissing his bearded cheek. "Play Nice."

My dad let out a nervous laugh. "It's snowing. I'm sure he was just helping her inside. Right? Grey? You were helping her inside because there was ice and it was slippery and you didn't want her to break her leg, and now you can let her go."

"Nah, there's no ice out there." I used my hold on her to pull her close, kissing her temple when she melted against me. I might as well make my intentions clear, right? I liked this girl and I wanted so desperately to be with her. "I'm for sure going to keep touching her." If me holding her hand was sending these people for a tailspin, I really hoped they didn't notice that hickey. "We're, like, together."

"You're *like* together?" Luca's dad raised an unimpressed eyebrow. "Since when? You've known each other for actual hours."

My mom's laugh matched my dad's. Super forced. "He's kidding. They're friends, and they had a friendly night at the studio and I'm sure he was a perfect gentleman." It wasn't a friendly night, and I was the opposite of a gentleman. My mom was losing it. "And now she's home, safe and sound, and not heartbroken." She pointed at Luca's face, her finger shaking. "She's smiling. Not crying. Everything is great."

I desperately wanted to point out to Luca that her satisfied smile was in fact a dead giveaway, but why kick a person when they were down. And by person, I meant my parents. "Do you need to sit down?" I glanced at my dad. "Get your wife a chair. She looks like she's going to pass out." Dad mouthed a threat to my life, but wrapped an arm around my mom's waist all the same.

I cleared my throat, holding up Luca and my still clasped hands. I did this now, I held hands with girls. Well, with one girl.

"This is what the kids call a, what was it, baby? A hard launch?" I winked at her when she giggled. I loved making her laugh. I loved that she thought I was funny and not a complete dumb-ass. "Yes, we've only known each other for a couple of days, but from what I hear, when you know, you know." I shrugged. "And I know. I really know."

"Luca? Kiddo, is this true?" Her mom looked like she loved me a little less today than she did last night when she was all but shoving her daughter into my grabby hands. "You're dating this boy?"

Boy? I leaned into Luca, whispering in her ear, "Would now be a bad time to correct your mom and let her know that you and I both know I'm all man?"

She elbowed me in the ribs with one of her beaming smiles. "Yes, we're dating."

"And she's staying in Dallas." Shit. I panicked. My plan to ask her later when she was naked and bouncing on my dick had apparently escaped me. I was really hoping Luca was into it and not mad at me for over stepping. "At my mom's studio. So she can work." I turned to look at her. "That sound good?"

"That sounds perfect." She glanced past me to my parents. "If that's okay with Maykin."

My parents were standing side by side, silent and blinking. Confused. My dad spoke first. "Are you pregnant?"

Luca giggled, she fucking giggled at my dad's inappropriate asinine question. "No. Not pregnant."

"Are you being kidnapped? Held against your will? Blackmailed?" My dad was a real comedian today.

She shook her head, then leaned further into my side. "Nope. Hard launch. We're together and I'd really like to stay, on my own volition."

"Well, then sure." My mom nodded, finally managing an expression that was somewhat normal. "If you would like to stay at the studio and work, I'd love for you to use the space. I would be thrilled, actually." She let out a deep breath, like she'd been holding in air and tension for the last twelve hours. My parents needed to chill the fuck out, maybe I could hook them up with that guy that brought all the MDMA to my rave?

Luca's mom and dad pulled her away from me, which I allowed because she'd said she was staying and that she was mine. I was feeling slightly calmer about the whole thing now. My parents seemed happy for me, and I still had two more weeks before classes started. I needed to run home and pack a bag so I could stay with Luca at the studio and—"

"I'm watching you, fucker."

I whirled around. "Jesus, Smitty. You move like a ninja." Shouldn't his old-ass creaky joints have given him away?

"If you hurt her, I'll kill you." His expression was dead-ass serious. Like not a trace of humor. "I'll drive you to the bayou where I grew up and I'll feed you to the 'gators. They'll never find your body. And you know the rule, no body, no crime. Do you understand me, kid?"

I nodded. "Yes, sir."

Luca came back to my side and I automatically wrapped my arms around her. Touching her wasn't even a conscious thought. It was a compulsion.

"Smitty, are you being nice?"

"Of course I am, *bebe*." Smitty completely transformed the moment Luca walked up. He was all smiles and crinkly sparkling eyes. I was pretty sure that was the mark of a sociopath, and I was utterly terrified. "You two ready for breakfast?" Smitty gestured with his hand for us to step in front of him. I winced when his hand gripped the back of my neck, giving me a shake. "I'm buying."

ARE YOU READY FOR THE 3rd GEN STORIES?

GUESS WHO'LL BE NEXT TO FALL HARD.

<u>PLAY LIST</u>

Keep On Loving You - Cigarettes After Sex

It Will Come Back - Hozier

Cool About It - boygenius

Running Up That Hill - Placebo

Go Down On You - The Memories

Motion Sickness - Phoebe Bridgers

MISSION: ACCEPTANCE

EMILY MIMS

CHAPTER ONE

Four-star general and former Secretary of State, Colin Powell once said, "'Pissing people off doesn't mean you're doing the right thing, but doing the right thing will almost inevitably piss people off."

If ever anyone could swear to the truth of that statement, it was San Antonio PD officer, Preston Ramos. In the last year, he'd managed to piss off just about everyone in his life. As it pertained to some of them, it was when he was doing the right thing, and as it pertained to others, it was when he wasn't. Most had yet to forgive him, and some never would.

Preston answered the last question his brother's attorney asked of him and was excused from the witness stand. He stepped down, exhausted from two grueling days testifying in excruciating detail about the two weeks he spent with an Army Black-Ops team chasing down his brother and his brother's partner in crime, who were dealing contraband emeralds for a corrupt Colombian official funding terrorism in America and elsewhere.

According to the prosecutor, Preston's testimony carried significant weight and had effectively sealed his brother's fate, assuring he'd receive a long prison sentence for his various crimes.

It had also permanently alienated Preston from the entire Ramos clan. "You're no son of mine," his father had told him. And Roel Ramos meant it.

The family had utterly and completely cut off Preston. No phone calls, no invitations to have a meal at his mother's table, no beer and football with his cousins, and no Christmas dinner.

Nada. Nothing. Because he'd told the truth and had done the right thing, and put the welfare of his nation before his loyalty to his self-centered family.

Never mind all the favors his father had called in over the years, most of them involving Preston using his position as a police officer to get the dirt on his father's business rivals. But he was done being his father's shill. Preston had dared to defy his father and tell the truth about his brother's crimes in a court of law, and for that he would never be forgiven.

It hurt more than he wanted to admit, especially with the holidays mere days away. And even though he wouldn't be spending them alone, he had to admit, not being with his family at this time of year sucked.

He walked past his brother, who was sitting at the defense counsel's table, inwardly wincing at the damage Jeremy Ramos had suffered during three days of brutal torture at the hands of the emerald cartel. Jeremy's once handsome face was now grotesquely scarred, and even after intensive physical therapy, he would never be able to walk normally.

Preston strode up the aisle, ignoring his father's hate-filled eyes and his mother's cold stare, and ducked out of the courtroom into the hall of the Fort Sam Houston Justice Center where he encountered more people he'd managed to piss off royally, most of whom hadn't forgiven him either.

Except for the one, and only one, who had.

He tilted his head in a perfunctory nod to the members of the Black-Ops team waiting to testify. They were an impressive bunch, even more so in their dress greens, attired for their appearance in court.

Paco Morales and Eagle Begay returned his nod with chilly ones of their own. Jazz Washington, who'd been hurt on a recent mission, sat in a wheelchair. He too greeted Preston without warmth.

Despite the success of the operation he'd participated in with them, the team had never forgiven him for the failure of an earlier mission that went sideways because he'd unfairly detained their team member Sabina Kaslov, causing them to be unable to rescue an attaché's family in Mexico.

Colonel Johnson's smile was a bit friendlier, but not much, and she asked him how he was doing, to which he answered the socially acceptable "fine." She was no fan of his either, and he doubted he'd be invited to dinner at her house any time soon.

But his attention was drawn to the woman sitting at the end of the row, the one and only person who'd forgiven him for his shortcomings. Sergeant Sabina Kaslov: his friend, lover, and, if she said yes to his upcoming Christmas proposal, his fiancée. Sabina's love was the only thing that had made the last few miserable months bearable, and he loved her more and more every day.

She spotted him and her face lit up in a sympathetic smile. He walked toward her and she scooted over to make room for him on the bench. He knew better than to hold her hand or kiss her in public. They needed to keep their relationship on the DL until after all the trials associated with the mission were finished. But she gave his hand a discreet squeeze as he sat down beside her. "How'd it go?" she asked quietly.

"It was tough," he admitted. "Jeremy's attorney did everything he could to make Jeremy look good and throw shade on Dominic."

Her face clouded. "We knew they were going to do that. I have no doubt Dominic's attorney will try the same tactic when his trial comes up." She looked at him. "Was it hard, testifying against your brother?"

"Wasn't fun. And you're going to have to do the same thing next month." Sabina's brother Dominic had been Jeremy's partner in crime.

"It's not costing me what it did you. Mom and Dad are pissed, but they haven't kicked me out of the family. At least not yet."

"They won't. They can't be too mad. Hell, they're planning to come over from Houston to celebrate Christmas with you."

"Us, Preston. They want to celebrate with us."

"They also want to check me out." Preston's lips twitched. "Your daddy own a gun?"

She snickered. "Not to my knowledge. But you never know."

The courtroom door opened and the clerk called for Sabina and cautioned the rest of the witnesses not to leave.

With the only friendly face in the crowd gone, he got out his phone and pulled up his reading app, burying himself in the latest James Patterson novel until Sabina reappeared a couple of hours later.

"The judge dismissed everyone for the day," she announced to the waiting witnesses. "The prosecutor said he needs to talk to everyone from the team who hasn't testified yet, and wants you to meet him in Colonel Bustamante's office in an hour."

"That's pretty much all of us except Sabina," Colonel Johnson said. "See you all in a few."

En masse, they headed for the elevator and out the door to the parking lot. Low clouds hovered, and the sky was spitting chilly rain. "It's cold," Sabina complained as she got into her new car.

"Where to?" he asked.

"How about that little burger joint on Rittiman Road? It's close and I'm hungry."

He followed her in his truck and in a few minutes they had double cheeseburgers and a mountain of fries sitting in front of them. "Mom and Dad are driving in on the twenty-second," Sabina said. "They plan to visit Dominic in prison the next day and spend the rest of the holiday with us." She grinned. "Our first Christmas together."

Which took some of the sting out of not seeing his family on the twenty-fifth. "The first of a bunch of them, I hope."

Sabina dug into her burger with gusto. That was one of the many things he loved about her. Her zest for life. She was an interesting woman, his Sabina. His soldier. His warrior.

Of Romani descent, her hair and eyes were dark, and her facial features were bolder and more arresting than classically beautiful. As a member of Bear's Brigade, an elite, covert unit, she was stronger and more muscled than the average woman, but, at the same time, she was sensual, desirable, and absolutely mouth-watering.

He'd made love to her countless times and knew every inch of her delectable body, and the more time he spent with her, both in and out of bed, the more he wanted her by his side for the rest of his life.

Which explained the Christmas gifts he'd chosen for her. He'd found a locksmith who'd crafted a sterling silver key to his front door, since part of his proposal was going to be an invitation to move in with him, and he'd also bought a gold ring in a striking cutout design that would lay flat against her finger, but extend from knuckle to knuckle.

It didn't look like an engagement ring, which was deliberate, since they weren't advertising their relationship, but he hoped she'd wear it on her left hand until he could place a wedding band there.

He wasn't too sure how he was going to go about creating a memorable proposal, but he had almost a week to figure something out that would involve her parents as part of the occasion. Maybe her mother would have some ideas.

They were finishing up the pile of fries when Sabina's phone went off with Colonel Bustamante's telltale ring.

"Uh-oh," Preston said quietly.

"Maybe he's calling about the upcoming meeting," she said. "They may want me there after all."

She answered and listened quietly for a couple of minutes, her face growing solemn. "Yes, sir. I understand." She paused a minute. "I'll pick up my go-bag and be there in twenty." She clicked off her phone and looked across the table. "I guess you heard."

"Mission?"

Sabina nodded. At least she didn't have to call it a "training assignment," the euphemism used by the team when they were being sent on a mission.

Thanks to the operation he'd gone on with them, he had a better idea than most partners what kind of work the team undertook, and the danger they faced. Sabina couldn't ever tell him the specifics, where she was going or what she was doing, which was always somewhere out of the country, and inevitably dangerous. On the one hand he wanted to know where she was going, and other, not. He slept better at night being oblivious to the details.

"Yeah. We leave in an hour. He said we'd be gone between one and two weeks."

He tried to hide his dismay. "There goes Christmas together."

Sabina looked stricken. "I know. I'm sorry. I'll make it up to you when I get back."

"Sabina, you don't need to 'make it up to me.'" He made air quotes with his fingers. "You have a job to do and it's got to be damned important for them to send a team at Christmas. Don't worry. I'll be fine and we'll celebrate when you get home." He smiled weakly and gestured to the remaining fries. "Grab a couple more and get going."

Sabina bit her lip. "Are you going to be okay?"

"Honey, I'll be fine."

She downed a couple of fries and headed out the door.

Preston sighed. Would he be okay was a matter of opinion.

He was going to be alone for Christmas.

It sucked like a son of a bitch, but there wasn't much he could do about it.

CHAPTER TWO

Sabina swapped her dress greens for worn-out jeans and a navy knit pullover, then went into her front closet for the go-bag containing her clothes, her weapons, and her tool kit. *Damn, damn, damn.* Of all times to have to go on a mission. And all the way to Argentina to babysit General Vanderveer's tattooed do-gooding daughter while she smuggled in a wad of cash to donate to an Argentinian orphanage. Why couldn't the girl wire them the damned money like a normal person? Unfortunately, no one dared to say no to the general, not even Colonel Bustamante, so she, Vorhees, and Galinski were going down to Argentina to make sure the girl stayed safe.

Which meant Preston would have to spend Christmas by himself, which sucked for them. Big time.

Her tall, sexy, good-looking cop had tried to be brave, she thought as she threw her stuff in the car and headed for the colonel's office. But she could see the disappointment in his eyes. As totally shitty as his family was, he loved them. And being completely disowned, to the point where they wouldn't even talk to him, had hurt him deeply.

He'd been counting on Christmas with her and her parents, and now that was out. It was going to screw up Christmas for the Kaslov family too, and make what was already going to be a tough holiday even worse for her mother and father.

Speaking of. She started her car and called her parents. "We're both here," her father said. "What's going on?"

"Christmas hit a snag," she said without preamble. "I just got called away for a two-week training assignment, and definitely won't be back until after Christmas."

"Training assignment? At Christmas?" her mother asked disbelievingly. Her parents didn't know what she really did, and they seemed to buy into all training assignments the Army sent her on.

"Don't they have any respect for the holidays?" her father groused.

"No, they don't. But it doesn't have to be a total loss. Why don't you and Mom come over anyway? You can still see Dominic and spend the rest of your time with Preston."

Her parents were silent for a minute. "I don't think so," her mother said slowly. "The only reason we were coming was to see you."

Sabina winced. Things had been chilly with her parents since she didn't cover up Dominic's participation in the criminal activities he and Jeremy engaged. Since they'd been arrested, she'd seen her folks only a couple of times.

Things had been even chillier between them and Dominic. Her parents had seen him only once since his arrest, and that visit had been anger-filled in the extreme.

"What about Dominic?"

"It hardly seems worth a trip for a thirty-minute visit to have another shouting match with him," her father said with a tinge of bitterness. "We'll see you both in January."

At Dominic's trial.

"Okay," Sabina said quietly. "I'll see you after I get back."

Her father clicked off and she stowed her phone in the center console and slowed as she approached the guard post at the entrance to Fort Sam.

She couldn't blame her parents. They didn't know Preston, and she understood why they didn't want to see Dominic. They'd aged ten years since Dominic had gotten into trouble, and they'd been so deeply angry and disappointed by her brother's criminal behavior that she doubted their relationship with him would ever heal.

At least they were thawing toward her. She could only imagine Preston's pain. Her parents were angry and hurt, but they didn't shut her out. Preston's family cut him off like a diseased limb.

She parked and took the stairs two at a time up to the colonel's fifth floor office, where a good number of Bear's Brigade waited for the prosecutor, each with varying degrees of waning patience.

Colonel Johnson, sitting in one of the visitor chairs, was flipping through her phone. Eagle sat on the edge of Lacey's desk with his heart in his eyes as he chatted with the colonel's administrative aide. Paco and Jazz were debating the merits of soul food versus Mexican food, and Josh Galinski and Jason Voorhees had their go-bags with them and seemed to be totally fine with having to go on a mission over Christmas.

"You ready, Sabina?" Galinski asked.

"I suppose. Not real thrilled. You two seem happy enough, though."

"It's now a Christmas tradition with us. We went with the general's daughter last year almost to the day," Voorhees said. "Fell in love with this dude on the trip. Seems to be an occupational hazard with our crowd. Falling in love on missions."

Sabina smiled. "Kind of is. Except I'm leaving my sweetie all by himself for Christmas."

"Aww, poor widdle Preston," Eagle said derisively. "All by his wonesome."

"So the fuck what?" Paco rolled his eyes. "He's got a family. A damned rich one. He can eat turkey with them."

"Couldn't happen to a nicer asshole," Jazz chimed in.

"What is this, shit central?" Sabina demanded. "You're being jerks."

"That we are, and with good reason," Eagle said. "Look, I get that you love him or something, but to the rest of us he's still an asshole and always will be."

"Seems to me he's not the only asshole," Sabina snapped. "He's going to be all alone. He's not going to eat turkey with his rich family because they threw him out on his ass and won't have a damned thing to do with him. And Jazz, who I would've thought knew better, you're being an asswipe and I don't appreciate it."

"Aw, come on, Sabina. He won't be alone," Paco said.

"He sure as hell will." Sabina looked around at her fellow soldiers. "You clowns don't understand. You weren't there the afternoon his father declared Preston dead to the Ramos family. Back in the spring, when he went into the debriefing he told the truth. He didn't lie to make Jeremy look better. His father disowned him that day. Shouted it so damned loud everybody in the hall heard him yelling at Preston over the phone. Preston did what was right, and put the good of his country before the self-centered demands of his family. And for his service, he was kicked out of his family."

"She's right." Colonel Johnson looked up from her phone. "I overheard the conversation. His father was quite angry and said Preston was no longer a Ramos son. It was pretty brutal."

"They kicked him out?" Lacey asked disbelievingly. "Just like that?"

"Yep," Sabina nodded. "They did. Big time. He's dead to them. And if they were ever going to forgive him, he put paid to that yesterday and today when he swore to tell the truth in a court of law, helping the government secure Jeremy's conviction.

"He paid a price, a damned high price, for doing the right thing." She looked around at her teammates. "Any of you ever had to pay that kind of price for your integrity? How 'bout it, Eagle? Has your *shinali* disowned you? Jazz? Has your Granny Washington, or your cousin Felicia kicked you out of the family? Have any of you *ever* had to pay that kind of price for doing the right thing?"

They looked at one another, and finally appeared contrite. "I didn't know," Jazz admitted.

"Sounds like the whole family's a bunch of assholes. I guess he came by it honestly," Eagle said.

"You're such a moron," Sabina told him.

"I don't care if he is an asshole. I don't care if he's the biggest asshole in San Antonio. Nobody should have to pay that kind of price for doing the right thing. And nobody ought to have to spend the holidays by themselves," Lacey stated.

"Thanks. But, as the saying goes: it is what it is. I hope he won't be too lonely by himself."

"One of the hazards of being with a Bear's Brigade operative," Colonel Johnson pointed out dryly. "Have a safe trip, Sabina."

"Thanks, Colonel Johnson. See you all after Christmas."

CHAPTER THREE

Preston stood in the middle of his living room with his hands on his hips and looked around. It was nice, his little deco-style house. It had good bones, and clean lines, along with the geometric ornamentation that was so popular when the house was built ninety-five years ago.

He'd bought the place after his divorce, and had spent the last year and a half painting and remodeling, while and adding updates that respected the deco look.

He'd bought the bare minimum of simple furniture that complemented the style. But the furnishings were sparse: a sofa and a matching chair. A kitchen table and a bed. Not even a coffee table or a nightstand.

And there were no homey touches, no comfy pillows or pictures or anything personal anywhere. The bathroom was utilitarian in the extreme and the kitchen had the bare minimum of cookware.

The only thing that could be even remotely considered décor was the huge wall-mounted television every single man owned. It was the epitome of a bachelor pad. Despite the time and effort he'd put into the painting and remodeling, it was still a house. Not a home.

He wasn't sure Sabina would even want to live here.

Not that her place was much better. As a soldier, she traveled light, and he suspected most of her furnishings were part of the lease. But if he was going to invite her to share the house and make a home with him, he needed to make his house someplace inviting, a place to unwind and relax, a place where they'd make memories while spending time together.

Damned if he knew how to do that.

He shrugged and headed for the shower, leaving his SAPD uniform in a trail down the hall and across the bedroom. Maybe he could get some ideas online. There was a YouTube video with instructions on pretty much everything. It was a hell of a note. He was nearly forty years old and didn't know how to decorate his own house.

He supposed a lot of men didn't.

He took a hot shower and tried not to think about the next few days. Christmas was four days away and was looking bleaker by the minute. Sabina was on radio silence, and he hadn't heard word one from his asshole family. Not that he expected to.

He'd already offered to work the twenty-fifth so Mike Werner could spend the day with his daughter and lady love, but that still left a long, lonely Christmas evening by himself watching corny holiday movies on the oldies channel.

Maybe next year would be different.

He pulled on a long-sleeved tee and was running his fingers through his wet hair when the doorbell rang. A second of hope flared before common sense reared its ugly head and curiosity took its place. It wasn't Sabina, and it wasn't his mom.

UPS, maybe.

He looked through the peep hole, blinked a few times, then opened the door with his mouth still hanging open in surprise. Eagle Begay stood on his front porch holding hands with a pretty blonde Preston had met once before. Her name was Laurie? No, that wasn't right. Um, Lacey.

Eagle and Lacey both had tentative smiles on their faces.

What the hell were they doing here?

"Uh, hey guys. Come on in." He opened the door wider and gestured for them to enter.

They trooped in and he motioned them into the living room. "Can I get you anything to drink?"

"We're fine," Eagle said.

"What can I do for you?" Preston asked.

"We're here to kidnap you," Lacey said cheerfully, and smiled engagingly.

"Kidnap me?"

"Lacey's idea," Eagle said. "We're going out to dinner tonight before my *shinali* gets here tomorrow and thought you might like to come along."

"His grandmother's not much for restaurants, so we'll be cooking at Eagle's place until she goes home," Lacey added.

Sabina had probably put them up to this.

Nice of her, and nice of them, but completely not necessary.

"It's…it's okay," Preston stammered, trying to decline gracefully. "You probably want to spend the evening together alone. You know, just the two of you. You don't need a third wheel."

Lacey put her hands on her hips. "It's not okay. We'd like you to come. Besides, what are you gonna do if you don't come with us?"

"Actually, I was going online to look at some decorating ideas for this place. Make it a little more appealing. Someplace a woman might want to live."

"Inviting Sabina to move in?" Eagle asked.

"Something like that. I don't think this impresses her much." He gestured around the room. "It's pretty spartan."

Lacey's eyes narrowed and she looked around the room thoughtfully. "It is. But we can do something about that. Let me think a minute."

Eagle rolled his eyes. "Ramos, you did not say what I think you said to Lacey." He shook his head. "That was like saying sic 'em to a bulldog."

"Oh, hush, Eagle. I love to decorate. I really like to pretty things up and make a house or an apartment homey. So sue me."

"You like to pretty things up?" Preston asked, hoping for a little assistance, but wasn't going to ask for it.

"Love to. And Preston, you have a point. The furniture you have in here is great, obviously quality, but I've seen Bachelor Officers'

Quarters that were more inviting and welcoming than this place." She took another look around the living room. "Kitchen?"

He pointed to the door and Lacey disappeared. "Her thing?" he asked Eagle.

"Completely. Her apartment's all done up."

She reappeared shaking her head. "The kitchen needs some attention, too. Like maybe something to cook with. Something to eat on. What about the bedrooms and bathroom?"

Preston shrugged and pointed down the hall. He and Eagle had barely sat down when she reappeared. "How about instead of dinner we grab some take-out then hit a few home stores and spiff up this place a little bit?" Lacey asked. "Let's make it more attractive for Sabina."

He hadn't wanted to go to dinner with them, but this was something else entirely. Lacey was actually offering him some much-needed help. He'd be an idiot not to take her up on it.

He turned to Eagle. "Are you okay with spending the evening traipsing through home stores?"

"Won't be the first time I've gone with her," Eagle said dryly. "My apartment barely knows itself these days."

Preston's F-150 had a camper shell and could hold a lot of stuff. They climbed in and Lacey leaned over and named a popular cookware store in one of the malls. "We don't have to go broke on kitchen goodies, but Sabina's going to want a set of basic pots and pans if she doesn't have any," Lacey said. "Does she have cookware? Tableware? Knives, forks, plates, cups?"

Preston nodded. "She has tableware, at least some. But little in the way of pots and pans."

Despite the heavy traffic, they made good time and before long were standing in the middle of a high-end cookware store. Preston stared in consternation at the array of every cooking device imaginable, from the most basic to the most frivolous. Lacey was already sweeping down the aisle, loading gadgets into a basket. "I'm glad she knows what she's doing," Preston murmured. "Because I sure as hell don't."

"Welcome to the club," Eagle mumbled.

They waited patiently making small talk and Preston found himself liking Eagle. The man was articulate and funny, as well as friendly and surprisingly warm. He was easy to talk to, and Preston wished to hell they hadn't gotten off to such a rocky start on their mission together. Eagle was a man he'd like to have as a friend.

Lacey showed Preston her choices and he agreed they would work. He handed over his credit card and soon they were lugging her selections, which turned out to be considerable, to the truck. "Where to next?" he asked as they got back in the truck.

Lacey thought a minute. "Basic comfort. Stuff like end tables and a coffee table. Nightstands for the bedroom. A few throw pillows to soften things and curl up with for a nap. And pillow shams and a bed skirt to accent that gorgeous quilt in your bedroom. Family heirloom?"

Preston felt an unexpected pang. "My *abuela* made it for me and my ex-wife." He made a rueful face. "It's probably the last family heirloom I'll ever get."

"Well, shit," Eagle murmured.

"Anything else probably should wait for Sabina to choose for herself. I'd hate to buy a lamp she detests," Lacey said with a smile.

"I didn't know you could detest a lamp," Preston said.

"You can. Believe me, you sure as hell can," she assured him.

They laid waste to two more stores before Lacey was satisfied, it was well after dark before they pulled into Preston's driveway. "Now we have to lug all this stuff in," Eagle groused.

"That's right. And as soon as it's unloaded, you can go on a take-out run while Preston and I get it all unpacked and put it where it goes."

It didn't take long to get the camper unloaded. Preston and Eagle placed the retro coffee table, end tables, and nightstands where Lacy instructed them to, and then she sent Eagle on a pizza run while she and Preston dealt with the new pillows and shams for the bedroom and the beautiful new bed skirt. Preston crossed his arms and looked at his bed. "I like it."

"It sets off the quilt beautifully," she sighed. "Now let's see if the pillows for the living room work."

Of course, they did. Preston was admiring the effect when Eagle came in bearing two huge pizzas and a six pack of soda. They sat down at his dining room table with paper plates and dug into the pizza. "This is delicious," Lacey said as she practically inhaled a slice. "You get these often?"

"We do. There's not much else in the area. The Deco District's nice but it's kind of a restaurant desert," Preston admitted. "The grocery store's deli does a lot of office business. It's always busy."

"No worse than living on the rez," Eagle said. "We had practically nothing. *Shinali* would have had to drive forty miles. Needless to say, we did our own cooking."

"I thought we'd take her out while she's here, but Eagle says she wouldn't like it," Lacey said. The girl looked uncertain. "I'm a little nervous. I don't know how she's going to feel about Eagle dating a *bilagaana* woman."

"A what?" Preston felt his brows go up.

"A white woman," Eagle said. His eyes softened as he looked at Lacey. "She's going to like you, Lacey. Especially since, you know."

"I hope you're right," Lacey murmured.

Hmm. Eagle and Lacey were keeping a secret.

He gave a mental shrug. None of his business.

They managed to demolish both pizzas and all the soda. Lacey volunteered to help him put away the new cookware but he assured her he could manage. "I don't know how to thank you," he said as they gathered up their jackets. "Both of you."

"I didn't do much," Eagle protested.

"You kept me company in some scary places," Preston said with mock solemnity. "Lacey, you did a marvelous job. This place is ten times better than it was. I love it, and Sabina will too."

She beamed. "I'm so glad you like it, and I hope Sabina does. We love her, you know."

"So do I," Preston said quietly.

"I'm sorry you'll be spending Christmas by yourself," Lacey said. "I've had a few Christmases alone over the years when Dad was deployed and I couldn't get to either grandmother. They're not fun."

"I'll be fine," Preston assured her. "It's one of the hazards of dating a soldier. Especially one who does Sabina's job. It's part of who she is, and I respect her for it."

"Thanks for that," Eagle said. "Not every partner does."

Lacey gave him a big hug, and he and Eagle shook hands. He stood at the window and watched Eagle's taillights until they disappeared at the corner.

It all boiled down to Sabina, he thought as he pulled his shades and stripped down to his underwear. They had reached out to him because of her. It wouldn't surprise him if she'd asked them to come over and to take him under their wing. Spend a little time with him. They'd asked him out to dinner for her.

Surely, they hadn't done it because they loved him.

Still, he appreciated it, no matter their motivation.

Lacey was a sweetheart. Eagle was no fan of his, but the man had been warm and friendly, more so than Preston expected him to be. Actually, he seemed to like Preston. If only. Eagle was a decent guy.

Preston wouldn't mind having a friend like Eagle Begay.

CHAPTER FOUR

Preston dragged himself to his truck and clicked open the locks. He was tired, cross, and sweaty, and wanted nothing more than to stand under a shower and wash away the shitty day at work.

It'd been a few years since he'd worked the seven to three on Christmas Day and he'd forgotten how absolutely crazy unwrapping gifts and eating turkey made people. He'd started the shift with a bang, catching a domestic disturbance call involving a married couple, the husband's side piece and a loaded revolver, and it had gone south from there. He worked a couple of DUI car wrecks, given some speeding tickets to irate drivers trying to get to Grandma's house, refereed three liquor fueled dinner table fist fights over politics, dealt with an assault triggered by a barking dog, and even made three arrests for a slugfest over whose turn it was to carve the turkey.

And that was the day shift.

He felt for the cops on the three to eleven, and really felt for the ones working the graveyard, when the liquor had been flowing for even longer and tempers were even shorter and the crazies were seriously out in force.

No telling what kind of shit those men and women were going to face.

Traffic had been light for most of the day but was beginning to pick up. The restaurant parking lots were mostly empty, but the movie theater lots were packed and there was a long line at the ticket booth. He started to pull in and catch a Christmas Day release, but the only one worth seeing was one Sabina wanted to watch, so he'd wait and take her when she got home. Which left either downloading a page-turner on his reader or sitting through yet another evening of any number of schmaltzy Christmas themed movies, all of which the streaming channels were pushing. Maybe he'd watch the "guy version" of a holiday movie: *Die Hard.*

It didn't matter what he watched, nothing would help him missing Sabina, which made him feel even lonelier.

He stripped off his uniform and adjusted the shower to a comfortable temperature. He'd known exactly what he was getting into when he became involved with her, and he admired the hell out of her and the rest of her team for doing the job they did. Most of the time he was okay with the absences. This was the first one that had really bothered him, and it was because of the holidays. But he was a big boy. A lonely boy, but still a big boy, and he would survive.

He stayed in the shower long enough to wash away the miasma of the day and dressed in old jeans and a concert tee from a while back. It was too early for dinner, so he parked himself on the sofa and was looking at the new releases on his reader when his doorbell rang. Again, a flare of hope morphed into curiosity. It wouldn't be Sabina or his family. And it wouldn't be Lacey and Eagle. Damned if he knew who might be out there. There was only one way to find out.

He peered through the peep hole, couldn't believe what he saw, and threw open the door and stared for a moment. An uncertain looking Paco Morales stood on his front porch. "Happy holidays," Paco murmured.

Paco Morales? Preston didn't know quite what to think.

Paco was the last person he would've expected to show up at his place on Christmas Day. He'd have thought Paco was celebrating with his family somewhere. Or out chasing down a conquest, if he was really as promiscuous as Sabina once said he was. Besides, this tough soldier had as little use for him as Eagle did.

More of Sabina's doing.

Even as she was leaving for a duty assignment, she'd tried to take care of him.

He opened the door wider to admit Sabina's teammate. "Come on in, and I'll see what I can scare up for us to drink. After the day I've had, I need a beer and I bet you wouldn't turn one down."

"I wouldn't," Paco said. He stepped inside and looked around. "Nice place you have."

"Thanks. I have Lacey to thank for a lot of it."

Paco followed him into the living room. "Lacey? She did this?"

"The homey touches, yeah. She and Eagle took pity on me the other night and helped me with it some. Beer?"

"Sure."

Preston fished two beers out of the refrigerator. He handed one to Paco and sank down on the easy chair across from the sofa. "I gather you weren't sent on any training assignments this Christmas," he said.

"Not this year, but it's happened." Paco sucked down a third of his beer. "So happens this year Sabina and a couple of looies are the only ones gone. Which suits the colonels fine. Everybody else is enjoying the holidays."

"I'm glad for the others. Since I was going to be alone, I took another cop's shift today so he could spend it with his daughter and his lady-love." He swallowed a mouthful of beer. "A boring shift it was not."

Paco raised his eyebrow and Preston shared a few of the day's highlights. "Sounds like you earned your money today," he told Preston. "After a day like that, you deserve a good meal. Want to go out somewhere for dinner?"

"I'd love to if there were anyplace open," Preston said. "It's Christmas Day. Every restaurant in town shuts down today."

"Not every restaurant. I know a couple of delis a middle eastern place and a Chinese restaurant or two that are open tonight."

"Chinese? Are they really open on Christmas?" Preston asked.

"They are, but I was thinking more of the kosher ones. They'll all be open. This year the twenty-fifth is also the first night of Hannukah and they're ready to feed us kosher-eating types." He smiled and winked.

Kosher-eating types. Preston blinked. "Jewish? You?"

"Proud member of the Tribe of Judah," Paco said. "Sephardic Jews from Spain via Argentina, and then San Diego."

"How about that. So you'd know where to eat today."

"I would. Every kosher restaurant and deli in town is ready and waiting to feed the Jewish community."

"Will they feed a Methodist?" Preston asked, deadpan.

"As long as you don't ask for a BLT or a ham sandwich," Paco said dryly. "Seriously, I like to share a traditional meal on the first night of Hannukah. With Sabina gone, I thought you might be free and up for a change of pace dinner-wise.

"Normally, I have plenty of friends more than happy to join me, but with the first night of Hannukah falling on Christmas Day, many of them are busy with their own celebrations, or are with their families in other cities."

"So you're kind of stranded tonight, like me," Preston said.

"Yeah." Paco nodded. "So, to prepare you for what you're going to have, our traditional meal has a lot of courses. Usually, we start with fish-balls called *quenelles* that are deep-fried, then simmered in tomato sauce," he said. "They're made with salt cod." Paco smiled. "Along with the fish, we have *bimuelos*, which are fritters, again fried, which is a theme at Hannukah since the lamp oil lasting for eight nights is adopted symbolism by using oil to cook all your food." Preston was fascinated. A whole world he didn't know, but was happy to learn about. "After the fish we have whole artichokes, prepared in oil, and are very spicy, then we have a veal roast with peas and a pilaf, and desserts. The most popular is similar to an American jelly donut, but lighter and the filling isn't gooey. They're called *sufganiyot*, and you guessed it, they're deep fried. That work for you, or are you a stickler for turkey and dressing on the twenty-fifth?"

"Actually, my family was more into enchiladas, tamales, and pozole," Preston said. "Not the same, but it sounds as if some of the food sort of overlaps."

"Yeah. Sort of." Paco laughed.

"Let me throw on a decent shirt, and I'll be right out."

Preston traded out the grungy tee shirt for a nicer one and ran a comb through his hair. He was surprised Paco was so friendly and forthcoming, and since Preston didn't want to be alone, he was more than happy to spend some time in someone else's company. Especially with all that great food waiting for him at the restaurant.

He followed Paco, and soon they were seated in a cozy restaurant surrounded by multigenerational families with tons of food on their tables, everyone eating and talking.

A smiling waitress brought them a menu and pointed to a chalkboard on the wall. "Everything on the regular menu is available tonight along with a traditional Hannukah meal. We're also offering kosher tamales."

"Kosher tamales?" Preston asked.

"There is such a thing," Paco said. "My mom used to make them for my *abuela*. You want to give theirs a shot?"

"Sure."

They ended up ordering the fritters, the artichokes, the roast with the pilaf, and a side order of tamales. "You don't eat kosher all the time, do you?" Preston asked.

"Hard to given my work, but I make sure I do on holidays," Paco said. "The rest of the time I eat the shitty food every soldier eats." Preston nodded understanding the dilemma. "Phil used to say I was a good kosher boy only on the holidays."

"I bet you're not the only Jewish soldier who does that," Preston said. "Who's Phil?"

Paco took a breath. "My husband. My late husband. He was killed on a brigade mission three years ago." Paco's eyes looked haunted.

Preston's stomach dropped. Then he thought, maybe Paco's promiscuity was a reaction to his grief. It would make sense. "Geez, that sucks," he said. "How long were you married?"

Paco took a deep breath. "Four years. We were together for a couple of years before that. Not enough time," he whispered, and it seemed more to himself than to Preston. "How about you? Bachelor?"

"Divorced. She was more interested in the Ramos family money than she was me. Five long years of never-ending fighting. The divorce was a relief."

"Ouch." Paco made a face. "All I have left of Phil is memories, but at least they're happy ones."

"Tell me about him."

The waitress delivered their dinner, and over mouthwatering food and perfectly fried almost everything, Paco waxed eloquent about Phil and how happy they'd been. "We were the envy of our friends," he said. "Damn few couples have what we had."

"How about your family? Did they like him?"

Paco rolled his eyes. "Not exactly. I took him home a couple of times. My mother was nice enough, but my brothers were jerks. It was one thing for me to be gay, and another entirely to be married. After the last visit I promised Phil I'd never make him go back. I returned once after Phil died, and that was to bury my mother. May her memory be a blessing," he muttered.

"Did they disown you?"

"Not to the extent yours did. But it's uncomfortable since Mom and Dad are gone now and my brothers are such dickwads. Mostly, I don't bother with them, but I send my nieces and nephews gift cards for their birthdays, holidays and things like that. I miss my mom's kosher cooking. She put a South American twist on the traditional holiday meals."

"I bet it was delicious," Preston said. "I have no idea what Sabina and her mother were planning to fix. She told me not to worry, they would take care of everything."

"She ever say anything about her family traditions? Old Romani customs, family recipes, anything like that?" Paco asked.

"From what little she said, I don't think they had many. Her parents were so determined to be good Americans, they abandoned anything that could be even loosely interpreted as Romani. They went the American as apple pie route. She ever say anything to you?"

"Not a word. Not to me, and I don't think to anybody else in the brigade. As far as she was concerned, she was American. Even though everyone didn't always see her as such." Paco looked at him and raised his eyebrow.

"Guilty as charged." Preston felt embarrassment creep up his neck to his cheeks.

Paco made a face. "At least you seem to've seen the error of your ways. Gotta admit, I don't understand it, though. You had a real hard-on for her and her family, but not for anybody else. You didn't bat an eyelash when you found out I'm Jewish or that I'm gay. What was with the other?"

Preston shook his head. "My mom grew up in a neighborhood with a pair of Romani families in the midst of a feud that spilled over onto the neighbors, which left her with some issues she and my father cheerfully passed on to me.

"Then there's Sabina's brother Dominic, who seems determined to live up to every negative stereotype about the Romani. My father was under the mistaken impression that Dominic had swindled Jeremy out of ten million dollars. Not that my brother, hell, my whole family, isn't doing the same. They're the real life examples of every soap opera about crooked businessmen."

Paco cocked his head. "The question then becomes: have you really and truly been able to put the prejudice behind you? Do you still on some level have a problem with the Romani? I would hate to see Sabina hurt any worse than she's already been by the shit with her brother."

"And mine," Preston said darkly.

"And yours," Paco acknowledged.

Preston took a breath. "I better have. Moved past the prejudice, I mean. I'm planning to ask a Romani to marry me. Think about it. If she says yes, and I hope she does, my kids will be Romani."

"You're planning to ask her to marry you?" Paco asked. "And have kids? I guess that means you're over the prejudice."

"I guess it does."

"Okay then. You and Sabina. Married. With kids. Wow." Paco let out a breath. "Can you imagine the daughters you'll have with her? Oh. My. God. Warriors, every one of them."

"It's crossed my mind a time or two. Sabina's daughters. Hers and mine. Scares hell out of me and at the same time I want it— them—her so bad I can taste it."

"Good. That means you'll be a good husband and father. Do I need to give you the if-you-hurt-Sabina-we-will-bury-you speech?"

Preston sighed. "Paco, I'm going to hurt her and she's going to hurt me. That's what happens when you spend the rest of your lives together. But will I ever deliberately hurt her? Deliberately act like the asshole we both know I can be? Hell no. I love her too much for that."

"Good." Paco looked at him with satisfaction. "Did you buy her a ring?"

"I did." Preston described the ring to an approving Paco. "And as you saw, I think I have the house in good enough shape she'll be willing to move in. What I haven't managed to do yet is figure out a romantic proposal that she'll remember for the rest of her life. I don't have a clue what to do about that."

"Hmm. What were you going to do before she had to leave?"

"I hadn't figured it out. Something that would include her parents. That's out now."

"You have a choice. Plan A, you can still involve others. There have been some memorable public proposals over the years."

"You mean the banners towed by an airplane, or the proposals posted on a halftime-show jumbotron."

"And don't forget the Century Tree proposals up at A&M."

"What? We couldn't forget the Aggies." Preston laughed.

"I was thinking mostly those with family, or a special group of friends in attendance," Paco admitted. "You want to think in terms of one of those?"

"It'll have to be just us. The one thing we don't have yet is a mutual circle of friends. My friends were mostly my cousins, and other members of the family, and I've lost all of them. Her circle is the Brigade, who have no use for me, so I doubt they'll want to be involved."

"Plan B, then. You and Sabina. If it's going to be just the two of you, the possibilities are endless," Paco said. "A romantic dinner on the Riverwalk, or a sunset stroll on the McNay Art Museum grounds, or at a downtown rooftop bar with a view. How about dinner at the top of the Tower of the Americas, or sunrise at one of the missions? You could have a picnic at the Botanical Gardens, or in a pagoda at the Japanese Tea Garden. This town is full of romantic spots to pop the question. Or go out to Canyon Lake and rent a sailboat. Or climb to the top of Enchanted Rock and ask her there."

"Wow. You know all the romantic spots in town."

Paco's eyes misted. "Phil knew every one of them. We made it a point every so often to spend some just-us time at someplace special. I loved it."

Preston was taken aback. Who would've thought this hard-nosed, battle toughened soldier was romantic?

"So I need to take her to a really romantic spot to pop the question."

"It doesn't have to be someplace exotic. Phil and I were walking across the base. We ducked into the Quadrangle and were laughing at the peacocks when he turned to me and said, 'Let's get married.' I said, 'Sure thing,' and we got married the following month in a ceremony in our backyard with a few of our Black-Ops teammates,

Phil's sister and her family. Colonel Bustamante wasn't on board yet so it wasn't 'Bear's Brigade' yet."

"Lots of possibilities," Preston said thoughtfully.

"Of course, you can always do champagne and rose petals on your bed." Paco snickered.

"Nah, that's been done in every cheesy romantic comedy Hollywood ever made."

They bounced around a few more ideas. Their waitress brought the check and after a good-natured argument Preston let Paco pay for dinner. "I appreciate the company," Paco said when Preston thanked him. "I didn't want to be alone tonight."

That definitely makes two of us.

Preston was deep in thought as he drove through the lighter than usual traffic. Again, he found himself liking Sabina's teammate.

Paco was every bit as nice as Lacey and Eagle, and Paco had been a wealth of good ideas for romantic proposals. Which made the reality of the situation even sadder.

Despite Paco's kindness, Preston doubted they would ever become friends. He knew Paco hadn't forgotten the bad blood between them from before. The question was why Paco had reached out to him at all.

Preston was almost certain what Paco did was for Sabina's sake, or because she'd asked him to. Whatever the reason, the man had taken a lot of the sting out of what had promised to be a lonely day, and Preston appreciated the hell out of it.

CHAPTER FIVE

Preston leaned back on the sofa and held the ice pack on his eye, hoping the cold would lesson the inevitable bruising he would have from the punch he'd taken this afternoon trying to break up a brawl between two rival biker gangs in the parking lot of a convenience store.

It'd been a miracle that none of the fifteen or so bikers were packing, but the bastards were good with their fists, and Preston and his fellow officers had taken a few blows in the process of breaking up the fight and arresting the perps.

He'd taken a couple of mild painkillers for his aching eye and his sore ribs, and was seriously considering a whiskey chaser whenever he could get up the energy to go pour himself one.

He shifted on the sofa and groaned. It'd been three days since Christmas, and he'd worked every one of them, covering shifts for officers who wanted a little more time with their families.

He admitted to himself that his motivation wasn't entirely altruistic. If Sabina was home next Christmas, he might be calling in this year's favors for more time with her. He wondered where he and Sabina would be as a couple by this time next year.

He still hadn't settled on where or when, but he was definitely proposing as soon as she got home. They probably wouldn't marry right away. Her brother's trial was coming up in January and there would be the inevitable appeals. And for the sake of the government's case they would have to keep their relationship on the DL for a bit longer. But not too much longer, he hoped. He'd like to be married to her by this time next year. Then, maybe, they could have a Merry Christmas for real.

Although this one hadn't been nearly as bad as he'd expected it to be. He'd been lonely, but not nearly as lonely as he would've been if Eagle, Lacey, and Paco hadn't taken pity on him. It'd been nice of them, and to his surprise he'd thoroughly enjoyed hanging out with them.

He credited Sabina for having them come to his rescue.

He held the bag to his black eye until it started to warm up. Time to refresh the ice and maybe pour that promised chaser. He swung his legs off the sofa and was headed for the kitchen when his doorbell rang. Hope flared as he turned and hot-footed it toward the door. Maybe Sabina's mission was over and she was home. He sure hoped so.

He peered through the peep hole, then pulled open the door and hoped his astonishment didn't show. Colonel Bustamante stood there with a gorgeous woman who must be his lady-love, Felicia Castillo.

They looked at him solemnly and he took a sharp breath as a horrible thought crossed his mind. "Is Sabina all right? She didn't get hurt, did she?"

"No, no," the colonel quickly assured him. "Last I heard, all was well on her mission."

Preston sagged with relief. "Thank you for that. You both looked pretty serious."

"We're looking serious because of you," Felicia said. "I'm Felicia, by the way. You look like you got the hell beat out of you today."

"Kind of did. Made the mistake of getting between two angry bikers fighting over a parking space." He backed up and motioned for them to come in. "I was headed to the kitchen for more ice and a whiskey chaser. Can I get you anything?"

"We're fine." Colonel Bustamante and Felicia stepped in and the colonel shut the door. "Actually, we came to invite you to come with us to a brigade party tonight. We're getting together for our annual holiday party at Colonel Johnson's, and we like to include the brigade's significant others at her get-together. Your cell number's not public, but we were able to find your address online, so Felicia and I decided to come by and invite you in person."

More of Sabina's doing. It had to be.

Apparently, she'd gone all the way to the top and involved the colonel in her efforts to make sure he wasn't alone during the holiday season.

But it did surprise him that Colonel Bustamante cared enough about her request to do what she asked.

"Wow. That's really nice of you. Not sure I'd be much in the way of company, though, as sore as I am."

Felicia crossed her arms in front of her and looked him up and down. "You're beat up, all right, but the brigade's used to that. They do beat up all the time. They even do the occasional bullet hole."

"Look at it this way. You can either stay here, drink your own whiskey and hurt by yourself, or you can come with us, eat Colonel Johnson's Kwanzaa meal, and drink somebody else's booze and hurt with all of us," Colonel Bustamante added. "We'll even chauffeur so you don't have to drink and drive."

Preston wasn't sure he was up for a party. But Colonel Bustamante was Sabina's commanding officer and the head of the Special-Ops unit she worked for. Preston wasn't about to do anything to insult the man or his lady-love, especially since they'd gone out of their way to invite him. But he still couldn't wrap his head around why they'd go out of their way, as little as any of them liked him.

They must really hold Sabina in high regard. Or she threatened them.

He looked down at his sweats and over at the nicely dressed couple. "Give me five minutes to get into my party duds and I'll be delighted to join you."

He switched out his sweats for a new pair of black jeans and a collared knit shirt. The sun was beginning to set as he followed them to a brand-spanking new Chevy Silverado. "Nice truck," Preston said approvingly. "Brand new?"

"Merry Christmas to me," the colonel said sheepishly. "My son's pickup gave up the ghost a couple of weeks ago, so I passed along the one I was driving and brought this baby home last week. Felicia tried to introduce me to the pleasures of a sports car, but I'm still too much of a country boy to drive anything but a truck."

"And when he says truck, he means a *truck,*" Felicia said dryly.

They made small talk on the way to the party and learned the colonel was from the Valley and Felicia was local, and that the colonel's son and his partner were in town for the holidays.

They made their way through the evening traffic to the base and the colonel turned off into the historic section of base housing and pulled up in front of a gorgeous old Victorian. "Beautiful," Preston said admiring the structure. "Even more vintage than mine."

"Yours is not to be sneezed at," Felicia said. "Does it date back to the twenties?"

"Maybe nineteen-thirty or so," Preston said. "What's your favorite housing era?"

"Midcentury modern," the colonel and Felicia said in unison.

They trooped up the sidewalk and a good-looking young man who vaguely resembled Colonel Johnson met them at the door. "Howdy. I'm Lemar Johnson and I've been put on front door duty.

"Colonel Bustamante, good to see you. And the beautiful Felicia. Come in, come in." He shook hands with the colonel and kissed Felicia's cheek before turning to Preston. "Let me guess. You're either a friend of Tucker's or Sabina's sweetie."

"Preston Ramos. Sabina's sweetie."

"Lemar Johnson. Glad to meet you. Mom's mentioned you a time or two."

Preston stifled a snicker. He bet Colonel Johnson hadn't told her son about pulling a gun on him during the mission to Colombia. He glanced over at Colonel Bustamante and the colonel was also fighting to keep a straight face.

Lemar led them into the living room. "Say hello and make yourselves a plate of food. Mom does a traditional Kwanzaa meal and says that tonight everybody's from Africa."

"My Granny Washington says the same thing," Jazz Washington said from the wheelchair he was parked in. "In some cases, it's strictly honorary." He squeezed the hand of a pretty blonde standing beside him.

"And for some of us it's very real," Felicia said. She gave Jazz a kiss on the cheek. "How's it going, cousin mine?"

"Like you didn't see me three days ago," Jazz teased. He looked over at Preston. "Jesus, what happened to you? Piss off Sabina?"

"Got between two bikers and lived to regret it. How are you doing, Jazz? For real."

"For real? It sucks, but I'm healing. Carrie, this is Preston Ramos. You and Preston have the honor of being the only two civilians who've ever traveled with this daring, wonderful, esteemed group of warriors. Preston, my girl Carrie. Gotta admit, she was a lot more fun to go on a mission with than you were."

"Sabina might take exception to that," Carrie said. "Glad to meet you."

"She might," Preston agreed. He looked again at the smiling, affable soldier in the wheelchair.

Hard to believe this friendly man was the pissed off son of a bitch who'd decked him in Colombia.

He made the rounds with the colonel and Felicia, who introduced him to a few members of the brigade he'd not met. Paco and Eagle both greeted him with warmth, although Eagle was looking a little hang-dog, and Lacey was nowhere to be seen. Colonel Johnson was resplendent in a red and blue *karabela* dress, she told him was from Haiti. She'd greeted him warmly and exclaimed over his black eye. "Our drink of choice tonight should help with that." She handed him a stinger. "Traditional drink always served at a Kwanzaa party. Doesn't do a thing for the bruise, but you no longer give a damn."

Preston sipped and nodded his head. "Delicious. But it may take a couple of doses for me to feel better."

Colonel Johnson laughed and invited them to make a plate. "It's my interpretation of a Kwanzaa menu," she said, gesturing to the spread on the table consisting of collard greens, black-eyed peas, cornbread, jerk chicken, sweet potato pie, and gumbo.

"Looks like good old-fashioned southern cooking to me," Colonel Bustamante teased.

"Bear, you know better. Every one of these dishes has an African origin," Felicia pointed out.

Preston took another look at the delicious-looking spread. "That I didn't know," he said. "Sure looks good."

It was. The food and the company were great, and they were all as nice as they could be. Which he still didn't understand. They had more than done their duty. They didn't have to invite him tonight. But they had, and they'd made him welcome.

Quite a change from the chilly attitude from before Christmas.

He probably should take it for what it was and let it go. But as the evening wore on, his curiosity grew. They had done more than what Sabina had likely asked them to do. So why? Why were they being so kind to him? He didn't deserve it. His prejudice against the Romani had delayed a mission that'd caused three unnecessary deaths, and his brother was an international criminal. Sabina had forgiven him because she loved him. But these people didn't love him. They didn't even like him.

The why of it was sticking in his throat,

He finally got his chance to ask. The majority of folks had settled on chairs and the sofa, and were involved in a serious bullshitting session over the merits of the local microbrews. The two colonels were off to one side talking about their sons' post-college plans, and Jazz was wolfing down a second or maybe third piece of sweet potato pie Carrie had sliced for him.

Preston walked over to the colonels and waited until he'd caught their eye. "Got a question for you," he said.

"Shoot," Colonel Bustamante replied.

Preston took a beat to get up his courage. "Why are y'all being so nice to me? Why have you all gone out of your way to be so kind?" The colonels looked at one another but didn't say anything. "I mean, none of you like me. You think I'm an asshole."

"You are an asshole," Jazz said cheerfully.

"Jazz, that's terrible," Carrie said, horrified.

"Terrible but honest," Jazz said. "This pie sure is good."

"Glad you like it," Colonel Johnson murmured, trying and failing to hide a snicker.

"That's what I mean," Preston said. "You think I'm an asshole and for good reason. Yet the brigade has reached out, and don't get me wrong, I'm grateful. But I don't understand."

Jazz pulled his wheelchair a little closer. "It's like this. Sabina loves you, which makes you her asshole. We love Sabina, and you're her asshole, so that makes you *our* asshole. Besides, you think you're the only asshole here? Take a look around. We've got a room full of 'em."

The colonels looked at one another and laughed. Carrie rolled her eyes. "I swear, Jazz, I can't take you anywhere. Eat your pie."

He was *their* asshole? O-kay.

Colonel Johnson's face sobered and she put her hand on Preston's arm. "Jazz isn't wrong, but that's not all of it. Not by a long shot. They didn't know."

"Know what?"

"They didn't know how much your honesty cost you. What kind of price you paid for going in that courtroom and testifying against your brother," Colonel Johnson explained. "The testimony the prosecutor said nailed down a much-needed conviction."

"Oh. They didn't know about my asshole family." He turned to Jazz. "Now, if you want to meet a bunch of real assholes, I'll take you to the next Ramos family reunion."

"Thanks. I'll pass." Jazz made a face.

"It's like this." Colonel Bustamante picked up the thread. "Doing what we do for a living, yeah, it's a job, but it's also about serving our country and putting our nation first. We all raised our hand and vowed to do that when we joined the Army, and it's damned important to every one of us. I like to think we've done that, and to some extent we've all paid a price for doing so. Some a higher price than others." He gestured toward Jazz's bandaged legs.

"Some have paid the ultimate price," Preston said quietly. "Like Paco's husband."

"They have," Colonel Johnson said. "And you, you've done the same thing we have. You put your country's welfare above the demands of your family, and you lost them for it. You paid a damned high price for being a loyal American. Not a person in this room, not a person in the entire brigade has had to pay that particular price. You made an enormous sacrifice. And you overcame a lifetime of prejudice to love Sabina, which is damned awesome. That makes you one of us."

The room had gotten quiet. Then Jazz raised his hands and started clapping, and was joined by everyone in the room as they all rose in tribute. Preston felt tears gather as he looked around at Sabina's friends. His friends now, too. He had friends again.

He had a feeling they'd be the best friends he would ever have in his life. And he had Sabina to thank for them.

"Th-thanks," he stammered, not sure what else to say.

He was saved from having to say anything more when the doorbell rang and a tired-looking Sabina came in, trailed by two equally tired-looking young soldiers holding hands.

"Holy shit. You're home," he barely got out as he jumped over an end table and met her at the door. She threw her arms around his neck and he picked her up and swung her in a circle. "I missed you so much." He bent his head and laid a long, sweet kiss on her lips.

"I missed you too," she said when he finally came up for air. "Colonel Bustamante texted us and told us to come. He said you were here."

He turned to the colonel. "Thanks."

Colonel Bustamante smiled and nodded.

Preston turned and caught Paco's eye. "You think I ought to switch to Plan A?" he asked.

"You have the ring and the key?" Paco asked.

Preston's face fell. "I don't. They're at home."

"Aw hell, Ramos, fake it," Paco laughed. "Give 'em to her later. By all means, go to Plan A."

Preston knelt in front of Sabina and the room got quiet again. "Sabina. I love you. I can be a real idiot, and I'm not worthy of you, but if you'll have me, I'd love for us to spend the rest of our lives together. Will you marry me?"

Sabina's eyes widened and her mouth made an "O." "You want to marry me?" she squeaked. "A house, kids, the whole bit?"

"I do. A house filled with warrior daughters just like you. We can even throw in a dog. How about it?"

Sabina's initial surprise transformed into the biggest smile he'd ever seen from her. Her eyes glistened, and she smiled before she said, "You better believe I'll marry you."

Preston stood up and whooped. "Did you hear that? She said yes. *Sabina said yes.*"

The room erupted into claps and cheers, but he barely heard them. His attention was focused on the magnificent woman standing in front of him. He bent his head and took her lips and kissed her with all the love he held in his heart. He was so eager to see where the next months and years would take them, and was happy he'd done this surrounded by their friends in Bear's Brigade. They could have done this alone. But it was so much better with their friends by their side.

***

Sabina lay curled up next to Preston, her head on his shoulder and her fingers in his chest hair. They'd made love for most of the night, pouring out their emotions while making plans for the future. She held up her hand and looked at her ring.

"You like it?" Preston asked, kissing her temple.

"I love it. It's different."

"That was the point. It doesn't scream we're engaged."

"And I can wear it while I'm breaking into houses on the missions." She snickered. "I love the key, too. My lease is up in a couple of weeks. Maybe we can move my stuff next weekend."

"That would be awesome. I can hardly wait to wake up beside you every morning."

"That'll be perfect. Maybe Mom and Dad will want to stay here when they come."

"Oh, shit. Should I have talked to your father before I proposed?"

"Nah. I've been grown and gone a long time. We will call them tomorrow, though."

"That works. Thanks, by the way."

"Thanks for what?"

"Thanks for taking care of me over Christmas."

Sabina looked at him, puzzled. "How did I do that? I was gone, remember?"

"I mean beforehand. When you asked the brigade to befriend me over the holidays."

Huh?" Sabina sat up and looked down at Preston. "I didn't ask anybody to do anything."

"You had to." Preston ran his hand down the side of her face. "They knew what happened with my family. You must've asked them to look after me. Take me out for a meal, invite me to the party."

"Preston, I did no such thing. I did tell them what your family had done to you. But that was all. I don't know anything about them taking you out. I didn't even know they had, and I didn't know anything about your being at the party until the colonel's text." She looked at him. "What did they do?"

"Eagle and Lacey came by to take me out to dinner, but we went shopping instead and Lacey helped me pretty up the house. We got nice pots and pans, and throw pillows. A coffee table, and the nightstands you didn't notice since we'd been," he grinned, "busy. We got stuff I hoped you'll like."

"I'm sure I will. Lacey has great taste."

"And then Paco came and got me on Christmas Day. Only it was the first night of Hannukah too and we had the most amazing Middle Eastern kosher Hannukah food, and kosher tamales. Then tonight, Colonel Bustamante and Felicia picked me up for the party. I was sure you'd asked them all to be nice to me."

"No." She shook her head. "I didn't. I said you were going to be alone and I was worried about you. But I swear, that's it. Lacey and Eagle, and Paco, they came up with taking care of you on their own. I sure as hell appreciate it, but I didn't instigate anything. Same with tonight. The invitation to the party came from the colonels without any input from me."

Preston stared at her, and remembered what they'd said to him at the party. "I'll be damned. I thought you were behind all of it."

"No. What they did, they did it on their own. They did it because they were thinking of you, Preston. Not as a favor to me."

"Huh. They reached out to me on their own." Preston marveled. "I'm kinda shocked."

"I'm not," she said. "Not really." She cocked her head and looked down at him. "The brigade is all about acceptance. That's why they were so mad at you in the beginning, because you wouldn't accept me and mine.

"But you changed, and then you sacrificed the love for your family to do the right thing. You accepted me and you accepted the values they...we hold so dear. Why wouldn't they accept you?"

Preston pulled her down, wrapped his arms around her and kissed her with everything in him.

She loved him, and in loving him gave him a world he hadn't experienced, but would forever embrace with his arms opened wide.

THIS STORY IS PART OF THE BEAR'S BRIGADE SERIES

A HOME FOR CHRISTMAS

JOAN BIRD

CHAPTER ONE

The wind buffeted against Casey's car as she drove down the two-lane mountain road. Dusk muted the surroundings with a soft rosy hue. In the hour before she'd started winding through this mountain pass, she'd seen several ranches in the distance. Signs made from iron were attached like banners to either side of posts supporting large gates, marking their names at each entrance. "Galloping Acres" was one. Another, "Twisted Spur."

The names had been a diversion because for most of the trip she'd ruminated over her life decisions. Like selling most of her belongings and her house. Truth? She was trying to forget by running away.

Let it go, Casey. Just let it go. But it wasn't easy. Images of a young man's cracked skull and prone body floated in front of her, a mirage of a life she'd ruined while derailing her own.

She stopped thinking about the injured kid, but then found herself trying to shake a vision of her "lived-with-for-two-years" boyfriend. Turned out he was a frog, and no amount of kissing would ever turn him into a prince. "Biggest jerk of all time," she muttered as she swiped at a tear threatening to spill down her cheek.

Casey drew a slow even breath. "One—two— three—" and then exhaled, "One— two— three." She repeated the exercise four times and was rewarded with a sort of calm. In fact, her eyelids had grown heavy and she prayed for some form of civilization to pop up on the horizon.

208

Cresting a hill, she saw lights in the distance. "A town? God, I hope so." She reached for her frozen coffee drink. A gigantic mistake. The contents had melted, and squeezing the cup to grab it popped the lid. Blended mocha went flying, on the dash, the radio— and why not? All over her shirt and jeans.

When she refocused on the blacktop, a shape loomed. A cow? "Holy…" She didn't finish the expletive as she tried to avoid the large animal. The cup dropped from her hand when her reflexes pushed into hyperdrive. Casey jerked the steering wheel to the right in an effort to avoid hitting the cow. Then she hit the brakes, and though the road was dry, she heard the tires hit dirt. Within seconds of seeing the solo cow, her car was airborne, and Casey's brain filled with staccato thoughts. *Is this it? Damn. I'm sorry, God.* And, *No, I'm sorry, everybody.*

She only hoped it didn't hurt to die.

CHAPTER TWO

Sam was tired. Three days of driving back and forth to the local auction had taken its toll. He still needed to get home to confirm that Rick Sanders, his ranch foreman, made it through another day without any major mishaps. Glancing at the dashboard clock, he stifled a yawn.

"I could stop for a burger and a beer." Spoken aloud, the words felt like company, and stopping meant he wouldn't have to figure out what to eat at home. Doing quick math, he confirmed he'd still have a few minutes with Rick to map out the next day.

After that? It would be feet up in front of the fire with a book and a bourbon.

The neon sign over the Dusty Boot Saloon and Grill came into view, and he slowed, turning left into the parking lot. A blast of north wind caught him as he stepped out of the truck, and he debated grabbing his down jacket, but it would be warm inside, so he slammed the door and walked toward the entrance.

Sitting at the bar, nursing his beer, he walked through the auction results in his head. The sale had gone well—eighty-two head of Angus beef sold at a premium price. The buyer's check was folded in his shirt pocket. He didn't need the money, but the satisfaction was rewarding. Having millions wasn't something you blabbed around when you wanted a new life.

It was becoming an old story: software start-up, moderate success, selling the company outright to one of the tech giants in Silicon Valley. Just like that, overnight, he'd sold most of his stock for the option of changing his world. And then, Briarwood found him five years ago when he was out exploring properties. Small town, big ranch, few people.

It wasn't a bad thing, and he didn't feel guilty of gentrification. Still, although he'd made friends, he didn't toss around his wealth, nor share much about his past. If anybody cared enough? They could Google him.

Dragging a French fry through a dollop of ketchup, he signaled the bartender for his tab. Maxine trundled toward him, a ready smile on her face. "You done, Sam?"

"Pretty much, Maxie."

"Hmmm." She grabbed his plate and immediately swiped the area clean. "Either you are or you ain't, Sam. Done, that is." From an apron pocket she pulled his check and slapped it down on the bar top.

"You're right, Maxie. Glad you're here to keep me on my toes." He gave her a thumbs-up and got the expected reaction. The barkeep's smile split her face, and dimples popped out on her full cheeks. Walking away, she added, "And don't you forget a hefty tip, Sam."

***

The last two hours had been apocalyptic. Well, it felt that way. Turned out she'd taken the road less traveled. Casey made a mental note thanking Robert Frost for "The Road Not Taken." It had been a daring choice—one made as she'd mapped out her trip to Denver. A road map and a whim led her to take the route that ended in the accident. The result? She'd had to sit shaken, hungry, tired, cold, and totally freaked out for almost an hour before the tow truck arrived. And in that time? Not a single car passed. She thanked all that was holy that despite being in what felt like nowhere, she'd had cell service. As it turned out, the civilization she'd spied in the distance before trying to kill herself by putting her car into orbit was a very, *very*, small town.

Now she stood outside the bar and grill recommended by her towing escort, and whispered another prayer for food and warmth. Inside, and once her eyes adjusted to the dim light, she read the "seat yourself" sign, figuring food would cheer her up, and a double shot of something would calm her down.

The kicker was she *still* needed to find a place to stay for the night. The mechanic with "Hi, I'm Frank" stenciled on his work shirt heralded dismal news about any repairs. He must have sensed her despair because he'd added that maybe he could get her some kind of loaner by tomorrow afternoon. It meant she'd have to come back to this nowhere burg, but at least she could spend Christmas in civilization.

Casey sucked in a deep breath and headed toward the bar. With continued concern about finding lodging, she glanced down at her phone browser, failing to notice the man standing next to the bar.

"Umph." She'd walked into something. It was upright, broad, and human. "Sh…"

"Indeed." Her impediment to forward motion had a deep voice, so—human *and* male. Shocked, she watched as his hand grabbed her phone away. She jerked her head up in time to see a maybe-cowboy-person put her phone behind him on the bar.

"Hey." Casey tried leaning around him, her right arm reaching for the device, but that turned disastrous because now she faced him with maybe two inches of space between her body and his chest.

"Give me my phone." She took a deep breath and squared her shoulders. "Now, buster."

"Buster, really?"

It wasn't that bright in the bar to begin with, so Casey only got a quick glimpse of his eyes before he set a well-worn cowboy hat on his head and its shadow settled over his face. She was used to quick assessments, had check-listed things rapid-fire in her mind for over nine years in law enforcement. It was a skill she didn't resent. Her career, though? A different story.

The stranger shifted his stance and leaned back against the bar, his broad chest and shoulders acting as a wall against recovering the phone. "The name's Wagner, ma'am. Sam Wagner."

"Which doesn't change the fact that you need to give me back my phone." She started profiling him in her head. Hazel eyes? A clean, short haircut had all but disappeared beneath the big-brimmed hat. Shirt tucked in, no food stains anywhere. So, he wasn't a slob. She didn't back away, instead putting out her right hand, palm toward the ceiling, she demanded, "Phone. Now."

"Well, maybe. But—" He held up an index finger. "One, it's rude to slam into someone because you're walking and texting at the same time." Holding up another finger, he added, "Two, you didn't say please."

She bit back a snappy comeback. Okay, she didn't have one. He was tall, dark, and handsome. *Good lord, how trite can he be?* Annoyed, she said, "I wasn't texting."

"Right."

"I was searching the web."

The sharp bark of laughter caught her off guard. "Oh, well then, that's different." His deep voice was soothing, but she refused to be sucked in by the sexy tone or his good looks.

"Well, of course it is." Casey paused, and it dawned he was being sarcastic. The grin on his face was unmistakable. "You're teasing me."

"Maybe, yeah. Just a little." Turning, he shifted his weight, opening up access to her phone, but before she could grab it, he did, holding it above his head.

"Jesus H…"

"Rude, and irreverent. You from California?"

"Yes. But what has that to do with returning my phone?"

"Oh, it's nothing really. Just a vibe."

Searching her brain for a rapier-like quip, once again she couldn't come up with anything. She wasn't used to being so flustered. "Okay, I'm sorry I slammed into you." Casey forced herself to sound apologetic. "Now, can I please have my phone back?"

"After an introduction—yes."

"To you? Ms. Pickett."

"No, your real name."

"Now who's being rude?"

"Sorry. I wasn't making fun of your name." Her phone kidnapper paused but didn't release her captive cell. "So why so intent on the phone?"

"It *is* Pickett. And I needed to look something up."

"How important was it?" He had the innate ability to raise a single eyebrow. Despite the shadow over his face, she could see that his nose was straight and well-shaped, and his mouth—Casey gulped—was perfect. Kissable. A hint of day's-end stubble added to, rather than detracted from, his unbearable good looks. She shoved her hands in jean pockets and studied her tennies.

Without warning, his right index finger tipped her chin up and she had no choice but to look at him. "It's good manners to look at the person you're talkin' to, ma'am."

"Damn you." Casey's cheeks burned. There was little doubt he was goading her, or maybe he enjoyed embarrassing damsels in distress, a title for which, at the moment, she qualified. The last five minutes had provided her a new hypothesis—it was a mistake for a single woman to walk into a Western motif bar in the middle of Podunk-nowhere and bump into a damn obnoxious cowboy.

"So, Ms. Pickett, ma'am—" His gaze locked on hers as he released her chin from captivity. "What were you looking up?" He smiled again, "Maybe a dry cleaner?"

"Someplace to…" She cut off her response, horrified by the realization that her open jacket revealed the blended mocha catastrophe and returned to the study of her shoes. No way was she telling him the truth; that she was looking for a motel, or an Airbnb, someplace, anyplace, to stay for the night. The fact she'd already searched the town, and nothing was available, didn't stop her from looking. Feeling his stare, she looked up, and lied. "A word. I was looking up a word for the day. You know, improve my vocabulary?"

"Weird." He cocked his head, "What word, if I might ask?" The cowboy seemed genuinely interested.

"It's taciturn."

The bark of his laughter drew attention from the handful of patrons in the bar, and she wondered if the place ever got crowded.

He shifted his weight again, "And you think—" He pointed an index finger at himself. "I'm taciturn?" His grin was devastating. Casey's knees nearly folded under and her mouth went dry. All she could do was nod. He continued, "So, you believe I'm reserved? Non-talkative? Reticent?"

Braving his direct look again, she managed an answer. "I do. Yes, in fact, I do."

"Ma'am?"

"Please. Please. Stop with the ma'am. It makes me feel like I should run home, put on a gingham apron, and start slaving over a hot stove on your behalf."

He seemed to be thinking, and his expression made Casey hold her breath. "Ms. Pickett, I think that's a great idea." He put his hat back on the bar, and she caught the glint of laughter in his eyes. "But let me assure you, I am neither reserved, nor reticent, about much of anything."

He was so close, Casey actually thought he was going to close the gap and kiss her. A flash of wishful thinking that he would had every nerve ending in her body firing, and she was once again unable to speak.

"Ms. Pickett?" His tone was nonthreatening. Casey returned to the real world where she was carless and being accosted by an irritating cowboy who smelled like horses and leather, and of hard work and hay. She was aware people in the establishment were watching, and yet she still couldn't move.

"Where's home?"

Still working to regain her composure, she answered honestly, "Here, I guess. Here until my car is repaired."

"You break down?"

"No, I wrecked it." Tired, upset, she felt the tears forming in her eyes. *I will not cry, I will not cry, I will not cry.* The mantra failed. Moisture had pooled, spilled, and slid down Casey's cheeks, ensuring complete humiliation. He studied her with a frankness that made her feel naked on top of being mortified, angry, furious—she was about to make an exception to the general rule that she didn't kill people.

"You look a little like you want to shoot me, ma'am."

"A little? How about a lot? I met the sheriff of this town, sir. She seems pretty tough and independent. Sheriff Hudson, yes, that was it. I just bet she'd see things my way after reviewing the facts of this encounter, you stealing my phone and all."

He shrugged. "Fine with me if you file a report. Results though? That may be—just might—be awhile. This ain't the big city."

"Really." She could be sarcastic too. She squared her shoulders, stepping back from the cowboy. "The town 'mechanic'—" She used little air quotes around the word, however overdone the gesture might be, "said it will be two to eight weeks."

"That's a big window."

"Ya think?" She took a deep breath, angry for being forced into snarky and immature. "I'm sorry. It's just so frustrating. The holidays are just two weeks away and I may not have a car."

"You had it towed to Bailey Automotive?"

"If that's the name of the only auto shop in town, then yes."

"Well, I've got some clout with Tink Bailey, maybe I can get him to speed things up." Of course, he'd know the shop's owner. The accident happened in what must be the smallest town in the universe. And what kind of name was Tink? The cowboy broke into her head-chatter. "But if you have to stay, we should get you settled into the Pine Tree Inn."

"I'm sorry, I don't know you, and—"

"Like I said, it's Sam. Sam Wagner."

"Well, Mr. Wagner—"

He cut her off again. "Sam."

She took a deep breath, counting to ten in her head. "Mr. Wagner. The Pine Tree Inn is booked up. I'm told there's a cattle auction nearby, and the *only* hotel around here is booked for the next few days."

"Then you're homeless." His smile was back, and she was annoyed that he thought her predicament was funny. The cowboy was alternating between so-*not*-taciturn and somewhat withholding. Plus, with the hokey accent bit, she suspected he was a big faker. All of it made more confusing by the fact that he seemed genuine in his concern.

"I'm not homeless, I just don't have any place to stay while my car gets fixed. I was also planning to look for car rental places when some big ape stole my phone."

He sat back down on his barstool, making them eye to eye. Turning from her, he sipped at a beer, then spun back, face-to-face. "No rooms at all? As my away-at-college daughter would say—that sucks."

Casey heard herself responding, while her brain did a somersault. "I lost my bearings when the tow truck brought me here. I was on Highway—" She didn't remember the name of the road because her reaction to him was making her daft. *Damn, he's married? What a moron, Casey. Damn, damn, triple damn. And no ring? What a shit.* She raised her arm, and pointed. "That way, out of town, up the hill."

"I'm sorry."

"You should be, I mean, I wrecked my car, I'm stranded in some not-a-town, in the middle of so-totally-nowhere, and…" Casey hadn't realized just how great the toll of nearly dying had been. So much she couldn't even remember the name of the town, -wood, something. "What is this place, anyway?"

"Briarwood." Flat, matter-of-fact. Like everyone in the world must know the where, how, and why of this hole-in-the-wall.

She continued as if the answer didn't matter. "And like I said, *your* only hotel is completely booked. And it's freakin' cold outside, and…"

He placed an index finger against his lips, and she stopped like a child in kindergarten being reprimanded by the teacher.

"Okay." He stood again, and this time she registered his height. He had to be six-two, maybe taller. "We can take care of everything. And I'm sorry I've been giving you such a hard time." He leaned across the bar, grabbed her phone, and held it out to Casey. She didn't take it. "Well, now who's reticent, Ms. Pickett?"

The smile returned to his face, only this time she didn't think he was teasing. Still, he'd been a Class A cad, and Casey wasn't inclined to let him off the hook. "How, Mr. Wagner, how are you going to fix things?"

"Sam."

"Cowboy."

He laughed; it sounded genuine, not mean, and she relaxed, but just a little.

"The fix is simple. You're coming with me, and I'm going to put you up at my house."

"Just like that?" He was crazy. "Like hell I will."

"Hell is what it'll be like for you if you have no place to stay in December at this elevation. And yep. Just like that."

"And I'd do this why?"

"Well, for starters, you don't really have much choice. Briarwood's not a big city, and though we're growing, there's still just one hotel, which you've already discerned is booked solid."

"How's this any of your concern?"

"You need a place to stay. Temperature is predicted to drop into the twenties tonight, and though it would be a terrible idea given the likelihood that you'd freeze to death doing so, you don't even have a car to sleep in. My ranch isn't far from here, and my home is large, four bedrooms in fact." He crossed his heart. "I promise, I can be trusted."

"Right."

"Ask Maxine."

"Who's Maxine?"

"She owns this fine establishment." The cowboy turned his head toward the end of the bar. "Hey, Maxie." He returned his stare to Casey.

She tried to focus all her experience into the seconds it took this Maxine person to travel the length of the bar and stop across from the cowboy. Her brain kept humming that the situation was too weird, and she should turn and run.

"Hi. I'm Maxine." Too late. The bartender's hand stretched across, and because it was the polite thing to do, Casey reached out to shake it, offering up only her first name. The woman's grip was strong, her hands rough, but her smile was warm. "What you need, Sam?"

"She doesn't trust me, Maxie."

"Oh dang. Sam? Casey, is it? Sam's the best person I know. I trust him with my kids *and* my dog. He's a gentleman too."

Sam didn't turn back to face Maxine. His grin widened. "I offered her a place to stay for the night, but she's leery. Can't say as I blame her."

"Nope, you can't, Sam. But here's the thing, ma'am, Sam's a good guy. He's got a terrific daughter—well, she's not home from school yet, but you won't be out there alone. He's got several hands, a foreman, and best of all?"

Casey waited, wondering *what* in this situation could possibly have a "best of all."

"Sam's got a live-in housekeeper, and *she's* not going to visit her grandbabies in Denver until Christmas Day."

"I'll be damned if I'm staying here, of all places, until Christmas Day."

To Casey, the desperation she felt sounded more like rudeness. And what choice did she have? She was faced with the biblical "no room at the inn" and it already felt freezing outside. "I can wait in the bus depot."

"Can't do that, darling." Maxine seemed impervious to what was being asked of Casey. "There *is* no bus depot."

"You're kidding, right?"

"No, ma'am." Simultaneously from Sam and Maxine.

"Dammit." She'd been in this Briarwood place for over two hours and her use of cuss words had grown exponentially with her frustration.

Sam walked past her to the alcove. "This your stuff?" He opened the door, picked up one of her suitcases, and said, "It'll all fit in my truck, ma'am, so let's go."

Of course, he had a truck. Mumbling a string of bad words under her breath, she walked toward her unwelcome benefactor. "Fine. I'm coming." She had no choice, but if Casey heard one more "ma'am" directed at her, she was going to puke all over his dashboard.

CHAPTER THREE

Sam couldn't help but wonder about his unfortunate but feisty passenger. He'd been glancing at her off and on during the drive. She, on the other hand, stared straight ahead. He was thankful he'd driven the new truck instead of his favorite old metal can of a V-8 because they were warm and safe. In fact, too warm. Sam turned the blasting heat down and hummed quietly to his satellite radio.

He was curious about Ms. Casey Pickett—beyond curious. There was no ring on her finger, no white band of skin to allow a deduction that she'd ever worn one. And she was as skittish as a young colt in a thunderstorm. She had guts though.

According to his dashboard, the temperature had dropped to forty-two degrees. It made him glad they'd be at the ranch before he had to worry about ice on the roads. He didn't figure he could get her to open up, at least not now, so he started singing aloud. Christmas was his favorite holiday, even if his daughter, Natalie, wasn't home from school yet.

"Sleigh bells ring, are ya' listening, in the lane, snow is glistening, a beautiful sight, we're happy tonight, walking in a winter wonderland." He glanced over quickly, hoping for a reaction from his truck-mate.

Nothing.

He figured they were getting near where her wreck must have been. People who didn't know the road often lost control coming down from the pass because their cars had picked up speed and there was a tight S curve right before the grade bottomed out into the long ribbon of highway that came and went through Briarwood. His eyes on the road, Sam asked, "So, are we near where you had your accident?"

She sat up straight and looked out at the darkness, seemingly trying to judge the location of her wreck. "I don't think so." The reaction revealed that she *was* paying attention.

"Hmm, well, about a mile up is a common site for accidents because of the curve and downhill speed."

"That makes sense, but I didn't lose it on a curve."

"No?"

"Nope. I abhor the mundane, so I almost hit a cow instead."

Sam burst out laughing despite the fact that it wasn't funny. Hitting a large animal could get you killed. It also meant a loss for some rancher. He started to express that thought when Casey snapped, "It's so not funny, cowboy."

"No, it isn't, but your delivery was."

"Oh." She turned her face away and looked out the window into darkness. "What's the temperature now?"

"It's dropping quickly, about three degrees in the last few minutes—" He looked at the gauge. "Thirty-nine degrees."

She shivered and returned her stare to the road ahead.

"We're almost there." As he said it, he hit the blinker, slowed the truck, and turned left at a wide swath of pavement covering the first fifteen feet of road up to the gate. Stopping, he put the truck in park, undid his seat belt, and jumped out.

***

Casey watched as her captor-maybe-benefactor ran to the large gate. A blast of cold air had whirled around her inside the cab until the door slammed. Like earlier when she'd noted the various ranch names along the highway, she was staring at an arch fastened between the posts holding up the gate. Large letters forged out of iron read *2WRanch*. Of course, she was curious about the name, but even more so about the man.

It was obvious he was comfortable in his skin. She couldn't fault him for being confident, articulate, and apparently generous, but she hoped the confidence didn't segue into arrogance. Arrogant men, her pet peeve. Full-of-themselves males. She'd dealt with male egos throughout her nine years in law enforcement, including four as a detective, but there was no time to revisit the past now, because the door of the truck swung open, letting in another blast of cold air.

"Ok, hang on." He pulled the door shut and drove the truck forward without his seat belt. Casey thought about writing him a ticket, but he jumped back out and jogged toward the gate behind them before she could voice her intentions. He was back in the cab within a minute, seat belt on, and with the truck idling leaned toward her.

"Had to close the gate behind me." He smiled. "Can't let any of my livestock get out to the highway. Big steer, cow, and of course any bull could cause a wreck, you know."

He turned his attention back to the road, but not before she caught a glimpse of the smirk on his face, visible as it was with a cloudless sky and a full moon. Casey didn't hesitate: leaning across, she gave him a knuckle punch to his bicep.

"Ow." He slammed on the brakes hard enough that her seat belt snapped tight, then added, "What the hell was that for?"

"Teasing me, and don't you deny it." It sounded bitchy, but she didn't apologize.

For a few seconds he rubbed his arm as if mortally wounded. She could just make out the words to a tune emanating from the radio he had turned down earlier. "Baby, it's cold outside…" *No kidding.*

"I am sorry, Ms. Pickett. You've had a rough day and I'm giving you a hard time."

"Indeed." She slammed her arms together across her chest.

Cowboy Sam reached across the console, his hand accidentally brushing her knee in the process. A flash of wanting him to brush against her again struck like lightning and then was gone. He popped open the glove box. "Here." It was a brain warmer. "Peace offering?" She took the soft wool cap into her hands. "Put it on, it's only about six minutes to the house but this will keep your ears from freezing when you get out of the truck."

"I'll look ridiculous."

"Nah." But then he smiled. "Yeah, maybe."

Casey pulled the cap down over her ears and tried to judge his reaction; like, was he laughing at her again?

"You look cute."

She snorted, then turned red—the heat of embarrassment flushing her cheeks. With a deep breath she changed the subject. "You said, cow, steer, and bull a minute ago like there was a difference."

"There is." He took his foot off the brake and the truck started forward again. "Here's a little cattle ranching one-o-one. A cow is a female that's had a calf, a heifer on the other hand, female, no calf. A bull, I'm sure you know, is for breeding, i.e., they make more cows. Finally, a *calf* can be male or female." He stopped. "You getting this so far?"

"Oh, get serious. I know what a bull is for Pete's sake. And a steer must also signify a male. Like the bull." She felt brilliant.

"Well, Casey, that would be right except for one itty-bitty difference."

"And what would that be?"

"Steers can't reproduce." He reached over and patted her shoulder with a "there-there." "They've been snipped."

The heat returned to her face, and she wished instead of a full moon, the sky was full of dangerous thunderheads so a lightning bolt would hit the hood ornament and fry the truck, putting her out of her misery. He'd said they were close to his home, but she closed her eyes anyway, putting an end to further cattle talk.

CHAPTER FOUR

Casey must've dozed. But for how long? Two, maybe three minutes? The truck coming to a halt turned on her brain, and she immediately missed the safety of her snooze. She began to study her surroundings.

The house was lovely. There was a long covered front porch that even had one of those swings hung by two chains. Christmas lights strung along the eaves added a welcoming glow. The driveway was circular, and she could see buildings off to the left, including what she presumed to be a barn.

Cowboy Sam was coming around the front of the truck, but she beat him to offering her any help by shoving the door open and jumping out. Bad idea. She felt weak and wobbly, and nearly went down. Strong hands cupped under her arms, holding her up.

"Dammit, cowboy, I can manage."

"I disagree. Have you forgotten you almost hit a cow and wrecked your car?" He let go of his support, and she straightened her spine.

"Are you teasing me again? Because if you are, it's getting old. And now, thanks to you, I'm not sure it was a cow. You know, it could have been," Casey smiled, and added sarcasm to her tone, "a heifer, a steer, or a bull. It wasn't a calf though. Nope."

He laughed at her joke, and pulled the largest of her suitcases out of the bed of the truck. "You're an interesting woman, Casey Pickett. I'm looking forward to becoming better acquainted."

"Well, that is so not happening. I'll be leaving in the morning, cowboy."

"Is that you, Sam?" Casey turned her head to see a woman backlit by interior lights coming down some porch steps. "Sam Wagner, you had me worried sick. I thought you'd be back from the sale at least two hours ago."

"Sorry, Emma. I stopped in at The Dusty Boot for dinner." Nodding in Casey's direction, "Picked up a stray on the way." She wanted to smack him for the comment, but bit her tongue. "We're putting her up for the night."

Instead of a smart remark, Casey turned to face the woman, seeing a moment of surprise on her face. She was tall and slender, mid-sixties maybe? This must be the housekeeper. Remembering the brain warmer, she whipped it off her head, shoving it in her coat pocket.

"Hello, dear. Welcome. I'm pleased to meet you, but we'll freeze out here, so let's get acquainted inside." She studied Casey's frame as if assessing her for auction. "Hmm. Did you eat, young lady? You must be hungry, come on. Except you, Sam Wagner, you grab any luggage first." Without hesitation, she looped her arm at Casey's elbow and started walking her up the stairs. "Dear girl, I've got to hear everything." She giggled, adding, "Sam Wagner never brings anybody home."

"Well, what about his wife?"

"Dear me, he doesn't have one. Not in ten years. Long story. Again, did you eat? I bet he didn't offer you dinner."

"He didn't, actually. And I haven't eaten since breakfast."

"Sam Wagner, you ate and didn't feed this girl? For pity sakes." She said nothing more and, gently ushering Casey into a large entry, closed the door. "Sam will be along, but this time of year you don't leave doors and windows open for long."

Casey took a quick look at the surroundings. "It's stunning." Dead ahead was a staircase to another floor. The house was done in Spanish style, like many of the houses on the coast of California.

The walls were stucco and painted a soft beige. An arch separated the entryway and the living room, which was to the right and down two steps that ran the same width of the opening. Exposed beams ran lengthwise along the high ceiling, and she heard the snap of a crackling fire.

The housekeeper's voice tugged her out of further observation. "Where are my manners? I'm Emma Blake, but just call me Emma. Come into the kitchen and I'll whip something up."

"Thank you. I am starving."

"You're a very pretty young woman."

"I'm thirty-four." Uncertain why she'd blurted out that tidbit, Casey pinched the skin between her thumb and index finger to stay alert.

"That, young woman, is young. And you're too thin, but we can fix that in a few days."

Casey opened her mouth to protest, thinking she should let Emma know she was only staying one night. One single, solitary night. But the cowboy's voice echoed from behind her, interrupting any about-to-be notice of departure.

"Emma, you got any Christmas cookies?" Casey sensed him before he slid up to her right side her and whispered, "Emma makes *the* best sugar cookies in the whole world."

Hay and cows and hard work clung to him, and she liked it. His nearness gave her a fuzzy feeling accompanied by an urge to reach up and touch his face. When she turned, tilting her head to study him, he stepped even closer.

"You like it? My home?"

He was so close, she swallowed past the lump in her throat. "It's lovely."

"That's kind of you to say, Ms. Pickett."

"Casey, please."

"Only if you call me Sam."

"Okay."

"Say it."

"Sam."

His left hand somehow came to rest at the base of her spine, and with the touch a sensation struck that made her suck in a breath. "I like you calling me Sam, Ms. Pickett." Then without another word he gently pushed her toward an entryway through which Emma had disappeared. It was nice. Too nice. His touch. *Get a grip, Casey. One night. You're here for one night. I don't care if you have to hitchhike out of this town to leave.*

***

Sam stood quietly outside the bedroom Emma had readied for his houseguest. A light shone from under the door and he wanted to knock, see how she was doing, but two things stood in his way. For starters, she must be exhausted. He sat at the kitchen table sipping the bourbon he'd thought about, what, an hour and a half ago? The whiskey settled him, allowing him to watch as she'd devoured a hefty sandwich made from leftover steak, and knocked back two full glasses of Chardonnay. Add that to her drive, a wrecked car, and a complete stranger taking her in, and no doubt she was tired. Plus, he'd given her enough of a hard time that she probably never wanted to see him again.

Sam *was* interested. He figured that's why he'd felt so compelled to tease the woman. But recognizing his interest and putting a name on it eluded him. He hadn't been around a woman for quite a while—maybe getting burned so bad by his ex-wife made him defensive around females. He hadn't really had much in the way of relationships since Rachel left.

Dragging a hand through his hair, he reached for the doorknob. A voice in his head stopped him, and instead, he turned down the hall toward his room. The place he'd slept alone for a long time.

Okay, there'd been Mary Adams, a teacher. They'd dated for several months over four years ago. The sex had been satisfactory and they got along well enough, but there was no spark. Mechanical. It all felt mechanical.

He also didn't miss her when they weren't together.

He realized as he closed the door to his bedroom that wasn't true of one Casey Pickett.

And that realization intrigued him.

CHAPTER FIVE

A rooster crowed, and Casey opened bleary eyes.. The bed was wonderful and she didn't want to move, but as the room came into focus, her brain stirred up yesterday's events. She jolted to a sitting position.

Sam Wagner's house. She was in a stranger's house, her car was close to annihilated, and if it could be repaired, it might take all of forever. She had landed somewhere, nowhere really, and Christmas was less than two weeks away.

She also needed to use a restroom.

And she was starving.

Realizing the room was warming up, she tossed back the down comforter and wool blankets. The window let in bright sun, which made her head hurt. Casey remembered opening the blind last night to stare up at a million stars before she crawled into the bed. "Right. That was cool." She also recalled the two goblet-size glasses of Chardonnay she'd imbibed and stopped laying blame for the headache on Mother Nature.

Someone, she figured Emma and not the cowboy, had laid a terry cloth robe at the end of the bed along with a large bath sheet, hand towel, and washrag. A note set on the pile cleared up any mystery. "Bath is directly across the hall. Breakfast is at eight. Em."

"I knew I liked that woman." Casey slipped first one, then the other arm into the robe and cinched the fabric belt. Studying the room added to her impression of the ranch house. She remembered the window seat as comfortable from her stargazing. An overstuffed chair sat in one corner with a small reading table, lamp, and a stack of books on its bottom shelf. Her suitcase was on a luggage stand, and she felt relief that it wasn't open. It's not like she'd been kidnapped by thieves and axe murderers. Still, it was reassuring that her privacy was respected.

So she'd slept well and survived the night. Grabbing clean jeans, shirt, and undies, along with her sundries bag, she cautiously opened the door to the hallway. Nobody in either direction, good. Her watch said 7:15, so she had time to get down to breakfast by eight. Good thing, because the smells floating up from below were amazing. Casey closed her eyes for a moment just to appreciate the flavorful aromas.

"Ms. Pickett. Good morning." She jumped, and then opened her eyes. Sam Wagner was standing in front of her, but he'd obviously come from downstairs. "Emma makes a great breakfast. You'll need it. You've got lots to do today."

Dumbfounded, grateful for the robe, she tried to interpret what he'd just said, but it wasn't making sense.

"What *am* I doing today?" She was part terrified and part preoccupied. The man was intolerably distracting. His good looks alone could buckle her knees, but also, he smelled clean, soapy, like leather and a forest. Unlike last night, he was clean-shaven. By all the saints in heaven, she wanted to reach up and feel the closeness of his shave.

"Besides daydreaming you mean?"

Casey refocused her attention, straightened her stance, and dared a direct look at the man. She'd been right about his eyes. *Green. Not hazel.* "Yes. And I wasn't." She swallowed hard. "Daydreaming." Nope, she was fantasizing. Obviously, *not* the same thing.

"Well, ma'am, you're going to earn your keep."

"What?" He *was* crazy. "And, please, cease and desist with the ma'am bit."

"Casey." Deliberate. "You know, like room and board. Some chores."

"Like hell."

"Oh, it just might be—" The insanely sexy grin returned. "For you. A bit hellish, but you'll feel great after a day's work on a ranch."

"I will?" She was dumbfounded and, again, unable to deliver up any kind of smart-ass response.

"Of course. And you better get going, we don't wait meals around here." He winked at her, and as he walked by gave a most gentle pat to her rear end.

"You…you…" It wasn't there. The don't-get-mad-get-even retort she wanted eluded her completely. Her nemesis entered another room at the end of the hall and closed the door without looking back. Casey stood flabbergasted. She was going to have to shoot him after all.

***

As Casey entered the barn, Sam watched his guest from the stallion's stall. Emma had his instructions, so something worked, because she'd managed to get Ms. Casey Pickett to the barn.

A little skinny, but all the right curves accented her figure. Thick blonde hair was tied back in a ponytail that swayed left and right when she moved. It was pure enjoyment watching her unseen. Timid at first, then curious. She looked over a divider to study equipment she probably didn't recognize. When Clementine, their milk cow, mooed, she jumped a foot.

"How was your breakfast?"

She turned with a start. "Delicious, thank you. But it's not going to work. I'm not staying and I'm not working for you. For crying out loud it's not the eighteenth century."

"Aw, and here I thought for sure you'd enjoy being my wench."

"You are the *most* aggravating human being I have ever met. And I've met a lot." She spread her feet a bit and punched her fisted hands against each hip, challenging him.

"Entirely possible, ma'am." Sam ducked his head to avoid revealing a grin. Good thing too, because the water bottle that whizzed past his ear would have hurt. He moved quick, reaching her in seconds. "All right, Pickett, that's enough." When he tried to grab her arm, she stuck out a foot, then bobbed right, and next thing Sam knew, he was in the hay.

"I asked you not to call me ma'am, cowboy."

The situation was funny, it couldn't be anything else, and he started laughing. Staring at the beams high up in the barn, he took deep breaths to regain control. He wasn't mad. He was impressed. "Self-defense training?" He got to a sitting position and, seeing his hat to the left, planted it back on his head.

"Black belt."

"Damn, Pickett. I'm impressed."

"As well you should be." She'd relaxed her arms, and he tried to picture her in a white gi and bare feet. He erased the image that popped up in his head because it caused an immediate reaction below his belt buckle.

Casey walked toward him and reached out her hand to help him up, "Peace?"

"Sure." Sam took her hand, but he couldn't do it, couldn't let the opportunity to get even slip away, and so he tugged her down. She landed with a loud expletive on top of him. He rolled and flipped her beneath him with the same lightning reactions she'd shown a moment earlier. "Ms. Pickett, I'm going to show you some chores to occupy you around here until your car is fixed."

"I'll be damned if that's going to happen, Mr. Wagner." Her muscles had gone taut and he could feel her vibrate with anger. "And I'm not agreeing to anything from you. Ever." She inhaled, and the sensation of Casey's body against his made him more intent on convincing her to stick around.

"Why is everything an immediate no with you?" She didn't answer. "I mean, all I'm suggesting is you enjoy the fresh air and have some new experiences. It'll kill time and you'll get the best sleep you've had in your entire life." He knew she couldn't escape, and he thought he caught a glimpse of interest in her expression.

"How so?"

"Because it's hard work, Casey."

"I've worked hard all my life, cowboy. We didn't all grow up on big fancy ranches, you know."

He ignored the snip at his position in life. Another reason he kept his bank portfolio a secret. "I'm sure you have, but did some office job exhaust you into a deep sleep? Maybe you live stressed out." He stared down at her, not budging, thinking how pretty she really was. Her cheeks were flushed with embarrassment—well, more likely, from anger. Her eyes were blue pools that invited a person in for a swim, and he found himself wanting to kiss her.

"I admit, I slept like a log last night, but there were plenty of reasons for that besides slave labor."

"It's room and board. Just until your car's fixed. And if it'll make you feel better? I'll pay you ten bucks an hour."

***

Now it was Casey's turn to laugh. The entire situation was so ridiculous there was nothing else for it but to bust out laughing, which she did. Her belly pressed against his, revealing his flat stomach as muscle. She was in danger of melting into the hay; worse, she was in danger of saying yes to anything he asked. His eyes sparked with interest, and she noted what she had thought to be green in color was closer to aquamarine. She swallowed. "Okay, cowpoke. But the hotel said they'd have openings in two days. So, that's it. That's how long I'll stay."

She couldn't look away. His gaze was intense, uncomfortable, and she wanted him to kiss her, deeply.

"Okay, two days. That can be our deal for now." That damned smile that made her weak-silly was back. "Let's go then, the days are short this time of year." When he got to his knees, she squirmed out from under him. The physical closeness they'd shared had tripped something in her heart. Sam offered his hand to help her up, after which they stood too close for another few seconds. She held her breath until Sam said, "So, you wanna learn to milk a cow or not?"

How could she resist. "Serious?"

"Yes, ma'a—Casey." He turned and walked past the partition, allowing her a great view of his backside. *Damn*. She guessed milking a cow with Sam Wagner could be a good thing so she picked up her water from the barn floor and followed him.

CHAPTER SIX

They were sitting on his front porch, Sam in an old rocker nursing a beer, and Casey on the swing, rhythmically pushing her foot against the wood decking, as the swing launched her up and back while she took occasional sips from a glass of wine. The sun had just set and though it had been an unseasonably warm day, she pulled the big sweater Emma loaned her tighter around her torso.

It was her second full day working, and her third night at the ranch. She worried about her statement to Sam two days ago when she mentioned that the hotel in town would soon have rooms available. Would he bring it up?

She let the rhythm of the swing calm her concerns. Every joint, muscle, heck, *every* part of her body was sore. Even her eyelids ached. She was barely awake, and the chirp of crickets and bullfrogs making a racket from the small creek that ran alongside of the house, and Emma doing dishes, singing Christmas carols with the kitchen window cracked open a bit, lulled her into a near coma.

"You awake, Pickett?"

"Um, yes. Barely."

"So, you're tired. I told you so."

"Nobody likes an I told you so, ranch man, and I'm not tired, I'm practically dead." His laugh poured over her like warm butter dripping off a hot biscuit. She realized she'd started thinking in ranch life. And after only two days.

"Sorry." He seemed lost in thought for a second or two. "Rick, my foreman, says you've become an expert at pitching hay."

"My arms, shoulders, and back agree, sir."

"Sam, Casey. It's Sam."

"I know. I guess I'm just fighting liking it here—" She looked across at him, his earnestness capturing a little piece of her heart. No, a big piece. "Sam."

"You know the Pine Tree Inn should have rooms now. The auction ended last night." Direct, as usual, but Casey could tell Sam had trouble making the offer. Maybe he didn't want her to go?

"I know." She wanted to add, why not stay until the car's fixed? Casey didn't care if her car was a total loss even if it was her current home. She decided to brave what she was thinking. "I'm not sure I want to leave, Sam. I'm learning a lot, and I'd have to move everything, plus then I'd need to run for exercise, and eat where?"

"Lulu's place." He'd bent at the waist and rested his elbows on his knees, rolling the beer bottle back and forth in his hands. "It's good."

"But I don't want to hurt Emma's feelings. She's a fabulous cook, and yet careful about too much sugar."

He interjected, "If you don't count her cookies and pies?"

"Okay, there's that, but the hard work destroys those extra calories. And besides, eating at Lulu's? From what I hear, I'd just get fat."

"Not likely, bones."

"Hey."

"Don't worry, you're perfect." Casey nearly slid off the swing. Blood rushed to her face and she felt the blush, happy the porch was shadowed in growing darkness.

"I uh—" Nothing came out of her mouth.

He stood up and walked across to the swing. The beer in one hand, he stopped her swinging with the other. "Come on, cowgirl. We'll find you frozen stiff in the morning if you stay out here much longer."

Was he propositioning her? She hoped so. Casey let him pull her from the swing, but he didn't stay close. Instead, he ushered her inside. "Besides, we all know you're in it for the money." She started to punch his arm in the same place she had in the truck three nights ago, but he was too quick. Holding her wrist, he leaned in, "Good night, Casey. Take some aspirin and get some rest." He turned, and said, "I'm going out to check on the horses and Clementine."

Casey stood staring as the door closed and cut off anything further between them. He wanted to check on a cow more than be with her? That stung. *He wanted to kiss me.* She was sure of it.

"Child, he's a man." Casey startled, surprised by Emma's appearance into the alcove. "Sometimes they're slower than melting ice at ten degrees, and thicker than a fence post."

"I…"

"Like I said the first night you arrived, Casey, that man hasn't brought a woman to this house in a long time, not one he much cared for anyway."

"He's got a weird way of showing any interest." She tried smiling.

"Trust me. He's got feelings for you." Emma took the empty wineglass from Casey's hand. "Now, what you need is aspirin, a hot bath with Epsom salt, and some warm cocoa. The salt is under the sink in the bathroom. I'll be up with the cocoa and aspirin in a flash."

"Emma, thank you. I—"

"Just go. You know what they say. Things are always brighter in the morning."

Casey watched Emma disappear into the kitchen, praying the housekeeper was right about Sam. If not? She needed to pack her bags.

***

Sam stood in the barn and cursed himself. He'd hurt Casey. The pain he caused translated in her posture and the crestfallen look on her face. But sitting across from her on the porch, watching her swing two nights ago, he knew he was falling for her, vulnerable as she was. It scared the snot out of him, hence the cold-fish attitude since that encounter.

"Easy, Tilly." He picked up a brush and pulled it across the sweet mare's flank. The horse responded with a nicker and a head toss, then returned her focus to the hay box. He'd spoken to Natalie on the phone, explained he'd met someone he had feelings for, and she'd been ecstatic. He promised they'd talk more when she got home. Her last words before hanging up were, "Awesome, Dad. Can't wait to meet her."

Well, maybe he'd blown it. The attraction to her had been immediate. That and her apparent hopelessness. Maybe his behavior in the Dusty Boot and taking her home were because he needed to save something, someone. It didn't matter now, because he'd avoided her for two days, knowing how close he'd been to kissing Casey more than once.

With two days to think, he now had a plan. Somehow, he'd make his newest ranch hand understand everything. Sam would confirm that Casey would stick around and then—who knew what could happen from there?

CHAPTER SEVEN

The reliable ranch rooster crowed, but Casey was already awake. Incredibly, today marked her sixth day on Sam Wagner's ranch. Her body was sore, but she was getting stronger all the time.

Remembering how she'd rejected Sam's proposal that she work off room and board, how she'd whined like a spoiled child and spit out a stubborn retort to the very idea, her "Hell no" echoed in her head. She'd been so mad back then, enough that she demanded he take her to the airport the night after. Sam, instead, offered logic. Regional flights booked out months, and Denver was a ten-hour drive without guarantees she'd get anywhere given the holidays and weather issues.

Oh, she'd wanted to get away from the cowboy back then. Now, her heart wouldn't allow her to leave. God knew she'd tried to dislike him.

Now that she wanted to be close? It was too late. Since the night of the porch swing incident, Sam had been mostly invisible. Gone early, home late. She'd misread his cues, believing that night he felt the same.

Sam obviously didn't want her, and the sensations that raced through her body around him were apparently hers alone.

Damn, it stung.

He'd flipped from close to distant and she didn't know why. Two sleepless nights of running through every scene of the two of them together, and she still couldn't pinpoint anything that would turn him away. "What did I say, Sam?" She sat up, pulled the pillow onto her lap, and punched the thing several times.

Until that evening on the porch, every encounter, each exchange, had chipped away at the debate in her head against having feelings for the cowboy. He was funny, articulate, hardworking, kind, too handsome for his own good, and… The list was a page long. She'd typed it on her laptop, then tucked the machine back in her suitcase.

When she tossed in the night sky, fresh air, deep sleep, and a growing friendship with the man's housekeeper, Casey stayed, and she worked. And there was the food. Morning one, Emma served an aromatic fat-infested breakfast of fried eggs, crisp bacon, fresh biscuits, and a large glass of orange juice. The food got better each day. And the coffee. Whatever Emma put in the brew left Casey ready to run marathons.

Somehow, during her stay, pitching hay, cleaning out stalls, feeding and milking a cow—okay, she wasn't so great at the latter— had become a routine. One that made her feel good about herself.

She'd never slept as hard, never experienced feeling refreshed and yet so exhausted simultaneously. And more surprisingly, Casey had been so content, so much so that she almost forgot the cloud over her head.

At first, she thought she hadn't gone far enough away, but the need to distance herself from her old life had lessened a little each day. And it had to be because of Sam. Dammit, she *had* fallen for him.

She missed the feelings that accompanied his tendency to lean in to her, get close. Casey shook her head to escape an image of his eyes, sparkling with a tease, the man stacking bales of hay, his biceps pumped up with muscle that showed beneath the wool t-shirt that fit him like plastic wrap. There'd been times when they were so physically close, her skin tingled. She argued with her feelings based on his actions.

Three separate times she'd sworn he was going to kiss her.

But he hadn't.

The Devil knew she wanted him to.

The snooze alarm went off. "Shoot." She jumped out of bed, hastily making it—everyone did in this house. It was protocol to earn breakfast. Grabbing fresh clothes, she poked her head out and looked up and down the hallway. *All clear.* Then she stepped out to cross to the bathroom, and his deep voice nearly stopped her heart.

"Well, Ms. Pickett, slept in a bit, did we?"

She stood stock-still, like a deer that heard something in the forest. A quick inventory of her appearance drew a gulp. Sleep shorts, Santa socks, and a form-fitting Henley t-shirt that was too holey for in-public viewing. *Dammit, Sam.* She took a deep breath and turned to face him.

"Ma'am, I do believe you're blushing." The grin, the one that made her crazy, appeared for the first time in days.

"You know, cowboy, I'm getting tired of your incessant teasing, not to mention that ma'am sh..." She stopped herself and took a breath. "And for your information, I wasn't *sleeping in*, I was thinking. Serious and important thoughts, in fact."

"Oh. I see." He stepped closer. Excitement jumped like dry lightning from synapse to synapse in her brain. Her knees went weak, and she knew in an instant that her nipples were taut against the t-shirt. Embarrassment wrapped around her like spandex, and she felt hot. Casey was certain that if he came one centimeter closer, she'd disappear—nothing would be left but a puddle and her silly sleeping outfit on the floor.

"How would you feel about a ride instead of work this morning?"

"Oh, that would be great, can we go into town? I'd like to get something for Emma for Christmas."

"I meant on a horse."

"Oh."

"Can you ride?"

"It's been about ten years."

"Okay, well, you'll be fine then. You know what they say, it's like riding a bike."

No, it most certainly is not.

"Meet me in the barn in half an hour. Forget the shower, you'll want one

afterward." His gaze caught hers. "You're looking cute again, Pickett."

Then he was gone. She didn't dare turn to watch him leave. Besides, she was confused. Totally. Why the sudden reversal in his behavior? She'd yet to reveal her past, nor had she killed or maimed any of the ranch animals, broken a fence, or some antique in the house. Maybe it was a plan to kick her off the ranch.

Still, she'd swear in the moments before he walked away, once again, Sam Wagner wanted to kiss her.

Ducking in the bathroom, she reached for her toothbrush, wishing he had.

CHAPTER EIGHT

Sam was grooming Tilly again. A good horse, not too big, and one that wouldn't likely toss Casey Pickett on her delectable ass. He smiled to himself. After grabbing a couple bottles of water, he'd headed straight to the barn. The methodical movement of the brush, up and down, up and down, calmed him. He couldn't believe the woman made him so anxious.

He kept mulling over the pros and cons of starting a new relationship, then the misery of his first marriage would flood his mind. Except Casey wasn't Rachel. Hell, nobody could be like Rachel. Selfish, uncaring, always wanting to impress. Shaking his head against memories of the most toxic relationship of his life, Sam figured his temporary ranch hand also had baggage but hopefully she'd trust him enough to open up.

If they *were* headed for a "thing," there was also something he wanted to take care of. Especially since she'd mentioned the possibility of buying property nearby. Then again, if he let her go? There'd be no risk to his heart.

"Hello?"

"Here." He popped his head out of the stall. "Casey, hi. Come on, I'm going to show you how to handle some of Tilly's tack."

"Like you have any." Even sarcastic, she was cute.

"Tack, not tact." He laughed, finding it easier than it had been for years.

"If you laugh at me, Sam Wagner, I'm leaving."

"I'm sorry. And I'm not laughing at you, Casey. You're just funny." He motioned her over. "Okay. Come here." He could see she was nervous, so he reached out, took her hand, and tugged her into the stall. "Come on, it's not that scary. I thought you said you rode." He could feel her hand trembling.

"Yep. Ten years ago."

"Well, how long had you been riding when you quit?"

"Didn't quit." She ducked her head, then looked up at him again. "It was just the one time. A trail ride. And before you accuse me of lying—" Sam noted her drawing a deep breath. "I told you the truth. You didn't ask for any specifics."

"You're right." He smiled, trying to put her at ease. "Okay, we'll go slow." He grabbed a saddle blanket and pushed Casey gently to the mare, her backside to him. "This is Tilly. She's sweet." Leaning around Casey, he said, "Take the blanket and put it on her back."

He wished he could see her expression, but she managed to get the blanket on the horse, having to reposition it only a little closer to the withers. Sam didn't push further, speaking quietly to Casey about approaching a horse as he finished saddling and bridling the mare.

In twenty minutes, they were astride the two horses he'd chosen for the ride. He had to force down longing when he'd given her a leg up, accepting that being so close to her without pulling her against him, kissing her, was making him nuts. Now she looked terrified. In a low, calm voice, he gave her basic instructions as they walked toward a trail that looped away from the barn, past a small pond, and back to the corral.

Plodding along in silence, Sam watched, noticing when Casey had relaxed somewhat. At the pond, he dismounted, and after helping her down, his hands making contact with her waistline, he dropped the reins on the bank, letting the horses drink. The simple task of helping Casey dismount again ignited a physical reaction that was anything but emotional.

Stepping away from her, he untied the blanket attached to his saddle. Laying it on the ground under a tall, broad pine tree, he waved her over. "Come on, sit."

***

"Uh, not gonna happen." Casey stared at Sam, she hoped with a look of incredulity on her face. She was so *not* getting on a blanket with the man. Of course, she wanted to, so much. Too much. But he'd been a jackass for days, including not showing for dinner, which was rude to Emma.

"Come on, Casey. I've got water if you're thirsty." The sound of Sam's voice almost made her cave; she longed for his nearness. But he'd been cruel, and since she'd no idea why, she didn't budge.

"What are you running from, Casey?"

"Nothing." He'd stepped closer. *Do you know that drives me crazy, cowboy?*

"Liar." His hand came up and tucked a lock of her hair behind an ear. What was that country song? Something about God driving a car, no, taking the wheel. Country music was on in the barn most of the time. She supposed the storied tunes were growing on her.

"I'll figure it out at some point. So why don't you just tell me."

Feeling inept, dangerously under his influence, a whiff of his scent, man, cowboy, hot. "Can I see your rifle?" Actions were better than words.

He looked befuddled. "You wanna shoot me?" But then he walked away, pulled the gun out of the sheath behind his saddle, and when he returned, handed it over.

Casey grinned. "Maybe." Studying the gun, getting the feel for its weight, she could feel his eyes on her, no doubt curious. Maybe Sam was gauging the crazy woman he'd invited into his home. "A Remington V3 semiautomatic. You have predators round these parts?" She thought the hokey accent was a nice touch.

"I'm impressed." His damn grin rattled Casey. "But 'round these parts'? You're acclimating, Pickett. And yes, we have bear, coyotes, and mountain lions." He took off his hat, brushed it against his jeans, and finger combed his hair.

She refused to be distracted even if he was damn near irresistible.

"Okay." Looking for something to shoot at, she picked up two pine cones, one the size of her hand, the other about two inches long and narrow. Ignoring Sam, she paced, counted her strides, and placed the cones on top of a boulder. She looked back at him, "This about one hundred feet?"

He nodded and she retraced her steps.

You can do this, Casey. She repeated it like a mantra because it'd been over a year since she practiced with a rifle, and eleven months and sixteen days since she'd fired *any* weapon. A fact tattooed on her heart because it was the day her career ended.

She felt beads of perspiration forming on her forehead, her armpits were damp, and she figured without the shower she stank. Good, maybe then he'd leave her be. The tucking-her-hair-in bit had sent Casey's libido into orbit. *Breathe.* Placing the rifle butt against her shoulder, she aimed, prayed, and fired.

The small cone disintegrated; tiny pieces flew up and away from the boulder. She heard and ignored Sam's whistle. Re-aiming, she fired a second shot. The larger pine cone popped up and disappeared behind the big stone. Relieved, Casey turned and faced Sam.

"I'll be damned."

His smile was infectious, but she'd revealed a piece of her past. She risked her chance at a relationship with her cowboy, because for sure, if he knew why she'd landed in Briarwood, he'd be the one running. Bending, she picked up the empty shells and stopped a foot shy of Sam, still thinking her past *was* awful enough to scare him off. She guessed he was the kind of man who didn't tolerate lies or secrets. "Here." She shoved the rifle at him, which he took in one hand, and the empty shells in the other.

**

Watching Casey, Sam could tell she had something else to say, so he stood silent, waiting.

"I was in law enforcement. A detective."

He let out a second whistle. Sure, he knew she had some kind of secret because she'd landed in Briarwood, homeless and tight-lipped. One of his guesses was she might be running from the law.

Wrong. She *was* the law. Or had been.

His other supposition had seemed the more likely, that she'd escaped a bad relationship. He turned away long enough to lean the rifle against the tree.

"Are you going to say anything?"

"You're a hell of a shot?" He pocketed the empty shells, noticing her blush, like she was embarrassed. For what, being an ex-cop? "Admittedly, the revelation was a surprise. You want to talk about it?"

"Maybe." She paused. "Except why would I? You've been giving me the cold shoulder for days. Did I do something wrong?"

He wanted to pull her into his arms and hold her close. What the heck was happening?

Casey Pickett was happening. She was tall, maybe five-eight, and wiry in a good way. Plus, she was pretty. He figured her for thirty-four, maybe thirty-five? Not so far from his forty-two that they wouldn't work.

"For now, please believe I had my reasons." She shrugged, offering nothing more. "So, did you quit?"

"Sort of." She'd been staring at her boots. When she looked up, her eyes held sadness and were filled with a well of tears ready to spill. "I should have. Before I got fired."

"What would warrant that?"

"Oh, nothing in particular. Unless you consider maiming a teenage kid, leaving him brain damaged." She crossed her arms, hugging herself.

Sam watched as first one, then a flood of tears slid down her cheeks. He couldn't take it anymore and pulled her against his chest. He could feel the rigid tension in her muscles, but she didn't protest.

"He had a gun aimed at my partner. I saw it, so I fired, aiming for his shoulder—he spun around when he got hit and fell." Casey took a breath, then let the air out slowly against his shirt. It felt right, having her in his arms. "He slammed his head on a curb."

Sam rubbed her back gently, hoping she'd relax. Waiting, certain she had something more to say. "His parents sued, of course, excessive force, abuse of authority, misconduct, it was a long list; their son was perfect." She hiccupped and he felt it against his chest. She raised her head. "I mean, let's just forget the kid had robbed a liquor store. There were witnesses, the store had cameras, but they were important, and wealthy—so much rhetoric. 'Not *our child*—blah, blah, blah.'" She snuffled. "Anyway, as a result of smashing his head into concrete, the kid was in a coma over a week. I don't even know now if he's completely recovered."

Sam waited. It was obvious she blamed rich parents for some of her predicament. The thought of all the dollar signs in his portfolio drifted by. He needed to tell her the truth.

"No surprise. The city was facing a multimillion-dollar lawsuit, and I was named as a defendant."

He studied her face. "Still, I don't get why that would get you fired. It sounds like a clean shoot."

Another big snuffle, and she pulled away. Like a child, she wiped her nose with a sleeve. "I—the boy's injuries. I mean, I shot him, Sam." Casey dropped her chin again. "I kind of fell apart. Then the family told the city's attorneys if I was fired, they'd drop my name from the lawsuit." She stilled for a moment, then added, "My attorney says I'll eventually get my pension, but I couldn't stay there. I was alone and miserable. I sold my condo—" another snuffle, "most of my stuff." The color of her eyes intensified because of the tears, but he didn't budge from his position. "When I said I was homeless, Sam, it was true."

He wanted to console her, but when he stepped close again, she held up her hand to stop his approach. "We should go."

Her shoulders squared as she walked to the horse. He was proud of her when she pulled the reins back over Tilly's head, grabbed the stirrup, slipped her foot in, and used the saddle horn to hike herself up. He moved quickly then, and with the rifle sheathed, he secured the blanket and mounted up.

Casey was trotting down the trail back toward the ranch, bouncing up and down like an amateur. He wanted to make her laugh, but even when he caught up with her, she said nothing else all the way back to the barn.

CHAPTER NINE

Sam understood why Casey wasn't sharing more, and he'd concluded a) he wanted her, b) was falling in love with her, and c) needed to gain her trust. Especially given what she'd told him that afternoon. The best way he could think of was to disclose his secrets. Okay, not really secrets, but still… A crummy marriage, a witch of an ex-wife, and a boatload of money.

Given her apparent view that "rich" people ruined her life, his money could be an issue. He'd kept his wealth under the radar for years. Maybe it was guilt at making millions.

Ten years ago, he'd been thirty-two, his daughter, Natalie, was eleven, and his marriage had been in trouble for a long time.

The mirror reflected back his image. "She's younger than you, old man." Nothing he could do about it, so he checked his attire. Jeans, white cotton shirt, single pocket, snap buttons, and a bolo tie, which had a square turquoise set in a silver clasp. He nodded, thinking his clothing appropriate for the evening's activities.

Emma was picking up Natalie from the regional airport, and though anxious to see his daughter and hear about her third year at Stanford, he was worried that after their ride today, Casey would be a no-show for the tree-decorating tradition.

Then again, if things went according to plan, if she showed up, he'd have at least twenty minutes alone with his newest ranch hand.

***

Casey spent extra time getting ready. The shower had helped wash off all of the dirt, and *some* of the pain of confessing her past to Sam. She wanted to smell good but not in an attention-getting way, so she'd used her bergamot body butter. Putting her nose to a bare arm, she sniffed. "Not bad." She wanted Sam to find her delicious, irresistible, to want her despite the flaws.

The need to look her best was tied in part to Sam's daughter coming home, but mostly because she was in the throes of falling in love. Which was why she'd opted for the dangerous little black dress. That, and the fact Emma said the family dressed for the occasion. Casey glanced at the big mirror in the foyer, trying not to be hypercritical. The fabric, a spandex blend, hugged what curves she had, and she worried it might be too much.

She stepped down into the living room, reminding herself she'd be leaving soon enough. There was no end to irony because now, of course, she didn't *want* to go. It was a hell of a predicament. The big stink she'd made about staying at the ranch even *one* night felt like eons ago, not just six days.

And it *was* hard not to be angry at Sam what with his not joining her the last two nights on the porch, skipping breakfast in the kitchen, cutting out on dinners. Until this morning, and the invitation for the ride, he'd been MIA in general.

Sam's invitation to join in the family tradition decorating the tree was before his disappearing act, *and* the morning ride. *Does he even still want me here?*

She stared at the big tree, tall and stately, but still empty of ornaments. She enjoyed the white lights strung carefully amongst the many branches. Still, her continued efforts at settling her emotions failed. She sighed, then whispered to the tree, "I could use a drink."

She looked around the room: exposed beams, supple leather furniture, and a dark wood coffee table adorned with three iron reindeer of various sizes placed in a garland of fresh pine.

"That little black dress, ma'am? Stunning, but not exactly ranch fare."

Sam.

Damn stealthy cowboy. She sensed him standing directly behind her, smelling woodsy with a hint of fresh soap. His nearness made her already frazzled nerves tingle. Blood raced through her veins, sizzling like a live power line.

She turned to face him. He was stupid handsome, and she wondered if a few Hail Marys would keep her from simply fainting to the floor.

Sam held out a flute of champagne, which she took, slugging half its contents with her first sip. The mirth in his eyes suggested she was busted for being nervous. He'd dressed up a little, or maybe it was a lot for him. What did she know? Until six days ago, her preconceptions of life on a ranch were based on reruns of old westerns on TV.

The reality was far different. She long presumed all cowboys were good-looking, and of course, that wasn't true. Except God help her, Sam was. She took a deep breath at the same time he bent to place his glass down on the coffee table, turned back to her, and stepped close.

"You smell delicious." Casey almost choked on her second swallow of champagne when his words mirrored her earlier thoughts. She kept the flute in front of her, thinking it could act as a defense to any advances.

And who was she kidding?

She wanted him. All of him.

"I'm not trying to embarrass you, Ms. Pickett." His eyes smiled, and since he was only inches away, she fell into his gaze, heart pounding, a throbbing ache in her core. She held her breath, longing for a kiss.

"Hey, Dad? I'm home. Are you in the living room?"

Casey took a sharp breath and stepped back from Sam, watching as he turned, a spectacular grin breaking out on his face. "Natalie?"

The girl was stunning—tall and slender like her father. Her hair was more auburn than Sam's, and her skin coloring confirmed a life in California sunshine. She bounced down the stairs, a thick ponytail bobbing as she hugged her father. "I missed you. I really, really missed you, Dad." Natalie Wagner buzzed with joy as she turned, "And you must be Casey. Dad's told me so much about you. You *are* staying through to Christmas, right?"

Wrong. Casey put out her hand and was rewarded with a firm grip of a handshake. "It's still up in the air, Natalie. But thank you for the kind invitation." Her head was spinning because Sam had obviously spoken of Casey to his cherished child. She tilted her head, trying to get rid of a buzzing between her ears.

The young woman's eyes twinkled. *So much like Sam.*

"Oh we'll talk you into it." She turned to her father. "Won't we, Dad?"

"We'll try, Nat. We'll sure try," Sam answered. Turning, and so only she could see, he winked at Casey. When she started breathing again, Casey chugged the rest of her champagne.

CHAPTER TEN

Sam watched as his daughter bounded back down the stairs in black slacks and a tailored red blouse. She'd only been gone twenty minutes, and with Emma back, coming in and out of the living room with more champagne and munchies, he'd no time to follow up on his plan. No opportunity opened up within which he could explain his behavior, nor express his feelings to Casey.

He'd already filled Natalie in. As father and daughter, and the years spent without his ex-wife on the scene, they were too close for him not to. Plus, with both women in the house for the holidays, he couldn't have kept his feelings for Casey from his daughter. To his delight, Natalie was happy he might have at last found someone.

As the evening went on, Emma brought sandwiches and Christmas cookies to the living room, while Natalie unwrapped ornaments, sharing with some of the unveilings tidbits about their origins into the Wagner household.

At some point, Sam noted Casey's demeanor had shifted from uptight to relaxed. He even got close enough to help her with an ornament. Their hands brushed, making his heart race. She felt the same, he was sure of it. He told himself to be patient about getting Casey alone.

But after two hours of decorating, laughing, and drinking champagne, Casey and Natalie headed up the stairs together with his daughter yammering about plans for the week leading up to Christmas.

Not quite the evening he'd hoped for with his houseguest, but at least Casey now agreed to stay through Christmas. It gave him time. Sam even thought to speak with her one more time tonight, but the women were sitting on a window seat, giggling like teenagers when he'd headed to his room to shower off pine sap and dust from ornament packaging.

He needed some shut-eye anyway. After all, he had a ranch to run.

***

Casey had been adamant she was leaving the next morning, and she'd been so sure Sam was going to kiss her the moment before Natalie flew into the living room. Because of those few minutes under his spell, she gave in to Natalie's pleading that she stay.

Besides, where would she go?

Thankfully, her best friend had reached her earlier yesterday morning. The young man she shot was recovering, the paper had written an article about Casey being a solid cop. Exonerated, Casey could go home. But she didn't want to, and now she'd had a little too much champagne and her eyes were heavy. Needing sleep, she said good night to Natalie, agreeing they'd meet at breakfast. However, the ache that began with the cowboy's almost embrace hadn't diminished. With a hand on the door to her room, she noticed his door ajar down the hall.

Okay then.

Debating go or stay, she knocked back the last of the liquid in her flute, realizing she'd lost count of how many glasses she'd imbibed. And why care? Alcohol-fueled courage pushed Casey to Sam's room. She lifted a hand to knock just as the door swung open, and Sam, exiting with some obvious purpose, slammed into her.

He didn't back away.

She could hardly breathe.

Her heart pounded so hard she was sure he could feel it through her dress against his naked chest. She gulped at the fact he was shirtless, but almost burst out laughing at the flannel Santa pajama bottoms tied just below his belly button.

Casey loved him. Six days. Time didn't matter; she couldn't measure her emotions against the hours in a day. She was in love with Sam Wagner. Flashes of events tripped and raced around synapses, pulling up memories of each small moment. "I'm sorry, Sam. I didn't mean to walk in on you unannounced."

He tipped her chin up the way he had the first time they met. "I'm not sorry, ma'am."

She tugged back a little, pretending she wanted to get away, but his gaze held her rapt, and she leaned into him, instead. A smile played at the edges of his mouth

Casey didn't realize she'd closed her eyes until a calloused finger again pushed loose hair off her face. "You smell good, Casey." He purred her name. "But I think I like it more when you smell like my barn."

"Well, I *have* been mucking stalls for a week. Horse just gets under your skin, I guess." She paused, waiting, hoping for an explanation of his behavior.

"I need to explain something, Ms. Pickett."

"Like you said this morning, you had your reasons for shutting me out."

"Yep."

"And?"

"I was scared, shaking in my boots. I couldn't rationalize the *how* of my feelings. I mean, it was zero to sixty in all of three days." He kissed her forehead, and it felt like fireflies were lighting up her insides.

"Okay. So?"

"You're not going to make this easy, are you?"

"Nope."

Sam ran first one index finger, and then the other along the slender spaghetti straps of her dress. "It's not much of a dress. And it hugs every bit of you." He continued to run his fingers up and down the straps, skin against skin. Casey was losing it. Nothing in her past prepared her for the explosion of sensations the simple motion was causing. "But then you know that, right?"

She studied his face, the shadow caused by the bedroom light on behind them making it hard to read his expression. "We're being honest, right?"

"Well, that's a good way to start a relationship. So they say anyway."

She stopped breathing. He was so close, he'd used the "R" word. It took super strength just to nod her head up and down, and whisper. "Truth. Yes."

He stepped back, and the distance, though less than a foot, caused her to shiver. "I don't want to move too fast for you, sweetheart."

She wanted to say WTF aloud and jump him, the endearment increasing the pace of her already racing heart. Inhaling deeply, she collected herself and asked, "So what's the 2WR brand stand for, anyway?"

"That's out of nowhere. But it's two Wagners, me and Natalie, so…."

She interrupted him. "Oh. I guess that makes sense." Damn, but she was nervous.

"It does, but don't try to dodge what's happening here."

"Wouldn't dream of it, ranch man."

"You've come a long way, greenhorn."

"More than you know, sir. Being homeless and all, I'm thinking of buying a piece of property—there's that large parcel that abuts your property line you talked about. You have *your* eye on it, I think."

"Yep." He stepped into her again, cupping Casey's face with both hands. She couldn't look away. "Fact is, I already bought it."

"You shit."

"God, woman, you are so romantic. Anybody ever tell you that?"

"Maybe." She didn't look away. "How could you afford it? Emma says you run the ranch on a shoestring budget."

"I do." He grinned. "I like to see if I can do it without dipping into my millions."

"Sure. Whatever you say."

"Okay. Don't believe me, at least I told you."

She tried to picture the cowboy-rancher-drop-dead-gorgeous man standing inches from her as filthy rich. *Was* it possible? It didn't matter, so she refocused on Sam. "So, you bought *my* piece of land."

"Indeed. And maybe I bought it so you and I could work something out."

"Like what?"

"Like maybe that's another reason why I was off the ranch so many times in the last few days."

"I hadn't noticed."

"Bull—"

"As opposed to a steer, heifer, or cow, right?"

"I'm going to enjoy sparring with you for the next forty or so years, Pickett."

Casey blanched. "Years?"

"Yes, ma'am."

She punched him, not hard, just to let him know "ma'am" was still not allowed.

"Sure, as partners. As in maybe we could ranch the land together. My experience, your hay pitching skills." He raised one eyebrow and she saw the smile creep back.

"Oh, that sounds too much like you want a hired hand, Mr. Wagner—not a partner."

"Maybe, but if it doesn't work out, the sheriff's looking for a new deputy." He pulled her against him again, and Casey could feel the rumble of his laugh vibrate against her body. Her pulse raced, and the need for him settled deeper within.

Six days?

Her feelings for the alternately aggravating then endearing cowboy couldn't be this strong, and yet...

"I don't want you as a ranch hand, Casey." It was almost a growl, deep, guttural. "I want you as a woman. I want you in my life." He paused, his eyes flashing with obvious desire. "In fact, I'm thinking maybe it should be the 3WR brand." She swallowed the lump in her throat as he added, "I'm falling for you, Detective."

The awkward shyness she'd often felt around men lifted. It had been an affliction that made no sense given her career. She had a black belt, awards for firearms skills, she'd fought for her life hand to hand on multiple occasions, and there was a three-inch scar on her right thigh from a bullet. Experience that should have given her confidence, yet hadn't.

Casey reached up and slipped first one, then the other strap of her dress from her shoulders, never skirting her cowboy's gaze. "Sam. I'm going to lose it if you don't k—"

His mouth found hers, gentle at first, then exploring. When he stopped, pulling back a little, a sudden pang of emptiness threatened.

The grin returned. "I seem to remember you called me taciturn, and that—" He traced a finger from her neck down to the top of the bodice of her dress. Heat seared her skin. "That, I am definitely not, ma'am."

"Stop with the 'ma'am' cra—"

This kiss was deeper, and instead of just desire, she felt emotion. He rested his forehead against hers, and she knew she didn't care if her car was toast. Flashes of being exhausted at the end of a day, playing Scrabble in the evening, drinking lemonade, a front porch swing, and old trucks danced across her brain like a rock skipping on top of a pond.

"I'm just going to say it, Casey. I'm not even falling anymore, I'm *in* love with you." He lifted her into his arms, walked into the bedroom, and kicked the door shut with his foot, heading toward the bed. "Crazy, right?"

"Not so crazy." She had nothing left to say.

"Ms. Detective Casey Pickett. Can I show you just how I feel?"

"Please, Mr. Sam Cowboy Wagner. Please do."

She touched where his heart would be, thumping his chest with her index finger. It felt like she'd just come home after being away. A home for Christmas. "And I…" Another kiss overwhelmed her, so she finished the sentence in her head, *I love you, Sam Wagner.*

And so she did.

HAPPY HOLIDAYS, EVERYONE

THE VOW

ELLE WRIGHT

CHAPTER ONE

Jaden

What started as a well thought out straight-line gameplan, went completely FUBAR. I sank into the sofa, dropped my head, and linked my hands over the back of my neck. My phone rang and I almost ignored it, but when I saw "Dad" on the screen, I knew the call was more than serendipitous, it was a gift.

"Dad."

In that one word, I must've communicated everything I felt. I heard him suck in a deep breath before, in a rapid-fire bark, he shouted, "What happened? Are you awright?"

"Nothing. Everything. Yeah, and no."

For a beat I heard nothing, then Dad chuckled.

"Nothing funny about this, man."

"Lay it out for me, son."

"Was in the bedroom packing for my deployment—you know, I was scheduled to be on the USS Theodore Roosevelt for at least six months—when the doorbell rang and a seaman hand-delivered my change of orders. I'm not leaving San Diego."

"Huh. You know why?"

"Yeah. Called CNO Admiral Franchetti and said, 'Hey, Lisa. What's up with this shit?'"

Now Dad was outright laughing. "Okay, boy. I take your point." He threw out one last chuckle, then got to the heart of the matter. "What does Zahli have to say about this?"

"Zahli's in the lab today. I don't expect her home until tonight, when she'll be shocked as hell to see me."

"You should call her."

"Right. That'll make her day. 'Hey, Zal, guess what? You know how you thought you'd have the apartment to yourself for the next six to eight months? You'd be wrong.'"

"Yeah. Okay. Better to have that conversation in person."

"What conversation. The one where her life, which has already been fucked, gets more fucked by the guy who promised to give her what she needs for the next couple of years. Or the one where I tell her we're going to have to move to a bigger place because there's only one bedroom and bathroom, and both of them are supposed to be hers." I leaned back against the sofa and let out a long-ass sigh.

"Right. But you've been sleeping on the pull-out for the last coupla months. Keep doing that."

"Two months was supposed to be a temporary thing since I was being deployed, and let me tell you, it's been far from ideal. We share a bathroom, the closet, and the bureau, which are in the bedroom, and I get up an hour before dawn, and she gets home most nights after ten."

"So get a bigger apartment."

"She'll have a shit hemorrhage."

"Is that a medical term, Doctor Schuyler?"

"Seriously, Dad. You know all this already. You and Mom were in the room when Zal was so royally pissed, she threw a pillow at me when I told her not to work. That I'd take care of the rent, utilities, and food. And that was after she blistered my ears for two months until I convinced her to marry me so she'd have health insurance and support from the Navy if she needed assistance when I'm deployed."

"Boy, she has us. You know we'll always take care of her. And you're a tough bugger. You'll survive her shit fit. Get a bigger apartment."

"And another car."

"Well, damn. I forgot about the car."

"Yeah. I wouldn't care if I had the money put away, but I'd had less than enough to live on while doing my residency, and it's only been three months since I started getting my Navy paycheck. Telling Zal I have to buy another car will surely bring out all her sweetness and light."

That got me another chuckle. "You're friends. You'll work it out."

"Old ground, Dad. You know she doesn't consider us friends. Everything I do or say winds up in a fight or a lecture. The world according to Zal is: I was best friends with her dead brother, and I'm the type who feels guilty so I've taken her on like a charity case. And, the only reason I'm doing anything for her is because of how close I was to Raffie. That fuckin' asshole who had to become a Navy SEAL and wound up getting himself killed."

"Awright, boy. There's no reason trying to retread a worn-out tire."

"Ain't that the truth."

"You feel any better?"

"No. But thanks for letting me drop all my shit on you." I ran my fingers through my hair. "I didn't even ask. Why'd you call?"

"Ah. Right. Your mother wanted me to tell you to remind Zahli to come early for Thanksgiving."

"I was supposed to be airlifted to an aircraft carrier, and wouldn't have been able to communicate with Zal for at least twenty-four hours. They talk at least three times a day. Why can't Mom tell her?"

"Boy, I've been living under the same roof with that woman for over fifty years. I have absolutely no idea why she does ninety percent of the things she does, and I know better than to ask."

This time, I was the one who laughed.

***

"Aaaahhhh." A shrill scream tore me out of an exhausted sleep. I scrambled to find the lamp on the end table next to the sofa, and when I turned it on, I saw Kahli on the other side of the counter that separated the kitchen from the living room/dining room. She was backlit by the over-the-oven light, and was holding a huge knife in one hand, her phone in the other.

Of the many things I admired about Kal, her commitment to overcome any problem or obstacle was one of my favorites. She was creative and inventive. If I'd given her enough time, she would've fashioned a homemade grenade.

"Kal. It's me."

"I can see that now, Jaden," she snapped. "When I walked in all I saw was a dark lump on the pull-out, and I knew you'd left so I thought someone had broken in."

"Is everything all right Miz Saab?" a voice came through the speaker on Zal's phone.

"Shit. Sorry. Yeah. Everything's fine. It's my husband."

"Is he…supposed to be there?"

"He had orders to deploy today, and for some reason he didn't. Since I hadn't been *informed*," Zal said sarcastically through her teeth in a tone I'd heard way too many times, "I thought—"

"Someone had broken in," the 911 operator said.

"Yeah. Sorry," Kahli mumbled.

"Don't be. Always best to call us. You good now?"

"I am. Thanks."

"No problem." The operator disconnected and Kahli put her phone on the counter, and the knife back in its drawer.

While Kal was talking to the operator, I'd picked up my sweat pants, pulled them on, and walked to the dining room side of the kitchen counter, where I stood watching her watch me.

Her head tilted to the left, something she'd done since she was a young girl right before she asked a probing question. "What are you doing here?"

"This afternoon my orders changed. I'm staying in San Diego."

She leaned back to see me better. Her gaze latching onto mine. "And you didn't think to call me to tell me this huge news?"

"What happened to 'Unless someone I love is on the way to the hospital or is in the hospital, don't bother me when I'm at school?'"

"This type of thing runs concurrent with that statement."

I couldn't help my lips quirking. Kal's rules were flexible only when she decided they were. If I'd decided my change of orders more or less fit the spirit of breaking her no-call-while-in-school rule, I would've been subject to another ear blistering.

"I'm thinking you should provide me with a list of other instances that 'run concurrent with that statement' to keep myself out of the Kahli shitter."

"Lovely. Such a kind and thoughtful way to communicate you don't care enough to keep me informed of the important stuff that impacts our lives."

"Kal, as much as I'd enjoy going a few rounds with you, I have to report to the Naval Medical Center by zero-five-thirty." I looked across the kitchen to see the time on the microwave read 11:35. Realizing how late it was, I went from wore out to ticked off. "What the hell are you doing coming home so late?"

Her head jerked back and her beautiful espresso brown eyes went wide. "Excuse me? Since when do I report to you?"

"Don't throw that bullshit at me. You promised you'd leave campus no later than nine-thirty since you assured me there were still a number of students around, particularly folks leaving the lab at that time. You leaving at eleven means you're not keeping yourself safe. So, yeah. Now is when you report to me."

She tilted her head back as she leaned into the counter so she could keep her squinty gaze locked to mine. "I was safe. Alex walked me to my car."

Alex? Who the fuck was Alex? She never mentioned an Alex before. I knew the names of all the students who were in her study group, her lab partners, and most of the other Masters' candidates in her class.

"Alex short for Alexis or Alexandra?"

"No. Alex is Alexander Weinfeld. He's a PhD candidate who's doing similar research in the aerospace field."

"Is he? Please, tell me more."

"I thought you had to get up early to be at the hospital by five-thirty."

"Amazingly, I caught a second wind." I stared at her, and I swear, when she sank her top teeth into her full bottom lip, she was fighting a grin. Like this shit was funny. And like I needed to see her biting her lip when that was supposed to be my fuckin' job.

"There's not much to tell." She shrugged. "This was only the second time I saw him in the lab. As I was packing up, we got to chatting, and he offered to walk me to my car. End of story."

"So you let a strange man walk you late at night to a dark parking lot."

She let out a weighty sigh. "The pathways and the parking lots are well lit, and he's not a strange man."

"Isn't he? You met him for the second time tonight. Anyone else in the lab know him? Did you ask around about him? Ask to see his credentials? From the look on your face, the answer is no. So, yeah, Kal, he's a strange man, and you *were not safe*."

There was a light in her eyes she got when she was amused. Seeing it right now made me want to find this fuckin' PhD asshole and rearrange his face.

I was so far from amused, it wasn't funny.

"Okay, Jaden. I won't leave after nine-thirty, and I'll ask around about Alex Weinfeld."

"You're damn straight you'll leave by nine-thirty because I'll be picking you up at nine-thirty."

"Excuse me?"

"I need the car tomorrow, so I'll take you to school and pick you up."

She shook her head. "I don't think so. You won't be able to get away in time to get me to class."

"I'll make time."

She flicked her hand in front of her face. "Don't worry about it. I'll text Lissa and tell her I need a ride. She'll pick me up and drop me home."

"I'm not in the habit of repeating myself. I said, I'll make time."

"And I'm not a seaman who has to take orders from Lieutenant Schuyler."

I pinched the bridge of my nose and counted to ten. "I'm not ordering you, Kal. I'm trying to take care of you."

"Ugh. I don't need taking care of, Doctor. I'm perfectly fine." She motioned her hand between us. "You and I will work out a car sharing schedule, and Lissa and I will switch off driving. Easy fix." She pocketed her phone and walked around the counter. "You need the bathroom?" I shook my head, too pissed to speak. "Fine. I'm going get ready for bed. Good night."

She marched through the living room, skirted the pullout, went into the bedroom, and closed the door quietly. Five minutes later she came out in a pair of red paisley harem pants and a cropped red hoodie.

Shit. She wasn't wearing a bra. Like I needed to see the bouncing evidence of her rockin' body. I had to bite the inside of mouth as I talked myself out of getting hard.

She stopped and stared at me. Her shoulder length thick dark brown hair was piled on top of her head in a messed-up knot that moved when she walked. Tendrils were tucked behind her ears, and the arm of her glasses was tucked in the zip of her hoodie in anticipation of removing her contacts.

"I thought you needed to wake up super early," she said in an accusatory tone.

"I do."

"Then why are you still leaning against the counter with your arms crossed over your chest?"

"I'm decompressing."

She scrunched her adorable nose as she blinked rapidly. "From talking to me?"

I wanted to say that wasn't talking, it was sniping, but I knew the comment would escalate things to a level I didn't feel like engaging in. "No, Kal," I lied. "It's been a hell of a day." That was no lie. "One minute I'm packing to leave, the next I've got orders to stay. I have no idea what's going on, and I've got to get up earlier than my usual zero dark thirty so I can be at the Medical Center for who the fuck knows why at five-thirty in the morning."

"Okay," she whispered. "Sorry. I didn't think about how thrown off you must be." She gestured to the pullout. "Go to bed. I'll be reading, so it'll be quiet."

I nodded and headed to my "bed" as she walked into the bathroom and closed the door.

CHAPTER TWO

Jaden

Of course, sleep eluded me. I kept replaying everything Kahli said, as well as every one of her gestures and facial expressions. A few things struck me as odd, but in a good way. She didn't seem upset that she wouldn't have the apartment to herself, and she seemed totally fine with sharing the car with me. I hoped I wasn't seeing things I wanted to see, or misinterpreted what I saw and heard, but she seemed pleased I hadn't deployed.

I reached back to five months ago when I was getting ready to start my "payback" years to the Navy. They'd put me through medical school, and when they didn't have a placement for my residency, they provided authorization for me to participate in a civilian match, which was a five-year residency in orthopedic surgery at Loma Linda. The deal I signed up for was: when I was done with my residency, I had to give them my time and expertise for four years, and go wherever they wanted me to be anywhere in the world.

Kahli had just finished her bachelor's degree at UCSD, and was going to start her Masters year in September. My smart Kal had been accepted into the five-year BS/MS program, which was a contiguous Bachelor's/Master's Degree course of study. That's when I suggested we get married. I told her the truth about the health insurance, and the support the Navy would provide when I was deployed. But the real reason I wanted her to marry me was because I wanted her under my protection. Safe and comfortable, and exclusively mine.

My apartment was in a nice newer building in a good neighborhood in Point Loma. She'd have my car, and only a twenty-five-minute drive up the five freeway to UCSD. She wouldn't have to worry about rent, food, gas money, or anything, except school.

She was wrong about me feeling guilty about Raffie dying. I was pissed the fuck off he was dead. We'd been friends since we were five-years-old. I knew him inside and out, and though I loved him like a brother, he'd done a lot of asshole shit over the years. And him deciding to go into the SEALs was the ultimate selfish prick thing to do. We fought about it plenty, but there was no stopping him. At least he remembered to designate Kahli as his survivor, so when he left her all alone at least she received the Navy's one-hundred-thousand-dollar death gratuity, which paid off most her undergrad student loan.

Their parents had saved for their higher education, but it wasn't the whack they needed to cover all the costs. The Naval Academy cost Raffie nothing, but UCSD cost about thirty thousand a year. Raffie gave Kahli all the money their parents had saved for both their educations, which was about forty-thousand dollars. She refused to dip into whatever was left over from their life insurance payouts, insisting Raffie bank the money in case either of them needed it for an emergency down the road.

Between the death gratuity and her parents' education fund, she'd had enough to pay off her undergrad loans, and barely enough to pay for the one year of her Master's program.

So yeah, I did my version of a knight in shining armor by giving her a good place to live without worries about having enough money to live on.

But I'd been keeping a secret nobody knew. Not even Raffie. Or more to the point, especially not Raffie.

In looks and personality, Raafe Saab was the dark to my light. Raffie was a trouble magnet, and since we were kids, I ran interference so neither of us got into too much hot water. As we got older, Raffie switched his talents to girls, and I made sure he didn't do anything stupid or irresponsible. Neither of us were particularly virtuous, but Raffie took bad boy to a new level.

It didn't surprise me he wanted to go to the Naval Academy. He was self-aware enough to recognize he had a short fuse and was an adrenalin junkie. He knew he needed structure to channel his more destructive personality traits.

But the one place Raffie shined and never faltered was with his little sister, Kahli. We were seven when Kahli was born, and Raffie guarded her like a Rottweiler. With her, he was tender and caring. He called her his *awhara*, his jewel. And as far as Raffie was concerned, nobody touched his jewel. Ever.

So, when Kahli turned eighteen, telling Raffie I'd fallen irrevocably in love with his precious jewel of a sister was out of the question. Then the stupid fucker went and got himself killed, and finally, though it sure as hell wasn't the way I wanted to get it, I had a clear shot.

Except, the jewel turned out to be impenetrably hard with about a thousand sharp, pointy, edges.

Which led me to tonight.

I hoped with everything I was that I didn't misread the signs.

Maybe, just maybe, Kahli felt something more for me than friendly gratitude.

I knew I could work with that more.

***

Kahli

Why did he have to walk around the apartment with his shirt off? And go commando when he wore sweat pants? Like I needed a reminder of how perfect he was *everywhere*, and how unbelievably tempting he was. There was no ice cream flavor in the entire world that could, in any way, taste better than Jaden Heathrow Schuyler.

Heathrow, btw, because that was where his folks banged in a bathroom, and decided that was the day he was conceived.

I had no direct experience tasting Jaden more than the pecks on the cheek we exchanged over the years. But I had a really expansive imagination, and I'd known and loved him all my life.

He was always in our house, especially at dinner time. Neither of his parents could do more than grill hamburgers, hot dogs, and bake potatoes. In direct contrast to their limited culinary abilities, my father cooked like a master chef. He made the best *sfiha* – flatbread open-faced meat pies, *kibbeh* – Lebanese meatballs with bulgur wheat, and lots of other dishes, including his fantastic *knafeh* - shredded phyllo with heavy sweet syrup, cheese, pistachios, and rose water.

From my earliest recollections right through their college years, the boys had bottomless stomachs, and both Jaden and Raffie grew like weeds. By the time they were sixteen, both of them were over six-two. Jaden was always an inch taller than Raffie, who was bulkier than Jaden.

They doted on me, and treated me like a princess. They took me out for pancakes, or ice cream, and even suffered the mall to take me shopping for girly stuff like hair clips and nail polish. But I knew as early as when I was six-years-old that I was going to marry Jaden.

And here I was, married to Jaden, who was sleeping on the pullout in the living room. *Gah.*

I knew he loved me like a sister, and cared about me all the way down to his big, sweet heart. But I wanted him to need me like air. Ravish me because he couldn't keep his hands and mouth off me. And love me the way I loved him. From the depths of my soul.

Of one thing I was certain: Jaden was passionate. When we fought, which I made sure happened often, his face was expressive, his words heated, and his voice dropped lower than its usual low, and got raspy. I knew this was kind of freaky, but I got off watching his Adam's apple bob up and down when he got supremely pissed off to the point his deep blue eyes shot fire.

Tonight, I'd been inspired and ecstatic. He was home. He wasn't going away for six months to somewhere he could get hurt. This was the perfect opportunity to implement my *Get Jaden in Bed with Me* plan. So to move that plan along, I invented Alexander Weinfeld.

It would've been too obvious if I'd started walking around the apartment in silk teddies and lace underwear. I needed Jaden to come to the realization that he loved me all on his own.

The kind of deep love a man felt about the woman he asked to marry him.

When he had "proposed" it was more a business plan than a declaration of love. His reasoning had been carefully delivered with logical points. But while he was laying it out for me, there were times I saw and felt him get caught up in the idea of marrying me, and in so doing, he revealed crack in his "brotherly" shield. He'd stumbled when he spoke, and Jaden never stumbled. And he'd stared at his sneakers a lot, like he couldn't look me in the eye.

I knew him, and could read his emotions in his beautiful blue eyes. That he wanted to hide them from me told me way more than any of the less than brotherly glances I'd caught him sending my way over the past few years.

Alex Weinfeld was the perfect foil. Smart, but not as smart as Jaden, yet smart enough to present a challenge. Clearly interested, since he talked to me in the lab and walked me to my car. And available due to his similar research interests, which gave him proximity Jaden had no control over.

Yeah, this was definitely a bit of poking the bear, but I had to do something.

I wanted my husband to be *my husband*.

And I'd do anything and everything to make that happen.

CHAPTER THREE

Jaden

At zero-five-fifteen, the on-duty gate guard told me to report to the Director of the Naval Medical Center's office. So here I sat waiting for Captain Elizabeth Adriano to call me in so I could find out why my orders were changed, and what she wanted me to do.

Thirty minutes later I was walking to my car still shaking my head at what she'd told me, and shared when she sent the patient's file to my tablet. Late yesterday morning, the son of one of the base commanders had been in a horrific accident on the eight freeway when a semi-truck rolled over onto his top-down convertible, crushing one of his lungs, his stomach and liver, and twenty-six bones in his body, including both femurs, knee caps, tibias, fibulas, and ankles. Insult to injury: he was San Diego State's starting quarterback.

The commander insisted on having the best Navy orthopedic surgeons attend to his son, Axel, which was why my orders had been changed. I was one of three Navy orthopedic surgeons in San Diego, and one was deployed. The other, Dr. Harley Weaver, was already in surgery working on Axel at UCSD Health's trauma center in Hillcrest with two of their trauma surgeons.

There was too much damage for the three surgeons assigned to Axel's case to handle all that needed to be repaired. Two had been working on him since he'd arrived at the hospital yesterday, and they'd barely made a dent. Harley told Captain Adriano he needed me to attend Axel to make sure there were enough of us to rotate through all the work that needed to be done to put this guy back together.

I met Harley and the two other surgeons at zero-six-thirty and we spent an hour going over what'd been done, what more needed to be done, and we started mapping the alternatives to achieve results while figuring out the best way to keep Axel alive through all these procedures. Everyone acknowledged this was the first round of multiple surgeries that Axel was going to need before he could start the lengthy journey to truly healing.

From what I saw from the imaging, and what I learned from the other surgeons, we were in for a long haul.

I wasn't going to be deployed for months.

***

Kahli

At nine-thirty at night, as Lissa and I were halfway down the walkway between of the lab building and the parking lot, she stopped and let out a loud half-laugh, half-shout of, "Ha."

I stopped alongside her, angled my body into hers and asked, "What?"

She grabbed my chin and turned my head to face forward.

In the first row of the parking lot, leaning against his car wearing his leather Navy bomber jacket over his blue scrubs, Jaden had his arms crossed over his chest and his gaze lasered on me.

Lissa and I became best friends sophomore year, and we told each other pretty much everything. She knew all about last night's fight, and Alex Weinfeld.

"Seems the good doctor didn't trust that *Alex*," she snorted, "wouldn't walk you out to your car again."

"Shit."

"Hey. If I ever found a guy who looked at me the way Jaden is looking at you, I'd marry him on the spot."

I glanced down at my platinum wedding band, which was embedded with diamonds, stared at my finger and said, "I've never seen him look at me like that before."

"You never had *Alex* walk you out to your car before last night." She gave me a shoulder shove. "You best get your ass over there wifey or hubby's gonna blow a gasket."

I started talking as I was walking. "You knew Lissa was driving me home. What are you doing here?" *Hehehe.* Yep. I was intentionally winding him up.

"Where's your jacket?" was his response.

I had to think about how I should answer. If I said I left it in Alex's car when he took me to lunch, I feared Jaden would indeed blow a gasket. So I went with the truth. "I left it in Lissa's car."

He pushed away from his lean, walked right past me and headed to Lissa, who was standing by her driver's side door.

"Hey, Jaden," I heard her say.

"Hey, Liss." He tipped his head to her car. "Is Kal's jacket in there?"

Lissa opened her door, leaned in and pulled out my jacket. "Here you go," she said with a huge smile.

"Thanks. Drive home carefully."

"Will do." Still grinning, she waved at me, then got in her car.

Jaden waited until she drove off then walked back to me and held my jacket open for me to put my arms through. "It's the end of November," he said by way of explaining his gentlemanly behavior.

"It's temperature controlled in the lab. I didn't even notice the chill until you said something."

He nodded, grabbed my hand, and walked me to his car.

It took major effort not to trip, screech, or drool.

The last time Jaden held my hand was when we got married in his parents' backyard by an officiant named George. That hand-holding episode lasted as long as it took for Jaden to slide on my wedding band, and for me to slide on his. Before that, he'd held my hand at my parents' funeral when I was eleven.

I was so excited about this hand-hold, in my head I was doing the Alex jig and became deeply involved with self-congratulations. Therefore, I didn't notice Jaden had opened the passenger door and was waiting for me to get in.

When I realized we were standing next the car, I gave him a small smile and dropped down into the seat.

As he pulled out of the parking lot, he rumbled, "You're not usually this spacey. Something specific on your mind?"

"Not really," I answered in as casual a tone as I could manage. I glanced over, saw his jaw muscle jumping, and had to push my nails into my palms to keep from laughing. He thought my musings had something to do with Alex.

Then I realized I was being way too self-indulgent when I knew his day must've been shit, so I asked, "Did you find out why your orders were changed?"

"Yeah."

Hmmm. Someone wasn't feeling chatty. "Temporary delay, or total change of plans."

He turned his head and gave me a wickedly satisfied grin. "I won't be going anywhere for at least four or five months."

I wanted to do backflips at the same time I had to acknowledge he thought staying home meant he could make sure Alex didn't factor in my life. Either way, I got what I wanted. Months to make my husband *my husband.*

When we got into the apartment, I was able to take a good look at him in the light, and saw written all over his face, he was wiped out. "You okay?"

He threw his jacket on the back of the club chair. "Long fuckin' day."

My jacket joined his, and I put my backpack on the seat of the chair. "Wanna talk about it?"

For a quick moment, he looked surprised, which sort of made me feel guilty that every other conversation we'd had over the past few months had been a rip-roaring argument. But, from the moment he began his *let's get married* assault, I made it my mission to force him to admit he felt more than brotherly love for me. And getting in his face meant he had to react, and if it took a chainsaw's worth of me hacking at his armor, I was going to get in there no matter what.

I wasn't oblivious to the fact that my brother had hung a "Do Not Touch" sign around my neck when it came to Jaden—and all of the other guys in the world, but especially Jaden—and how after Raffie was killed, Jaden put his feelings in a vault and was all about taking care of me like a brother would.

Except a brother wouldn't ask me to marry him. He'd hover. He'd be all up in my business. He'd scowl at guys I dated, and he'd lecture me endlessly. But marry me?

Jaden was a wonderful person, but he and my brother had gone through women at a breakneck pace. A man with his appetites did not get married just to be a good guy who intended to take care of his dead friend's sister.

When he sat on the edge of the couch and clasped his dangled hands together, he lifted his gaze to mine and in his eyes I saw pain. "A nineteen-year-old kid is hanging onto to his life by a thread."

"Oh, no." I went to sit beside him. "What happened?"

Jaden told me about the accident, the commander's request, and how Jaden had been in the operating room working on this kid for nearly thirteen hours. "The good news is Axel is an athlete, and before the accident was in excellent shape. His heart is strong, and he's fighting to stay alive. The bad news is everything else."

"Did his father come by?"

"I was told his father, mother, grandparents, and two sisters were camped out in the waiting room the whole time we were in surgery. When Axel was finally back in the ICU, his parents stood at the window looking into his room until Harley and I convinced them to go home."

I put my hand on his knee. "He's fortunate you're one of his surgeons. I know you'll doing everything possible to make him whole again."

He laid his big hand over mine. "Thanks," he rasped out. "I gotta hit the sack. Harley and I are taking shifts, and I've got six hours before I have to head back."

Well shit. If I hadn't put the idea of Alex making moves on me in Jaden's head, he would've been asleep already, instead of driving up to UCSD to make sure I was where I was supposed to be, and was with whom I was supposed to be.

"You take the bathroom first."

He nodded, patted my hand then stood and went into the bedroom to get his stuff. While he was in the bathroom, I pulled out the bed from the sofa, and made it up with lots of pillows in case he couldn't fall asleep right away and needed to watch TV to unwind.

What I really wanted was for him to sleep with me so I could hold him and try to soothe away his shit day.

CHAPTER FOUR

Jaden

Sweet, attentive, caring, and helpful. Who was this woman, and what did she do with Kahli? Actually, to be fair, being sweet was Kahli down to the ground. She was one of the most astute and considerate people I knew. Except recently, with me.

As I exited the bathroom, I saw she'd made up the pullout, and was in the kitchen wrapping sandwiches. She'd held them up and said, "I'm putting these in the fridge. Don't forget to take them out in the morning so you'll have decent food handy to keep you going during the day."

If we were the "we" I wanted us to be, I would've gone into the kitchen and showed my appreciation by laying a deep, long kiss on her fantastic mouth. Instead, I'd said, "Thanks. Really."

She sent me a genuine smile, then told me to, "Go to sleep. You need your rest. I'll be super quiet. Promise."

On the tip of my tongue was *If you sleep with me, baby, I know I'll rest well.* Instead, I nodded, then waited until she went into the bedroom before turning out the light.

***

The night sky was coasting to dawn as I drove to the hospital, and by the time I got there, I'd eaten two of the best sandwiches of my life. I knew it was stupid, and I felt like a sap, but I tasted Kahli's care and concern in every bite. She'd make six sandwiches, and the other four would go a long way to sustaining me throughout the day.

I couldn't stop thinking about how she'd sat beside me and put her hand on my knee to comfort me, and I couldn't help but wonder how could I miss something I never had. Yet, I did. I missed sleeping with her every night and waking up next to her every morning. I missed kissing her for no reason at all, and for the express purpose of getting her wet for me. I missed her laughter, her smiles, and her warmth. I wanted her to love me so bad I ached from it.

As much as I'd prefer to sit in the car a few more minutes and indulge in some of my favorite Kahli fantasies, I had to get inside. I tagged my bulging-with-sandwiches laptop case, and made my way to Axel.

Even though they'd been here all day yesterday and well into the night, at a few minutes before six in the morning, the Commander and his wife were posted up at the window looking into Axel's room.

As I was raising my arm to salute, the Commander shook his head and held out his hand. As I took it, he said, "Thank you Dr. Schuyler. You and," he lifted his chin in the direction of the room where Harley, gowned, gloved and masked, was standing next to Axel's bed reading his charts on a tablet, "Dr. Weaver have helped my boy make it through the night. My wife," he reached out with his other hand and grabbed hers, "and I appreciate your dedication. We know he's not out of the woods, but with all of you working so hard to make sure he does, we have hope."

"Hold onto that, sir. It's what we're doing too."

He nodded, and I went to get a gown, gloves, and mask to confer with Harley before he headed home for a few hours.

***

A little after noon, I got a rare text from Kahli.

Hey. How's Axel doing? Have you eaten any of the sandwiches yet?

Warmth surged through me, and I couldn't help but smile.

He's maintaining, and given the state of his injuries, that's a good sign. And yeah, four so far. They're great. I didn't expect variety, so each has been a surprise.

And now I was chatting like a teenage girl. If Kal knew how easily she undid me, I might as well put a ring through my nose and hand her the lead rope.

I'm so glad he's hanging in there. I can't wait until he can talk to you. I bet his first words will be "thank you." ☺ So, I made pasta primavera. It's in the fridge along with a salad. There's a fresh kalamata olive loaf from Con Pane in the paper bag next to the pan I left on the counter. Use the pan to heat up the pasta. If you nuke it, it'll be rubbery.

Why was my wife sounding like *my wife*? My first thought was she was starting something with that asshat PhD dude, and this whole taking care of me thing was guilt-driven. But no. That wasn't Kahli. She'd tell me. She'd hate doing it, but she'd tell me. That's who she was.

I stared at her texts and decided she'd been moved by what happened to Axel, and since I was one of his doctors, she was tending to me on his behalf. Okay, yeah, that was a bit of a stretch, but I didn't dare entertain the idea that she was doing anything for me other than out of the goodness in her heart. Something she'd do for anyone. If I allowed myself to believe she had feelings for me other than wanting to hit me with a baseball bat, I was dooming myself for disappointment.

But... How delicious it would be to have her doing anything for me out of love.

Impulsively—which I wasn't in anything or with anyone in my life except Kahli—I decided to tease her.

Spoiling me?

No response. And now I felt like a fool.

Then those three stupid dots started rippling, and my stomach took a dive.

Flirting?

Okay. She wanted to play with me, I'd be more than happy to play.

And if I was?

More stupid rippling dots.

So it's true.

What's true?

The way to a man's heart is through his stomach.

My breath caught in my throat, and I had to remind myself I was a doctor and a Naval Officer. I couldn't start hyperventilating outside my patient's room.

. But damn. It wasn't a stretch to say Kahli was hinting she wanted into my heart. I had lay back. Not rush this. The last thing I was going to do was overwhelm her with all I felt for her.

Medically speaking, that's physically impossible. However…

Axel moaned loud enough for me to hear him in the hall. Quickly, I shot off a text to Kal.

Gotta go. Axel needs me.

***

Kahli

"Shit." I banged my phone against my knee.

Lissa glanced over, then asked, "What happened?"

"It was just getting good. He started flirting and was about to say something juicy, and then he cut me off."

"No," she said to the windshield drawing out the "O." "He ditched?"

"Not really. His patient needed him so he told me he had to go."

She made a *pffft* noise. "Not rubbing salt here, Kal, but when he's at work, it's not like he can duck into the copy room and pretend he's busy when he's fucking off and sexting you."

"Duh. I know that, Liss." I stuffed my phone into my backpack. "We have five minutes before we reach campus and I'm going to indulge in a quick but effective righteous sulk until the car stops."

Lissa laughed. "So noted."

"I mean, he was right there with me. I know he can be playful, and I was trying to draw that out of him. Keep it sexy light."

"Sexy light?"

"Yeah. Flirty without being overtly suggestive."

"In other words, teasing him."

I grinned at her, and she must've felt it 'cause she turned her head for a quick moment. "Exactly."

"Playing with fire, Kal."

"I certainly hope so. I want all the fire he keeps bolted down in that gorgeous body of his."

"Well, the upside is, you're married to him. Any and all reactions you're pushing for him to express will culminate in one of the rooms in your apartment."

"I need to culminate in the worst way."

She laughed. "I bet."

"He walks around the apartment without his shirt on, and he's commando under his sleep pants. Do you know what kind of torture I've been living with?"

"I've got eyes and a good imagination, Kal. Really, I feel your pain." She pulled into the parking lot, parked, then turned to me. "Keep up the sexy light. I have a feeling the good doctor will be seeing to your culmination needs soon."

She shut down the engine, and I opened the car door. Before I stepped out, I told her, "He better or I'll be a scientific first: the only human to implode and explode at the same time."

CHAPTER FIVE

Kahli

That night, I frowned when Lissa pulled into the garage under my apartment building. Jaden's car wasn't in our assigned slot.

She turned and must've seen the look on my face. "What now?"

I pointed over my shoulder to our empty parking slot. "Jaden's car isn't here."

"He's probably still at the hospital. Something must've happened when you guys were sexting. He'd said the kid needed him."

"Yeah. I guess. I wish he would've texted me to let me know what was going on."

"And break your no contact when at school rule?"

I huffed out a "humpf."

"Call him." I shook my head then nodded, then shook my head again. "Go on," she urged. "I don't mind waiting." She flicked her fingers over one shoulder then the other in a *I've got this* gesture. "I'll be your silent support partner."

I took out my phone, saw I hadn't missed any calls or texts, rang Jaden, the call went straight to voice mail, so I disconnected immediately. "He's turned off his phone."

"Does he take it into surgery with him?"

I shrugged. "I'm guessing no."

"What did he tell you to do if you had to reach him?"

"Um."

Her eyes went wide. "You don't have an emergency protocol?"

"Um."

"Shit, Kal. Even marginally friendly roomies have backup numbers for the just in case stuff."

"Okay. Okay. I'm a terrible wife and a horrible person."

"No, you're stupid in love with a guy who's stupid in love with you, and you've both being totally STUPID."

"What happened to silent support partner?"

"That shit went out the window when ninety seconds ago I learned how completely lame two highly educated, intelligent people can be when they love each other but are waiting for the other one to give over." She ran her fingers through her thick sandy blonde hair. "Geesh. Tomorrow's Thanksgiving. Are you going to sit like strangers at his parents' house giving each other the cold shoulder?"

"Of course not," I sort of shouted. "I've known his folks from before I can remember. They were family before they *became* family. And Jaden and I are…friendly."

Lissa started laughing so hard she laid her head on the steering wheel and held her stomach. "You two…" she drew in a deep breath, "suck at romance."

"Well," I deflated, "I can't argue that."

"Okay," she wiped under eyes, "okay. We're going to the hospital to find your *husband*, and we'll take it from there."

"At last," I muttered to myself, "a plan."

"Yeah," Liss grunted as she started up the car.

***

The security guard at reception was skeptical to the point of requesting two forms of ID before she called ICU to find out if Jaden was there. On the one hand, I appreciated the scrutiny, on the other, I gave her Jaden's name, my name, Harley's full name, and Axel's full name. I'm not saying some cyber stalker couldn't find that info somewhere, but what were the odds?

"Dr. Weaver will meet you in the waiting room outside ICU." She handed us visitor badges and a map of the hospital, then pointed us to the bank of elevators.

Sure enough, we'd barely exited the elevator and Harley grabbed my elbow and walked us to the waiting room. Before I could say a word, he put his hands on my shoulders and said, "He's been in surgery since twelve-thirty this afternoon. The four of us have been tag-teaming all day and into the night. Around eight-thirty, he crashed in the residents' bunks for about two hours, took a shower and came right back in. I was just heading out to get some rack time myself."

"Oh, no." I reached up to squeeze his hand. "Axel?"

"Is trying harder to live than anybody I've ever worked on. The kid's a fuckin' mess." He looked over to Lissa, then said, "Pardon my French."

Liss rattled off a couple of sentences in actual French, then concluded with, "and nowhere in there was the French you spoke."

Harley grinned and held out his hand. "Harley Weaver."

"Mélisse Babineaux, but everyone calls me Lissa."

Harley motioned between me and Liss. "Another rocket scientist?"

"In a manner of speaking. Kal leans more esoteric while I'm more mechanically inclined."

"Brainiacs," Harley said through a stifled yawn.

"Well, yeah." Lissa smiled. "You need sleep, brother."

"Yep, I do." Harley took my hand. "Don't be angry with him if he can't make Thanksgiving. Even if we repaired and re-repaired everything that needed fixing, we all have to be on stand-by."

"Of course." I nodded. "Tell him I came by, and to make sure he eats. I'll be back tomorrow."

"Will do," he said, gave my shoulder a squeeze, then walked us to the elevators.

As soon as the elevator car door closed, Lissa asked, "Is he married?"

I shook my head.

"With someone?"

"Nope."

"He's yummy."

"Yup. And a really good guy."

"I got that right away."

"You want me to give him your number?"

She bumped me with her hip. "Nope. I like to devise and execute my own strategy, thank you very much."

"A game plan?"

"My darling, Kahli. It's all about the game."

***

Skye and Hudson Schuyler had been together for twenty years when she "discovered" she was pregnant. She was thirty-seven and he was fifty. Until her pregnancy, they'd be inveterate wanderers. They'd converted a school bus into their traveling home long before it became fashionable, and saw no reason to get married since they'd pledged their love when she was seventeen and he was thirty.

Yeah, I'd had more than a few ick moments thinking about that, but by the time I knew them, they were married, lived in a nice house, and had stable jobs, as opposed to the vagabond, catch-as-catch-can life they'd lived before Jaden came along. No judgment, but I've seen the photos, and those two were only a couple of weeks away from joining Grizzly Adams.

Skye was a secretary at Rice Elementary School in Chula Vista, the town where Jaden and I grew up. Hudson worked at the best garden center/nursery in the world: Walter Anderson Nursery in San Diego.

Hud and Skye retired eight years ago, but they're busier than almost anyone I knew. Between all the causes they supported—they leaned waaay left, and had enormous hearts and souls—and all the artsy things they did, I'd get exhausted listening to their schedules.

At sixty-eight and eighty-one, neither showed any signs of slowing down.

Skye was still a terrible cook, and Hud grilled, but most of the time everything was charred. To make sure our meal was palatable, I prepared Thanksgiving dinner in their much larger than Jaden and my apartment's kitchen, and after everything was ready, they insisted on coming with me to the hospital to bring Jaden Thanksgiving and some family time.

At eight that morning, he'd finally called me, and from the scratch in his voice, I could tell he was wrecked. After hours and hours of trying, they weren't able to save one of Axel's legs, and had to amputate above the knee. My heart broke for Axel, his family, and all the people who worked so hard to put him back together. Especially, Jaden, who would take this as a personal failure.

"I'm coming over with breakfast," I'd told him, but he said he wouldn't have time to see me until the late afternoon.

Given that directive, at three o'clock, I loaded up the car with enough food for the Pacific Fleet, and Skye, who drove like a Formula One race car driver, got us to the hospital in record time. When we arrived, Harley told us Jaden was talking to Axel's parents as Harley came downstairs to help carry up the food to the staff breakroom on the ICU floor. We laid out so many large foil trays filled with everything Thanksgiving, there wasn't an inch of surface space left in the room.

While I was setting up the food, Skye walked out to the nurses' station to tell them to come get a plate and have some Thanksgiving.

When Jaden, who looked as wrecked as he'd sounded on the phone, finally walked into the breakroom, I didn't think, I jumped up and ran to him, wrapping my arms around his solid body, holding on tight.

His arms circled my shoulders and he pressed me so close, I had to turn my head against his chest so I could breathe.

I tilted my chin up and said, "Tell me."

He shook his head and whispered, "Later, when we're home."

Harley joined us for a while, and we ate and talked about anything that had nothing to do with Axel. After about an hour, Jaden went back to work, and we cleaned up, leaving the meager amount of remaining food for the staff.

On the drive to the apartment, no one talked until Skye pulled up in front of the building. Then Hud turned toward me, and talked through the space between the bucket seats. "You know Skye and I have led a life filled with love and gratitude. What you probably don't know is one of the things we're most grateful for is you being our daughter."

I felt the first teardrop trail down my cheek before I drew in a breath deep enough to keep from sobbing.

"Go upstairs, honey," Skye said. "We'll talk some more tomorrow."

I nodded, leaned forward and kissed each of their cheeks. Then I went upstairs to my empty apartment wishing with all my heart that Jaden would come home soon.

CHAPTER SIX

Jaden

We were done. There was nothing more to do for Axel but wait for him to recover, or worst-case scenario, for his body to give out. All along, that kid had been fighting like a champ, but his injuries were in a realm none of the team members had ever encountered all at one time. Certainly, his injuries were the worst I'd ever seen.

We'd agreed to put him in a thirty-six-hour medically induced coma in the hopes his body will heal enough for him to begin to truly physically recover, and then later withstand the trauma of knowing he'd lost his leg. He'd learn he'd have a difficult, long recovery road ahead of him.

For me, it meant that unless I got a trauma alert, I could go home, sleep, and spend time with Kahli.

Even if all she did was fight with me, I needed to be near her. To hear her voice, watch how animated she was when she talked about her lab work, eat her tasty food, and be tortured by her petite yet unbelievably tempting body.

Today was the Sunday after Thanksgiving, and I'd lost time. The only contact I'd had with the outside world was on Thanksgiving, and after, through Kahli's texts and phone calls. I didn't even see her when she came to pick up the car keys, which I'd left for her at the nurses' station. It made no sense to go home for an hour or two, so I'd showered and bunked in the hospital, and had told her to take the car since I didn't need it.

Now, I was sitting in an Uber listening to Ed, my driver, curse at the radio as a football team that was clearly losing, and, apparently, costing him some money. I closed my eyes, leaned back, and the next thing I knew, Ed was shouting, "Hey. Doc. Wake up. You're home."

I slipped him a decent tip, stumbled out of the car, and made my way up to our apartment where Kahli promised to have a full middle eastern spread waiting for me. I hoped she made falafel. Hers were the best. She'd told me the secret was to add some gigante beans to the chickpeas to give the falafel a richer flavor. I grew up with parents who were terrible cooks, and knew nothing about cuisine. But Kahli's dad was amazing in the kitchen, and she had inherited that talent from her father, from which I was the beneficiary.

Actually, when it came to Kahli, the benefits were plentiful. She spread her warmth, intelligence, and kindness to everyone in her sphere. I enjoyed being in her sphere, but if I was honest, I wanted to be the center of her universe, not just another satellite.

If I tried to talk to my parents about this—which I'd never do since they adored Kahli and would be pissed at me—they'd encourage me to tell her how I felt about her. They'd also browbeat me for carrying a torch for so long, especially since they knew how much she needed to be loved. Plus, my folks were all about sharing how you felt, and engaging in the free and open expression of emotions.

Frankly, my mother would tell me I was emotionally constipated.

This was my last thought before walking into our apartment where I was hit with the dining room table set like it was a special occasion. There were candles burning, and a bouquet of colorful flowers in a big blue vase in the middle of the table. And the smells coming from the kitchen made my stomach growl.

All that goodness receded to the back of my brain when Kahli came out of the bedroom with her shining hair bouncing around her shoulders. My gaze drifted down to her body-hugging peach sweater, and my mouth went dry at the same time my scrubs got tight. Her short denim skirt showed off her shapely legs, made longer by sexy, strappy high heels, and there was no way she missed my body's reaction.

"Hey," she said softly, her eyes twinkling as she walked up to me and laid her hands on my chest. "You must be starving."

Damn, she smelled good, and I loved the way her hands felt resting against me. And, yeah, I was starving, but my appetite had shifted away from food to other delicacies I've been wanting to savor for a long time.

I wrapped my arms around her waist and bent down to whisper in her ear, "Absolutely famished."

"Good," she whispered back, her voice raspy. "Go ahead and sit down. I'll bring out everything."

I was about to say, "I'll help," when her phone started ringing.

"Can you get that?" she asked over her shoulder as she walked into the kitchen.

I picked up her phone from the edge of the counter and saw "Unknown Caller." I answered anyway, and said, "Who is this?" I'd barely got out the "s" in this when whoever it was hung up.

Intentionally, I took her phone with me to the table. I'd barely sat down and the phone rang again. "Unknown Caller" again. I answered, said, "What," and the person hung up.

Kal was walking over to the table with a bowl of tabbouleh as she asked, "Who was it?"

"I don't know. An unknown caller who hung up twice the moment I spoke."

"Huh." She shrugged. "Put the phone on silent so we're not bothered by it. It's probably some telemarketer, or something like that." Then she went back to the kitchen and came back out with a huge platter filled with falafel, lots of triangles of pita bread, a bowl of hummus, cut tomatoes, dill cucumber, a small bowl of different kinds of olives mixed in with cubes of feta cheese, and some sliced lemons.

She sat next to me, grabbed my plate and started spooning up tabbouleh when the phone rang again. No, I hadn't turned it off. I wanted to know what the fuck was going on. "Talk, asshole," I shouted, and whoever it was paused for a moment before hanging up.

"Really, Jaden. Turn it off. Lissa wouldn't hang up, and neither would your parents. You're sitting here, so whoever's calling isn't important, or has the wrong number."

I hated myself for thinking what I was thinking, but I had to ask, "You sure about that?"

She sat back so fast her chair rocked. "Excuse me?"

"Maybe we should see if 'whoever' rings again, and if they talk when you answer."

"You fucking asshole." She jumped up and pointed at my face. "You think I'm fooling around with someone?" I raised my brows, but before I could answer, she yelled, "You bastard. For days, I've been turning myself inside out trying to find ways to soothe you and care for you while you're imagining me with another man."

I stood, and she stomped to the middle of the living room, put her hands on her hips and leaned forward. "You're so dense, I have no idea how you navigate life. Haven't you been paying any attention to me?"

The burn in my blood and roiling in my stomach seemed to be the right noxious brew to release the hold I'd been keeping on my spiraling and pent-up emotions. "How could I do anything but pay attention to you. But every time I try to talk to you, any and every fucking topic turns into a battle. I try to make your life easier. I try to support you and have your back, but nothing I say or do seems to be right." I ran my hands through my hair. "Why wouldn't I think you're interested in someone else. All you do is fight with me, and I have no fuckin' clue why. Every single day I wonder where your head's at."

"Really? You don't understand why I'm always fighting with you?" She shook her head. "You really are clueless. About everything." She sighed before saying, "But to be clear, so you absolutely know 'where my head is at,' I was eleven and waiting for my family to show up to an important science fair. They didn't show, and I was freakin'. Then the fair's almost done and Principal Adler comes walking across the gym, and she had two cops with her. We all went into the coach's office where I learned a delivery truck slammed into my parents' car, killing them and injuring Raffie.

"You were there, so you know." She stabbed her finger at me. "You know how I spent two weeks of my life in the hospital watching my only living family member suffer. And the first thing he did when he was discharged, the first fucking thing he did was make funeral and burial arrangements for our parents. He wouldn't let you or anyone help him, and he was driving everywhere with one hand 'cause he had a broken arm, and he was using his broken leg, which was stupid and dangerous. You have to remember what a joy it was for us to attend our parents' *double* funeral."

"Kahli, please sit down. You're—"

"Don't you dare say I'm too worked up. Especially in that condescending *I'm a doctor, I know better* tone."

I closed my eyes and breathed deep as I gestured with my hand for her to continue telling me things I knew in such detail they were tattooed on my brain, heart, and soul.

"Our folks had good life insurance, but it wasn't enough to keep the house, so Raffie, who was set to graduate high school in another month, at the ripe old age of eighteen, sells our family home, buys us a condo, and asks the Naval Academy to defer his entrance. Then, because he had mad computer skills, he gets the highest paying tech job he can find so he can support me."

Her chest was heaving, and I can tell she was out of steam. She plopped onto the sofa, and held up her hand with her index finger pointed in a *wait a minute* gesture. So I waited. Knowing what was coming next, but I had to let her get it all out. Maybe, just maybe, this is the storm that had to happen so we could clear the air and move forward. Together.

"Raffie stopped working and finally entered the Naval Academy only after he knew I got into UCSD. And what does he do when he graduates with honors as a Naval officer? While he's fulfilling his duty assignment, he's working everyone he can, and doing everything he can to get into the fuckin' SEALs. For two years he's gone way more than he's home, and last year my beautiful, kind, cool as shit brother got himself killed."

She looked up at me with tears welling in her eyes. "Every member of my family is dead. Do you honestly think I'd be happy about tying myself to a man who's looking forward to spending half a year on an aircraft carrier that's patrolling seas rife with terrorists?"

She must've seen me flinch.

"Yeah, Jaden. I know all about Operation Prosperity Guardian and the Houthi-led attacks on ships in the Red Sea. What I don't know is why you're so gung-ho to put yourself in the middle of all that. Especially after you browbeat me into marrying you knowing your orders are to go into the middle of a conflict where the terrorists use missiles."

I opened my mouth to explain that I had no choice, and since it was going to happen anyway, I figured I'd give her space and thought while I was away we could reset our relationship and slowly build it to where we could and should be.

But before I could get a word out, she launched herself from the sofa and jabbed two fingers into my chest as she yelled, "I'm not losing one more person I care about." Then she stomped away, and slammed the door to the bedroom.

Ah, hell no. We were nowhere near finished with this "conversation." I tried the doorknob to find she'd locked herself in. Already pissed the fuck off at being lectured about history I knew chapter and verse, while barely admitting feelings I was now sure she had for me, I didn't think about what I was going to do, I just did it.

I kicked the door open and stormed into the bedroom.

CHAPTER SEVEN

Kahli

The bedroom door crashed against wall and seemed to be hanging on by a thread. As I was backing up, Jaden, his face like thunder, crossed the room, his focus and aim on me. My back hit the wall and his big, hard body pressed into mine, and all I could think was *finally*.

His head tilted down and he held my gaze for so long I thought I'd faint from the intensity I saw there.

"You think," he rasped in a rough whisper, "I did all this," he threw his arm back toward the rest of the apartment, "as a stand-in for Raffie?"

Ninety percent no, and ten percent yes would've been my answer a few minutes ago. But I shook my head, because clearly his motivation was one hundred percent me.

"No," he rumbled. If possible, he pushed even closer, and there was no doubting what his body intended. "For years, I've loved you the way a man loves and wants a woman." *Ho-lee shit.* He bent his head further down until his lips were so close to mine, all I had to do was get up on my tiptoes to kiss him. "If Raffie was still alive, I would fight him for however long it took for him to *know*, I would love and cherish you for the rest of our lives."

Hearing his words, words I'd been dreaming to hear for so many years, I couldn't think anymore, all I could do was feel. So, even as the tears were coursing down my face, I grabbed onto his shoulders, pulled myself up, and did what I'd been wanting to do for most of my life. I kissed him. For about twenty seconds. Then he wrapped his long, strong arms around me and took over the kiss.

I knew he'd had lots of practice, so I expected him to be good at this, but for real, Jaden could *kiss*. His warm, firm lips pressed against mine as he tilted my head to where he wanted me to be. Slowly, he ran his tongue over my lips again and again, then he began to nibble on my lower lip and it felt so good, I gasped. As my mouth opened, his tongue slid inside, and I got to taste him for the first time, and found I'd been right. There was no ice cream, hell, there was nothing in the world that tasted as good as Jaden.

As he took the kiss deeper and wetter, his hands started roaming my back, slowly making their way down to my tush. When he squeezed hard, I got the message and did a little hop as he lifted me, which brought me face to face with the man I'd loved for as long as I had memory.

I wrapped my legs around him, and he pressed me even closer, still kissing me as a deep groan came up from his gut to his throat. I felt it. The whole of it. The pain of all the years he'd held onto what he'd wanted but couldn't have, and the sheer pleasure of releasing all those emotions.

He ended the kiss, but kept his lips on mine as one of his hands fisted in my hair. "You love me?"

"Always have, and always will," I whispered.

He backed up until he hit the bed, turned, leaned down, and placed me in the middle, then slowly he stood and did a thorough survey, his gaze lingering on my shoes. "Everything off but the shoes."

I got up on my elbows and told him, "Bossy."

"Baby, you're about to learn just how bossy your husband is."

I wanted to rub my hands together, then throw some sass to express my intention to torment him in the best possible way, but instead I decided to ask, "What if I say no?"

He grinned. "I was kinda hoping you would." He pulled off his scrub top and undershirt in one fluid motion. I took in his broad chest with its light dusting of blond hair that thickened into a trail down the center of his stupendous abs. He let me look my fill, and when I licked my lips, he divested himself of the rest of his clothes, and stood gloriously naked at the foot of the bed where he began stroking his hard, thick cock.

Seventy-three thousand thoughts careened through my brain at the same time: totally proportional body; he'll never fit; I want to wrap my lips around him and suck until his knees buckled; he'll never fit; all this is mine, and I'll make him fit because I'm not missing out on one millimeter of that gorgeous cock.

He leaned down, grabbed my ankles and yanked me until my tush was at the edge of the bed. He kneeled, pushed up my skirt, tossed my legs over his shoulders before lowering his head and began trailing kisses up from the back of my knee to the inside of my upper thigh. A fraction below my panty line, his kisses turned to sucking and licking so damn close to where I wanted him to be, I started writhing.

His grasped my hips and held me in place, his big hands keeping me still and he worked up from the back of my other knee to the same place on the inside of the opposite thigh, where he sucked and licked until I could take no more.

"Jaden," I called, my voice husky in a way I'd never heard.

"Hmm?" he hummed against my skin.

"Quit tormenting me."

He lifted his head and grinned. "I haven't even gotten started."

Before I could think of a good come-back, he lowered his head, pressed my thighs wider, then licked me through the lace of my apricot panties. To keep myself from flying off the bed, I fisted my hands in the comforter as he sucked, nipped, and nuzzled, the light scratch of the lace against my most sensitive skin making the torture more pronounced. When he moved the gusset aside and slid his finger inside me, my body clenched tight, readying for my release. I was so close, bare moments away from letting go when he removed his finger, and stopped.

"Hey," I shouted, angling my head to see down my body to his smug smirk.

Before I could think of what to say next, he flipped me over, yanked my tush up so I was on my knees, and then he covered my back as he pushed up my sweater. His large hands covered my breasts, and so, so lightly he slowly rubbed his palms over my nipples.

Holy hell, he was going to kill me with restrained pleasure.

The curl in my stomach arrowed down to between my legs, and again I was climbing. This time, the sensations were layered on top of his earlier assault, and I knew my release would be huge.

Then he stopped. Again. And I screamed, "No."

"Oh, yes." He sat back, pulled me onto thighs, his arms circling my waist, then with his chin, he pushed my hair over my shoulder and began slowly licking his way up my neck to behind my ear, and back down. His hot breath caressed my skin as he began to nibble his way up and down my neck.

So softly, I had to strain to hear him over my heavy breathing, he told me, "Only after I've gotten you so hot and so wet you'll be begging me to let you come, then, and only then, I'll fuck you every way I can fuck you, so you'll know you belong to me, and only me, until there's nothing left of us but dust.

And he did everything he said he'd do. For the next six hours.

EPILOGUE

Kahli

Skye was Wiccan, and Hudson called himself a child of the universe. Jaden was raised celebrating the full moons, and Yule, the day of the winter solstice. Skye embraced the Wiccan belief that the shortest day of the year marked *the end of the descent into darkness*, and the beginning of the return of the light as the days began to get longer after the solstice. So Yule, as with many spiritual holidays, was a celebration of light, and a time of reflection.

Since the Schuylers were my family, and my beliefs aligned well enough with theirs, on December 21st we walked the trails in the Torrey Pines Reserve, then went back to Skye and Hudson's house to eat way too much food, and open the presents we each bought or made for each other.

Skye had handmade a double wedding ring quilt in white and deep blue. "For my children," she said, "this pattern has long been a symbol of love and romance, which I'm so unbelievably happy you found in each other."

Before I could get too teary, Hudson handed me a set of car keys. "Don't go gettin' all choked up, girl. It's a clunker I fixed up so you have your own car until you kids have enough dough to buy one for yourselves."

As I was hugging Hudson, I got choked up, and he shook his head and laughed.

Jaden and I had talked a lot about what to get Skye and Hudson, who loved to travel but didn't do as much of it as they probably wanted. We checked out "spiritual sites" and figured they'd totally be into a trip to the Yucatan Peninsula in Mexico where they'd be able to visit *Chichen Itza*, the source of ancient Mayan culture dating back some two thousand years.

The minute Skye saw the tickets, she clapped and let out a "whoop" before she began telling us about the Mayans, and how they considered *Chichen Itza* a sacred site, and about the cenotes serving as a gateway to the Mayan underworld. We got a whole NatGeo-like mini-speech about how the natural sinkholes were believed to be sacred portals connecting the mortal world with the divine realm.

Jaden and I grinned at each other, knowing we'd given them a gift they'd remember forever.

It took me a while to figure out what to get Jaden. Axel was improving, but he'd had to have another surgery in the past month, and two more were scheduled for the first few months of the new year. So I did what I was good at: research. I located the best Orthotists and Prosthetists in the world. I called, researched some more, and compiled a pamphlet for Jaden with all the information I could find on each of the extraordinary Orthotists and Prosthetists. Even though I knew there were all sorts of databases with this kind of information, I wanted Jaden, who was beginning his career, to have more than rudimentary information filtered by other doctors who had their own favorites and biases.

When he opened the wrapping paper and saw the antique wooden box I put the pamphlet in, he said, "Kal, this is beautiful. I'm putting it on my desk, when I get one."

"Open the lid," I told him.

When he saw the pamphlet, he gave me a look I now saw often. Love, pure and true shined from his eyes. "Later," he mouthed, and I knew he would take hours to show me how much he appreciated the gift.

The last box on the coffee table was the largest, and was wrapped in shiny silver paper. Jaden got up, came back to the love seat and put the box on my lap. He gave me a nod indicating I should open it.

Carefully, I unwrapped the pretty paper so I could save it and the big white bow, only to find another wrapped box, this time the paper was white and the bow was silver. This went on for three more boxes, and each time I laughed at the silliness of it all.

Until I got to the light blue box. Anyone who knew jewelry understood where that box came from.

"If I may," he said, and I nodded. He took out the box, got down on one knee, and asked, "Will you marry me?"

The tears came even as I smiled. "We're married," I whispered.

"Yeah, we are, but I wanted to make sure you knew, really knew, I loved you when I asked the first time."

"I know."

"I'll take that as a yes." Then he opened the box and inside was a perfect princess cut solitaire diamond."

"Jaden," I breathed out.

"Can't have a wedding band without an engagement ring."

"Sure you can."

He shook his head. "Not my wife." He leaned in and wiped the tears from my face with his thumb. "My vow, Kal: You'll always know that I love you with everything I am."

Then he slid the ring on my finger, looked up, and grinned.

ELLE WISHES EVERYONE HAPPY HOLIDAYS AND INVITES YOU TO READ HER SERIES - THE LETTER CLUB

ABOUT THE AUTHORS

DIANE BENEFIEL

USA TODAY Bestselling Author, Diane Benefiel has been an avid reader all her life. She enjoys a wide range of genres, from westerns to fantasy to mysteries, but romance is her favorite. She writes what she loves best to read—emotional, heart-gripping romantic suspense novels. In her stories, she puts the heroes and heroines in all sorts of predicaments that they have to work together to overcome. Her novel, *Solitary Man* was a National Readers' Choice Award winner.

A native Southern Californian, Diane enjoys nothing better than summer. For a high school history teacher, summer means a break from students, and time immersed in her current writing project. With both kids grown and gone, she enjoys her leisure time camping, especially in the Sierras, and gardening, both with her husband.

Diane loves hearing from her readers.

Website: dianebenefiel.com
Twitter: twitter.com/dianebenefiel
Instagram: @diane_benefiel
TikTok: @diane_benefiel_romance
Pinterest: diane_benefiel
Facebook: /DianeBenefielRomance
BookBub: /authors/diane-benefiel
Goodreads: /author/show/8075321.Diane_Benefiel
Newsletter:
https://landing.mailerlite.com/webforms/landing/n1i2u8

Sign up for Diane's newsletter for sneak peeks and inside info on her new series.

M. TASIA

M. Tasia is a M/M romance author who lives in Ontario, Canada. She's is a dedicated people watcher, lover of romance novels, 80's rock, and happily-ever-afters (once the MCs are put through their paces, of course), who grew up with a love of reading.

She's a firm believer that everyone deserves to have love, excitement, and crazy hot romance in their lives. Love should be celebrated and shared.

Connect with M.:
mtasiabooks.com
FB: mtasiabooks
twitter: @mtasiaauthor
IG: @m.tasia.author
TikTok: @mtasiaauthor

L.P. MAXA

L.P. lives in Austin, Texas with her husband, two daughters, two rescue dogs, and one adopted cat. Stay tuned, there'll probably be more animals soon.

Writer, business owner, and office manager, L.P. says she loves to read as much as she loves to write. Reading a good book is her reward after writing one. In her spare time—ha!—she fosters puppies for a rescue organization based in Austin.

Connect with L.P.:
Website: www.lpmaxa.com
IG: @lpmaxa_author
TikTok: @lpmaxa_author
X: @lpmaxa

FB: pages/LP-Maxa/1442560722667127

EMILY MIMS

Author of over forty romance novels, Emily Mims combined her writing career with a career in public education until leaving the classroom to write full time. The mother of two sons, and lots of grandchildren, she and her husband split their time between central Texas, eastern Tennessee, and Washington, DC.

For relaxation Emily plays the piano, organ, dulcimer, and ukulele for two different performing groups, and even sings a little.

She says, "I love to write romances because I believe in them. Romance happened to me and it can happen to any woman—if she'll just let it."

Connect with Emily:

website: emilymims.com

IG: @mims_emily

TikTok:@emilywmims

FB: emily.mims.756

JOAN BIRD

Joan traces her roots back to Ireland, England, and Wales. Discounting any inherited pioneer courage, she recently left California, her home of forty-plus years, and her state of four generations, for the mountains of northern Arizona.

Instead of musing the fates of a hero or heroine along a foggy beach, she now hikes trails looking out to Granite Mountain or the San

Francisco Peaks. Petrified, sure, but she loves her small-town peppered with rodeos, lakes, pines, old trucks, and rocks - lots of rocks.

The transition made by moving truck instead of covered wagon allowed her to settle into writing full-time. While support from her four sisters, her children, their spouses, and a crew of grandchildren is a constant. Her cowboy-hero husband remains her best bud along with her Labradoodle, Doobie, who practices goofiness, toy-mongering, and provides constructive criticism of character arcs in exchange for walks.

CONNECT WITH JOAN:

FB: www.facebook.com/joan.m.bird

X: www.twitter.com/AuthorJoanMBird

ELLE WRIGHT

Elle Wright has been writing stories since she was a child, which led her to a career in journalism. She enjoys reporting life as much as making up a world she can control. She lives on the east coast of the United States where most of her large, noisy family resides. When she isn't in front of her computer, she loves to travel, garden, hang out with her dogs, and take in the brisk sea air that she's told is supposed to help calm her. She's been testing that theory for a while now.

CONNECT WITH ELLE

FB: facebook.com/elle.wright.1460

X: twitter.com/ElleWright18

IG: instagram.com/Elle_Wright_Writes/

www.BOROUGHSPUBLISHINGGROUP.com

If you enjoyed this book, please write a review. Our authors appreciate the feedback, and it helps future readers find books they love. We welcome your comments and invite you to send them to info@boroughspublishinggroup.com.

Follow us on TikTok and Instagram, and be sure to sign up for our newsletter for surprises and new releases from your favorite authors.

Are you an aspiring writer? Check out www.boroughspublishinggroup.com/submit and see if we can help you make your dreams come true.

Love podcasts? Enjoy ours at:

https://boroughspublishinggroup.com/podcast.

www.ingramcontent.com/pod-product-compliance
Lightning Source LLC
Chambersburg PA
CBHW020252200626
46816CB00001BA/255